THEIR TORMENTOR WAS GONE . . .

Mackenzie sat shifting his naked buttocks on the hard ground, and listening to the dwindling growl and rattle of the truck until finally the night absorbed it and there was nothing.

He looked slowly at the others.

Jay Painter was sitting up. A muscle worked at the back of his jaw. His thin body was a patchwork of tangled hair.

A gust of dry air spun Shirley's long hair around her face. She combed it away with her fingers and tossed it back with a shake of her head, an unconsciously impatient gesture. She was watching the darkness where the truck had disappeared.

Earle Dana writhed slowly, not really conscious. His leg was broken . . .

Unless they could find shelter and moisture in the desert, they were all condemned to die . . .

FEAR IN A HANDFUL OF DUST

JOHN IVES

A JOVE BOOK

Jove books are published by Jove Publications, Inc., 200 Madison
Avenue, New York, N.Y. 10016

For Gwynne

And I will show you something different from either
Your shadow at morning striding behind you,
Or your shadow at evening rising to meet you:
I will show you fear in a handful of dust.

—T. S. Eliot, *The Waste Land*

1

When the lights go off Calvin Duggai lies still and gapes straight up into the darkness while he absorbs the night through his ears.

He hears the slap of the bolt and the male nurse's footsteps pocking away down the corridor; he hears the squeak of springs, the rustle of bedclothes along the ward. He hears Joley's fear-of-darkness whimpering and someone's catarrhal snort and the empty bitter cough of an inmate's laughter.

Duggai's stomach churns. A tight ache spans his skull. Air conditioning pushes the rancid air around but does not leach it of the sick smells of fear-sweat and incontinence and incipient nausea.

Hate spins through him—just now it is unfocused, directionless. Its only restraint is purpose: he must will chaos away. He pushes the pain far back out of his awareness because everything needs to be precise now and he has no leeway for the carelessness that rage could cause.

He reviews the steps, isolating each move in his mind, visualizing, seeking weaknesses—here a point of risk, there a need for swiftness and silence. The rain came suddenly this evening: until then he wasn't quite ready; the pumping of blood through his temples has been very fast during the past few hours and now he must double his caution because the impatience of weariness may betray him otherwise. If anything comes awry then the entire scheme will collapse because they won't merely put him back in here, they'll take him back to the other place with its armed male nurses and its concrete walls from which there is no escape.

When he judges them to be all asleep Duggai lifts his legs off the bed and sits up until his bare feet touch the cold floor. The air conditioning rumbles and he listens beyond it, judging the sounds of men's breathing, turning his head slowly to catch every angle against the flats of his eardrums. There must be no alarm.

He puts his weight on his feet and strips the blanket slowly off the bed. He folds it because he can't have a loose edge drag against someone's foot in the dark. He pads down the length of the ward and carries the blanket into the bathroom, closes the door tight, shutting himself in, dropping the folded blanket to one side.

The silence is abrupt. In the absence of the numerous sounds of human life he now hears the drift of rain upon the roof overhead.

He moves confidently without needing light; long ago his feet memorized the dimensions. The faint hint of illumination defines the high vent window—heavier vertical stripes are the steel bars set into the opening. Even without its bars it would be too small for Duggai to wriggle through.

He crouches. Under the third sink his hands move with quick familiarity: a deft spanning and twisting of the wide fastenings until the elbow of drainpipe comes free. He upends it into his palm and the kitchen knife drops into his hand, a reassuring weight. He lays the pipe elbow aside on the floor with silent care; to replace it would take time and he has examined each step carefully from all directions and determined that there is no need to replace the pipe because they will know about the breakout anyway. It has taken him years in the other place and months in this one to work out the plan and fix each detail in his mind; this is the night he has aimed for and he moves swiftly without waste.

Four paces take him to the outside wall. With the blade he unscrews the four screws that hold the plywood panel over the cavity in the wall (access to the incoming hot and cold water pipes). It has taken several months' nightly work with fingers and the table knife to cut through the outside paneling and scrape through the stucco. Eight nights ago the knife went through free to the outside of the building and he knew he'd cut his way close enough. Since then it has been a matter of waiting: he has waited for a night black with rain.

He hikes himself up to the window, hanging on the ledge by his fingers, peering out. The rain is opaque. In his imagination he can see the lawn, the high fence, the trees beyond the fence. To the left he can see rain slanting into yellow light from a window farther along the building but that is a safe distance away.

On the floor he lies back and kicks the wall out.

The months of digging have weakened it. The three-foot segment of stucco gives way neatly to his barefoot kick.

He hears it break apart when it strikes the lawn fourteen feet below. A damp soft thudding of pieces. He lies absolutely still now, ears keening the night. The fresh smell of rain seeps in through the hole, dispelling the bathroom's disinfectant air. Duggai feels around the hole with his fingers, finds a jutting edge of stucco and breaks it off, sets it aside and puts the knife in his teeth and wraps the blanket around his shoulders; and goes out feet first.

He wriggles out belly-down and blind, his back to the night. Raindrops soak the pajamas to his legs. The cold rain makes him wince. He grips a pipe and lowers his body until he hangs full length against the outside wall, toes touching the rough surface. Without hurry he gathers himself. When he is balanced for it he lets himself drop.

But he didn't push out far enough away from the wall and the ground-floor windowsill cracks his knee just before he hits the ground. It upsets him and he sprawls, banging his knee again on a stone in the lawn. He lies still and breathes shallowly through his mouth and fights down the scream of pain. No one must hear him now. He must not be interrupted. He has four people to kill.

In the ticking dark rain he hears only the pneumatic swish of a car on the road some distance away. His eyes track it by the moving reflections of its lights on the underbellies of the clouds.

Pain slams through him in great battering waves. He waits for them to roll back. At the bright hot center of his thoughts is the plan, the next step; he tries to focus everything on that. But images of his enemies keep distracting him. The four hated ones. The doctors.

Now he moves experimentally to find out if he has broken the knee. The pain brings out his tears but he doesn't feel the grating of anything shattered. He is able to get to his feet and with a rough uncaring need to know he puts his weight on the bad knee. It holds. He limps, dragging the right leg across the grounds, carrying the knife and the blanket: these, and his pajamas, are his only possessions.

Near the end of the building behind him two windows are alight. None of the light reaches this far but even so the lawn is vaguely phosphorescent and his feet leave dark matted prints. He keeps turning his head, searching.

The knee is a great frightful agony. Rhythms of faintness beat through him. Now he is afraid for the first time—not afraid of men but afraid because he isn't at all sure he has the strength for the fence: can he do it on one good leg?

He does not see the fence at first but the sibilance of the rain gives way to a faint pinging and this sound, felt if not heard, determines the location of the fence for him. He extends a hand before him and gimps forward step by step until his splayed fingers penetrate the mesh.

He looks up but cannot see. Raindrops make him blink. But he knows this fence. Twelve feet high, heavy steel chainlink, and there are five strands of barbed wire running parallel at three-inch intervals, canted inward at the top. For all these months he has measured it in his mind and known that he can do it but that was counting on two good legs and now his fear takes the form of a great rage and he has to stifle a roar.

At the far end of the building a shadow passes across one of the lighted windows and Duggai's breath stops in his throat. He waits for the siren and the floodlights but knows this is only unreasoning fear: there won't be a bed check on the ward until dawn unless one of the crazies starts to demolish a bed or attack another inmate. On these wards such occurrences are not nearly as likely as they were in the old place, the Maximum Security Hospital. But the distinction has not made this ward any more bearable. They ought to kill a man rather than put him in a place like that. They do not understand, and their failure to understand is hilariously funny in its way because they are the ones who keep talking about understanding. We want to understand, Duggai, so that we can help you.

You can help me by setting me free of this place. This place is not fit for a human man. Such a place sucks the spirit from a human man. Put me in prison if you want: if I'm guilty by your law then punish me in prison. A man in a prison only needs to close himself off and wait out the time. Prison is not personal, it is just time to be passed. This place, all the picking and prying and

13

understanding, this place with its machines and the needles and the pills and the lunatic inmates—the examinations of my blood, my breath, my urine, my feces—you are like shamans using my waste in a clay pot to foretell things as if I were a goat, you leave a man no dignity.

You are turkey buzzards picking over carrion; you make me into carrion for your pickings. That is not life. That is not what a man can endure. Life is dignity. I come from a line of people who tortured our enemies as a matter of course but we tortured them in good faith and allowed them to die, in the end, with dignity intact. We did not dismantle their insides and poke around their manure while they were still alive to watch us do it.

We want to understand, Calvin. You want to understand by destroying. You put the needle in my arm to draw blood and study it but what you really want to do is put the needle in my brain and study my spirit: you want to draw me out of the skull into your syringe and study it in a laboratory beaker, a curiosity, like something people stare at in a zoo.

You've tried every way you know to destroy my dignity. Dignity is a man's only possession in the end. You have failed to destroy mine but if you keep me here long enough I will lose strength and you will succeed after all. I will be worse than dead. A man can die but dignity can continue to inhabit his spirit.

And I am not dead yet anyway. I have things to do first.

Hate keeps him moving. He clamps his jaw with the anguish of the knee. He folds the blanket carefully over again and then rolls it neatly and drapes it around his neck. He gets the knife back into his teeth and crouches twice and straightens, experimenting. It is possible to mask the pain with hate: just think about the four of

14

them. The muscles are working and that is what matters. He hooks his fingers through the chainlink mesh, testing it; he puts his toes into the wire and allows himself to sag, putting his weight on fingers and toes, feeling the metal cut into his flesh.

He knows it will have to be fast because he can't hold long; the wire cuts too fast. He releases the fence and steps back a pace, secures the blanket around his shoulders and goes into his crouch, spreading his hands until the palms touch the wet grass.

There is a flicker of light along the cloud bellies and he hears the hiss of another car going up the road on the hill. He feels chilled in the wet; his toes curl in the grass.

He makes the leap with all his strength. The stab of agony in the knee shocks him faint; he hears his own grunt of pain and clamps his lips shut on the knife, cutting his lip. His stretching fingers fumble against the mesh and he scrabbles for holds with his toes. The wire cuts into him. All his two hundred pounds are distributed on a few pieces of narrow steel wire and the effect is that of razor blades.

Pain is his existence, complete now. It does not increase when he removes one hand from the wire.

With the hand he snakes the blanket off his shoulders, shakes it out, unfurls it to its four-thickness fold, swings it overhead, slaps it blindly down, feels it drape over the barbed wire above him, feels across the blanket until through the cloth he finds a taut strand—the point of a steel barb bursts through the padding into his finger. He shifts his hand an inch to the left, between barbs, and clenches his grip.

He frees the other hand and both feet. Now he hangs full length by one hand from the blanket-padded barbed wire.

The rain beats against him. He gets the left hand up and gropes between the barbs. When he has his grip he

15

heaves his left leg high, hooks his heel against the blanket and feels it slide over the barbed wire. A prick of steel rakes his calf but he drags himself up with his weight on the puncture, thinking of the free earth beyond, propelled by his hate, visualizing the four faces.

For a moment he is poised on top of the wire, tangled in folds of the sodden blanket, and he flashes on a monkey he saw high in a tree in montagnard country with fragmentation bombs exploding all around. Then he is rolling, switching his handgrips frantically, his legs swinging off into space.

He hangs free. His toes bang against the outside of the mesh and he swings his feet out and lets himself drop.

He tries to land mainly on the good left leg but the battered knee takes part of the fall and he cries out faintly. The knife drops from his mouth. He is on both hands and one knee, holding the injured knee protectively off the earth; he sobs, his agony beyond control.

The four of them. They put me in here. They could have sent me to prison but they sent me here. When men invade your spirit and trample your dignity they must be destroyed. That is the Old People's law and I am still one of them, one of the people of the high desert. They must be destroyed and I must be the instrument of their destruction and it must be appropriate to their offense. You do not simply kill such people because that would leave their spirits intact to follow you forever. You must cripple their spirits first by dominating them, by proving to their spirits that yours is the stronger spirit, by inflicting upon them tortures that you yourself can withstand.

Duggai lets himself down onto his left side and scrabbles with his hand in the wet weeds but he cannot find the knife.

The need for speed and distance overpowers everything else now. He leaves the knife behind, drags him-

16

self one-legged across the gravel and stickers, makes for the trees.

He looks back. The lamplit windows are only faint smudges of light.

Freedom.

But to keep it he must make distance. Against the twisting needles of pain he hobbles over the top of the hill and into the forest beyond. Twigs and stones lacerate his bare soles.

Finally there is the road.

He remembers coming through the town manacled in the back seat of the Department of Corrections sedan seven months ago. It is not more than two miles to the edge of town. If he keeps moving he can be there in an hour even on one leg.

He puts his good foot onto the road and limps into the drenching darkness.

2

Mackenzie's corded forearms wrestled the steering wheel. Insects crashed into the Jeep's windshield, leaving smears; on the highway ahead lay a black watery heat mirage. A roadside sign flashed past: "Industry we do desire. . . . Interested? Please Inquire!" The painted letters had been faded gray by the sun.

He left the blacktop at the head of the pass. The Jeep rattled across the rails of the cattle-guard and Mackenzie put it recklessly down the washboard ruts of the dirt road. Everything shook; there was a clattering din. Impelled by haste he didn't let up until he passed the turn-off to the Recreation Area. Then the road narrowed and began to twist and he was forced to drop it into second gear.

He went grinding on up into the pines; the Jeep humped painfully over roots and rocks. Finally in thinning air he reached the fork. Little shingle signs pointed both ways: RANGER STATION. CAMPGROUND. He went through the trees toward the station.

Smyley was at the foot of the fire tower waiting. "Heard you coming a mile back. You trying to wreck the Jeep or just set a new land-speed record?"

Mackenzie got out. The dog came out from under the cabin and stretched lazily and came forward to have her ears scratched. Mackenzie said, "Good pooch," and started to unload the supplies from the back of the Jeep.

Smyley waddled over. "Let me give you a hand."

Mackenzie didn't want help but there was no way to get rid of the relief man until the Jeep was unloaded. They hauled the grocery sacks inside the cabin.

Smyley put his fists in the small of his back and flexed his spine, rearing far back. "Want some help putting it away?"

"No thanks."

"Just talk a blue streak, don't you, Sam."

"Sure." Mackenzie went outside and waited until Smyley gave it up and came out.

Smyley gave him an accusing look. "Some of us take kindly to company when we get a chance at it."

"Sorry, Smyley. I didn't mean to offend you. I'm in a solitary mood, that's all."

"What's bugging you, Sam?"

"This and that. Never mind."

"Tell me one thing, will you?"

"What?"

"Where do you go on your days off?"

"Here and there."

"Jesus Christ." Smyley rubbed his big belly and glanced down at Mackenzie's feet. "Nice old dog. She got a name?"

"I don't know. Maybe she did at one time."

Smyley got into the Jeep. "Somebody was telling me—did you used to be a doctor or something? Psychiatrist, they said."

"Yes."

"What the hell are you doing up here then?"

"My job." Mackenzie watched him shake his head in disgust and drive away. Then he went inside the cabin and unpacked the supplies. He gave the dog a Milk Bone and went up the ladder into the tower and did a binocular sweep of the mountain forests. He recorded the sweep in the log and checked the radio, broke open

19

the new decks of cards and laid out a double-pack board of solitaire.

The newspaper story kept intruding on his contentment. Finally he climbed down to the cabin and read the story again.

The dog heaved herself on ancient limbs to the larder and he gave her another Milk Bone. She didn't eat it. She took it outside, perhaps to bury it.

Once every three weeks I see a newspaper, he thought, *and I had to pick this one. Odds of twenty to one.*

He read it twice. Duggai was a sort of bad tooth that Mackenzie seemed compelled to keep biting and prodding with his tongue.

He went outside and the dog brought him a stick; Mackenzie spent ten minutes throwing it for the dog to fetch; the dog was too old to do more than trot after it. Afterward Mackenzie went back up to the tower, moving up the ladder with a grace that betrayed quite well-tuned muscular coordination for a physique barely shy of fifty years' age. It was just about all he had to do—calisthenics and isometrics. Otherwise sedentary in the fire tower he'd have gone to atrophy—constant head colds and bellyaches like Wilder or flaccid fat like Smyley, the relief man. Smyley was a reader; doing the circuit from tower to tower he always had his knapsack filled with paperbacks. Wilder was a deep thinker who worried a great deal about ecology and the world; with nothing to do in the towers but worry about Armageddon it wasn't surprising Wilder had heartburn and sinus trouble. *And me? I just get musclebound—in body and mind.*

Nevertheless he never could wait to get back to his isolated cocoon after a weekend's liberty. It was the frantic impulse toward his safe hermitage that always brought him home at top speed in the Jeep. *Comes right*

20

down to it, I'm happy here and how many can make that claim? He had to smile.

He still had the Sacramento newspaper; he tossed it on the desk and did a sweep of the mountains, searching through the glasses in a deliberate grid pattern until he'd completed the circuit. Down at the foot of the tower the dog was excavating to bury the Milk Bone at the foot of one of the stilts that supported the rickety fire tower. Mackenzie leaned out over the railing. "You're digging so close you'll knock the whole thing over, you stupid twrp." The dog wagged her tail briefly to acknowledge she knew he was talking to her. Mackenzie went back inside the glass enclosure and sat down with the newspaper.

KILLER SOUGHT AFTER ASYLUM ESCAPE

San Francisco, July 11 (API). Calvin Duggai, 27, committed to a state mental hospital for the criminally insane since his trial in 1972 on five counts of manslaughter, escaped Tuesday night from the California State Hospital at Cochino, in Marin County north of San Francisco.

In making his escape Duggai apparently tunneled through a second-story exterior wall and climbed over a 12-foot steel fence.

Dogs employed in the search failed to trace Duggai because of Tuesday night's heavy rain, which had washed the spoor away by the time the escape was discovered yesterday morning.

According to Highway Patrol Lt. Richard Loomiston, Duggai allegedly broke into a house one mile from the prison hospital before dawn Wednesday. He may have stolen guns as well as clothing and food from the house. Duggai's fingerprints were found on several objects in the house, which has been unoccupied for several days, its owners vacationing.

Lt. Loomiston stated that all leads are being pursued. A dark brown camper-body pickup truck, California license plates XVZ237W, was stolen at some time before dawn from a residence on the outskirts of Cochino, and the theft may be connected with Duggai's disappearance.

Police are emphasizing that if seen, Duggai should not be approached. "He is extremely dangerous and may be armed. Anyone having information about his whereabouts should immediately call local police or the Highway Patrol," Lt. Loomiston said.

Calvin Duggai is described by police as a Navajo Indian, height 6′ 1″, weight 205 pounds. Hair black, eyes brown, complexion swarthy. The fugitive has a three-inch scar on the back of his left hand extending from the wrist to the center knuckle.

Tracks left in the wet ground at the hospital indicate that Duggai may be limping as a result of his leap to freedom. Color and description of his clothing are unknown pending the return of the householders from whose wardrobe it was stolen.

In 1971 Calvin Duggai, a Vietnam combat veteran, was arrested and charged in Barstow after five men died in the Mohave Desert collecting spent shells on the Randsburg Wash Test Range during the Independence Day weekend.

Tire tracks and other evidence led police to Duggai's Barstow shack, where his pickup truck still contained 17 buckets filled with empty brass cartridge cases.

According to evidence presented at Duggai's trial, the six men—described as "scavengers"—had driven into the restricted Randsburg Wash range in the pickup for the purpose of collecting shell casings ejected from Air Force planes during gunnery practice. Such brass casings can be sold to scrap dealers for 55¢ a pound.

For several months prior to the incident, Duggai allegedly had operated similar scavenger hunts on various artillery and gunnery ranges throughout the Southwest.

During the hunt for brass in the desert, an altercation apparently occurred among the scavengers, after which Duggai drove away in the pickup truck, abandoning the five men in a desert area about 40 miles from the nearest road. The high recorded for July 3 was 123° Fahrenheit, and in his summation San Bernardino County Prosecutor Everett Sellas pointed out, "Those temperatures are measured at the weather station in the shade, and in the middle of the Mohave Desert there is no shade."

Tracks indicated the five victims tried to walk out of the desert. Four of them managed to cross about 5½ miles.

The fifth victim, Gilbert Rodriguez, 15, of Victorville, made his way several miles farther, surviving the first night by breaking open cactus with rocks and squeezing the pulp through his shirt. The desert heat claimed him before noon of the following day.

The five bodies were found by an Air Force helicopter after Mrs. Carlos Rodriguez of Victorville called police to say her son had not returned from a brass-collecting expedition led by Calvin Duggai.

In testimony at Duggai's trial, San Bernardino County Medical Examiner Dr. Philip Rawson stated that when the bodies were found, "They'd been picked fairly clean by buzzards and ants but we were able to piece the story together. Life expectancy in that desert is extremely brief, even for a healthy adult, if he isn't a trained expert in the techniques of survival. People's cars break down out there, they make the mistake of trying to walk out for help, and quite often they're dead in just a few hours."

Heat exhaustion and heat stroke are blamed for most summer desert fatalities of this kind. Dr. Rawson stated, "The blood almost literally comes to a boil."

It was established at the trial that Duggai had deliberately abandoned the five men without water.

In the absence of clear evidence of motive, Duggai was charged with five counts of second-degree murder in the deaths of the five scavengers.

Rumors that Duggai's motives involved Indian witchcraft and intertribal rivalry led Duggai's court-appointed defense attorney to successfully petition for a change of venue from Barstow. The trial was held in San Francisco in March, 1972.

A prosecution witness, Oro Copah, testified that his brother, Taxco Copah, one of the five victims and a member of the Yuma Indian tribe, had argued several times with Duggai about Indian "medicine" or witchcraft, each man claiming greater power for the spirits and demons of his own tribe. On two prior occasions, Oro Copah recalled, the arguments had led to blows. According to Oro Copah, the argument had not been resolved between them when the two men—Duggai the Navajo, Taxco Copah the Yuma—set out on July 3 in the pickup truck with their three companions.

According to the testimony of the surviving brother, one topic of argument between the two men had been whether Yuma medicine or Navajo medicine provided greater protection against the "demons" of the desert. In his summation at the trial, San Francisco Prosecuting Attorney Edwin Garraty suggested that the motive for the crime was probably to be found in this dispute. "Essentially what must have happened," Mr. Garraty told the jury, "is that Duggai and Taxco continued their argument throughout the trip into the proving ground, and finally Duggai must have said words to the effect, 'All right, let's find out just how powerful your medicine really is.' And left the five men to survive as best they could."

Duggai was found not guilty by reason of criminal insanity. He was remanded to the custody of the psychiatric division of the State Department of Corrections for an indeterminate period.

At the time of his escape Tuesday night, Duggai had spent five years and four months in two successive state hospitals, having been moved to Cochino nine months ago on recommendation of psychiatrists who judged that it was no longer necessary to confine him in the maximum security facility at Sacramento.

Duggai was born and grew up on the Window Rock Navajo Indian Reservation in northeastern Arizona. He is a graduate of an Arizona high school and attended the University of Arizona at Tucson for one semester. He was drafted in 1969 and served as an infantryman in Vietnam in 1969–1971. Prior to his medical discharge in early 1972 he underwent psychiatric treatment at Letterman Army Hospital in San Francisco for a condition that was described at his trial by Army psychiatrist Captain Samuel Mackenzie as "combat disorientation caused by an experience of involuntary participation in atrocities." According to the testimony of Capt. Mackenzie and three other expert psychiatric witnesses, Duggai was "not capable of distinguishing right from wrong," and was not legally responsible for his actions, and thus met the legal definition of insanity.

By last night police had widened the dragnet for Duggai to include San Francisco and the Bay Area.

Mackenzie looked at the grainy wirephoto at the bottom of the newspaper column. Like most mug shots it was barely recognizable: there was no life in the face depicted—it might have been a photograph of a death mask. It was a face that had closed up completely. He saw no sign of the bewildered pleading he remembered.

Mackenzie hoped they'd nail him. Maybe it wasn't Duggai's fault but Mackenzie disliked him nonetheless: he remembered Duggai as a figure of sinister menace.

He stayed in the tower until nightfall; every twenty minutes he swept for smoke with the glasses. When it was dark he climbed down and went into the cabin to eat. The dog followed him inside.

He didn't like the glare of a gas lamp; his light came from the cookfire and from a candle he'd stuck in the neck of a whisky bottle. He ate something that had come out of a can—five minutes afterward he couldn't remember what it was. He mixed the remains of it into a bowl of Rival and Friskies and fed the dog; afterward he went back up the dark ladder and had a look around for fires. He spotted three or four campfires on the campground but nothing disturbing. At midnight he made another sweep and then went to bed.

When he was half asleep he heard the dog stretch, her claws scratching the floor. He thought of the pneumatic brunette who'd wandered into the station two weeks ago wearing a knapsack and chewing a string of jerky out of a cellophane pack—wide-eyed and full of college-girl enthusiasm for ecological conservation and the healthy outdoor simplicities. She wanted to apply to

26

the Forest Service when she graduated: she saw no reason why fire rangers had to be men.

She wanted to know everything about the job. He'd answered her eager questions with a monosyllabic reluctance that only convinced her he was a lovable eccentric. She was ready to believe him heroic: she saw his isolation as a tremendous sacrifice. He did not disabuse her.

She fixated on the whisky-bottle candlestick as a symbol of his resourceful conservationist ingenuity. That amused him—he'd never thought of it as anything but a lazy whim—and he had laughed at her. His laughter in turn struck her as true communication and she was tearfully passionate, delighted she had been able to bring him out of his hermit shell, and he made love to her four times in the one night—the only time in his life he'd ever accomplished that.

In the morning she'd told him breathlessly that he had the great charm of one who didn't fit into an acquisitive society.

When she was ready to leave she became shy. "You *are* an Indian, aren't you?"

"Why?"

"You look like an Indian. You talk like one."

"Navajo," he told her, although it was only half true.

She left to go back to summer school at Pomona. Mackenzie had been relieved to see her go.

Where do you go on your days off?

Smyley, you stupid oaf, I go to whorehouses. Where the hell do you think a man goes after he's spent three weeks on top of a Sierra Nevada mountain in a fire-lookout tower?

Finally he fell asleep.

The dog woke him. He heard the thump of her tail against the floor.

It triggered all his warning systems.

Pitch dark. Nothing to make a dog wag her tail—unless there was someone else in the cabin.

A voice spoke.

"Yah'a'teh."

He recognized the Navajo greeting, the deep big voice in the darkness. The phrase meant *Hello* or *It is good* or just *Nice day ain't it* but it had been spoken in an irony of vicious rage and he knew that voice.

A match struck explosively. In its light he saw Calvin Duggai's big face and the huge revolver.

"Half your brains on the wall if you blink, Captain."

The dog lay drowsily with her head rising slowly. She stopped wagging her tail.

The breath hung in Mackenzie's throat. He watched Duggai light the candle in the whisky bottle. Duggai shook the match out slowly. The gesture was redolent with menace.

"Some watchdog you got."

Mackenzie watched him.

"What kind of dog is he? Beagle?"

"She. Retriever."

"Looks like a beagle to me."

"If you say so."

"Don't humor me, you son of a bitch." Duggai spat the words out like insects that might have flown into his mouth. His thumb drew back the revolver's hammer. The click of sound was abrupt and loud. With a taste of coppery fear on his tongue Mackenzie noticed, with bleak pointless recognition, that the handgun was a .44 Magnum. Big enough to smash an engine block.

Duggai gaped at him. It brought a great many things rushing back through Mackenzie's memory. That way Duggai had of staring sightlessly with his mouth slack.

The mahogany skin was suspended from massive cheekbones; Duggai had small haggard eyes high in his face and they were buried deep in their sockets like those of a sick dying man. Mackenzie saw pinched lines

28

of strain around the corners of the open mouth. Duggai wore Levi's and a quilted hunting jacket and heavy boots but he wore them uneasily as if unaccustomed to wearing clothes at all. They didn't really fit; the Levi's were too big at the waist, cinched in like a mailbag by a tight belt, and the jacket was tight on Duggai's shoulders.

"How the hell did you find me here?"

"Made a few phone calls to San Francisco." Duggai moved away from the candle—limping a bit. "It wasn't hard at all. Not as if you was really trying to hide or anything."

"I wasn't."

"It don't matter much." Duggai picked up the khakis where Mackenzie had left them draped across the table. Mackenzie watched him go methodically through the pockets, one-handed. Duggai emptied everything out and then tossed the trousers on the bed. He made the same search through the pockets of the tunic. Then he threw all the clothes on the bed and stepped back toward the candle, staying to one side so that his shadow didn't fall across Mackenzie.

"Put them on."

"You want help, Calvin? Is that why you came to me?"

Duggai pushed the muzzle of the .44 Magnum toward Mackenzie's face. It mesmerized Mackenzie.

"Put your clothes on, Captain."

When he was dressed he waited for the next instruction. Duggai saw the way his eyes wandered toward the candle. "Don't think about it."

The dog was sitting up watching. She hadn't moved from the spot—doubtless the tones of the two men's voices had warned her. She was a very old dog and she had learned to stay out of trouble. It was one of the things Mackenzie had discovered about her in the months since she had wandered up to the cabin and adopted him.

It was occurring sluggishly to Mackenzie that Duggai didn't have it in mind to kill him right away. Otherwise why have him get dressed?

"What do you want, Calvin?"

"Be daylight in a little while. We go then."

"Go where?"

"A place."

"How long will we be gone?"

"Long enough to settle things." Duggai looked at him, open-mouthed.

Mackenzie said, "I asked because of the dog. The dog's got to be fed."

"The dog gets hungry, he can wander on down to the campground. Somebody'll feed him down there."

"Or shoot her."

"Captain, shut up your mouth a minute."

Mackenzie tried to judge Duggai's intentions but he had no inkling. One of his many failures was that he'd never been able to get inside that mind.

The dog moved tentatively, shifting her hindquarters, finally getting to her feet. When that failed to alarm the newcomer she waddled slowly toward the bed where Mackenzie sat. She thumped her rump down to the floor and put a forepaw on his knee. Mackenzie scratched her throat. Anger of all sorts ricocheted through him but the most acute anger was on the dog's behalf. He said a silent so-long to her and wished her luck.

The candle was down to a stub, guttering in the bottleneck. But gray light came in through the window.

"We wait till the sun's up," Duggai said. "They'd have noticed us on the road at night. Down by the campground. They'd have wondered."

"Calvin, what do you want?"

Duggai's eyes seemed to mirror disgust and impatience. "What the hell do you think, *beligano?*"

Beligano. White man. The Navajo word rattled around his skull with all its associations. But none of them connected with anything that told him what Duggai might have in mind.

"Calvin . . ."

"Shut up your mouth."

The light grew. Duggai blew the candle out. For a little while the dead-candle stink filled the room. Duggai opened the rickety wardrobe cabinet and took a wire coathanger out. He stepped on the hook and pulled the wire out straight and tossed it on the blanket beside Mackenzie.

"Twist one end around your right wrist. Fasten it good and tight."

"Why?"

"Do it, Captain. Just do it." Duggai's voice trembled with rage.

Duggai watched him wrap the stiff wire around his right wrist. He twisted the end around the stem and held his arm up to show Duggai it was secure. The long piece of wire dangled stiffly from his wrist.

"Lie down belly flat now. Turn your face to the wall. Put both hands behind your ass."

"Calvin, I don't think this is going to . . ."

"Shut up," Duggai roared. In his fist the Magnum trembled.

He felt his wrists being slammed together and wired tight. Then Duggai rolled him over on his back. Mackenzie looked up at him, past the massive revolver. "What now?"

"Now we go."

The dog walked a little way with them until Duggai got angry about it. Mackenzie said, "Stay," and the dog

31

watched them go. From the bottom of the road Mackenzie saw her trot over to the foot of the tower to dig up yesterday's Milk Bone.

About a quarter mile down past the fork Duggai turned him off the road into the trees. They walked forty or fifty feet and a brown camper-body pickup truck came in sight parked back in the woods. To get this far off the road it had to be four-wheel drive. Mackenzie saw that it had Nevada license plates. Duggai must have pinched the plates somewhere. Clever enough. He couldn't see through the camper windows because red-and-white checkerboard curtains were down across them inside.

Mackenzie stopped, not sure what was expected of him; the muzzle of the Magnum dug into his back. "Keep going."

"Where?"

"Back of the truck."

The chill in the thin early air came through his tunic and made him shiver involuntarily. Duggai mistook the meaning of it. "You going to be a lot more scared after a while, Captain."

Mackenzie wanted it to be over with, whatever it was Duggai had in store for him. But Duggai was right: he was afraid. *I'm damn well terrified*, he admitted to himself.

He watched the big Navajo dig keys out of his pocket and run through three of them until he found the one that unlocked the back door of the camper. Duggai swung it open and gestured.

With his hands wired behind him he had to make three tries before he was able to get up into the camper without losing his balance and falling back. He stepped up on the pickup's rear bumper and stooped to go inside.

"Sit down there on the bunk."

It was a bare mattress in a frame against the alumi-

32

num sidewall. On the opposite wall were a compact bottled-gas stove and a tiny flap-table hinged down flat against the wall; there were booth seats on either side of the lowered table. The seats doubled as storage compartments. Camping gear was lashed down on top of them: blankets, a Coleman lantern, five-gallon water drums, canvas sacks that probably contained provisions. Overhead were narrow lockers. A long weapon case was suspended from cleats in the ceiling; probably a hunting rifle with a scope, hung up there out of the way so that it wouldn't bang against anything that would knock the sights off center. Forward in the cramped space above the cab a child-size bunk lay crosswise near the ceiling; this too was piled with lashed-down objects and sacks. There was a water tank in the back corner to which a shower head could be screwed by way of a fitting outside the truck. The windows were small—one on each side, one in the back door—and he saw that the curtains had been tied securely across them.

Duggai had a short piece of heavy rope coiled into a noose. Mackenzie hadn't seen him pick it up. "Raise your feet off the floor."

He lifted his feet and Duggai flipped the noose under them, adjusting it and gesturing. Mackenzie dropped his feet back to the floor inside the noose. Duggai pulled it up tight, forcing him to cross his ankles; then Duggai swiftly ran the rope back under the cot and threaded it through something Mackenzie couldn't see—a cleat under the seat or a metal cot leg. Duggai pulled the knot up tight. Then he took the cased rifle down off the ceiling. In the opening behind him birds flitted among the sunlit treetops.

"I don't guess you'll get loose right away."

"Is there a point to all this?"

"You'll figure it out for yourself by and by. Now just in case we stop for gas or a red light or anything I'm going to put a gag in your mouth. I guess you know

33

enough not to strain against it. Man can choke to death on his vomit with a gag tied into his mouth."

"Thoughtful of you."

"I want you in real good shape, Captain." Duggai put a wad of cloth in his mouth and tied it in place with a length of precut clothesline. Mackenzie had to acknowledge that Duggai was well equipped for whatever his scheme was: everything—rope, cloth gag, clothesline—was at hand when Duggai needed it.

Finally Duggai backed out of the camper. "You take it easy now. Think about what I'm going to do to you."

The door slammed. Mackenzie heard the lock shoot home. The truck swayed with Duggai's weight when the big man climbed into the driver's seat; the door chunked shut; the starter meshed; the engine chugged. After a moment the truck began to move, slinging Mackenzie from side to side on the cot.

Something skidded across the floor. It drew his attention. At first he couldn't determine what it was; then he recognized it. A thin transparent plastic raincoat, folded into a tiny packet and held together by a snap-band of the same material. Camper's emergency equipment.

The truck lurched across the uneven ground in low gear, the four-wheel drive whining. Mackenzie braced himself hard back against the wall to keep from being thrown off his seat.

The journey began.

3

Jay Painter came out of his classroom feeling hoarse. He fended off an eager student who tried to buttonhole him and escaped down the back flight of concrete stairs and emerged into the July sun to make his way through the flowing student throng.

A pair of handsome girls drew his attention. The big one had golden skin, darker than her unbleached hair—a surfbaby, California goddess, caricature of healthy athletic perfection. He thought wonderingly, She doesn't get much change from six foot.

The girl's companion was stouter, her skin pale, almost transparent; she walked pitched backward against the swaying counterweight of her pregnant belly. Associations caromed around in his mind and made him remotely bitter. He crossed the Stanford lawns toward the faculty parking lot and saw Elderslee getting into his car—enormous and shabby and old, a gray eminence crowned by a violent eruption of tangled hair.

Elderslee waved a thick folder of student papers at him as if in accusation. "We're fast becoming a nation of illiterates. I've got a list of flunkees longer than your face. It's disgusting."

"The television generation," Jay Painter said. Elderslee had written two books that had become definitive psychology texts. He loved disputation, hated humanity and loathed students; he loved human beings.

"Can I have ten seconds?"

Elderslee looked at his watch. "Barely. I'm on my way to a consultation."

"They've roped me into testifying on Tuesday."

"The Boley woman?"

"Yes. Can you arrange to have one of the lecturers take over my classes?"

"Certainly." The old man unlocked his Volkswagen and tossed the file of papers inside. "Incidentally, what's your testimony going to be? What are your conclusions?"

"I think she's feigning it. I think she's perfectly competent to stand trial."

"Feigning madness is itself a sort of madness."

"Not the kind that matters in court," Jay Painter said.

"Some of the other boys found her convincing enough. Jack Feinberg's going to testify for the defense, you know."

"There are a few too many inconsistencies in her performance."

Elderslee wedged himself into the car. He rolled the window down before he pulled the door shut; he looked up at Jay and squinted in the sunlight. "Doesn't it ever begin to strike you as a silly childish game of pointmanship? The prosecution parades its battery of friendly expert witnesses and then the defense follows suit."

"It's what keeps our art from becoming a science. But it keeps it alive."

"It's why I gave up testifying in criminal cases. Legal definitions of insanity are the real insanities."

"I can't argue with that."

"I'll ask Van Alstyne to cover for you Tuesday." The old man put it in gear and Jay watched him drive away. The car spewed smoke from its tailpipe.

When he approached the station wagon he saw himself reflected in its back window—wavering image of a thin tall man thatched with dark hair, wearing a faint stoop and an aura of melancholy and what he fancied to be the look of confidence that came of knowing one's way around in the world. As he drew closer he bent down to study his face in reflection. He could find no sign of the uncertainties that bubbled within.

He wasn't sure whether to be heartened. Was it strength or weakness to wear a cloak of intact assurance over a body secretly racked with inadequacy?

I suppose everybody does it.

He got in the car.

Palo Alto was thick with traffic and he was ready for a drink by the time he got home. He parked the wagon in the driveway under the palm tree because the lawnmower was still scattered in dismantled chaos on the garage floor. Down the street a brown camper-body pickup truck was parked at the curb; he hadn't seen it before and wondered briefly to whom it belonged.

He heard faint splashings and went around the side of the house and found Shirley floating in the pool on her back, kicking her feet each time her legs started to sink.

"Hey you."

"Hey yourself." She stood up in the pool and waded to the edge; he gave her a hand up and kissed her carefully so as not to get his suit wet.

"I want a drink."

She said, "I haven't got the nerve to make myself another martini, but if I hope and pray . . ."

He found her empty glass by the aluminum chaise and went inside. Her papers were strewn across the kitchen table and he paused to glance down at one of them.

37

*. . . but everyone has their own way of dealing
with these problems. According to Dr. Herbert
Kalbstein the most unique aspect of the schizoid
syndrome is when the therapist first contacts the
patiant's undermind.*

The term paper was ever so neatly typed. The page was
covered brutally in the red scrawl of Shirley's pencil.
Everyone and *their* were circled and joined by a red
line: "Grammatical agreement." *Most unique* was circled: "Tautology." *Is when* was circled: "Illiterate."
Contacts was circled: "Not a verb." *Patiant's* was circled: "If you can't spell, use a dictionary."

He made the drinks and took them out to the pool.
Shirley was on the chaise removing her swimming cap
and shaking out her soft rosewood hair. Freshly washed,
it shimmered in the sun. "I shouldn't drink this damn
thing. I've still got a dozen papers to do."

"What's the point? Elderslee was just complaining
about our nation of illiterates. We all might as well hang
out shingles as remedial writing tutors. I saw your edit-
ing job in there."

"Don't get me started on that again."

He stood hipshot with his feet slightly apart, jingling
keys in his trouser pocket, regarding her white bikini.
"You're very seductive in that outfit."

"I know."

"I'm feeling vaguely shitty."

"Why?"

"General malaise. I must be regressing to sophomor-
ics. The 'what-does-it-all-matter' phase. Like some idiot
writing rancid poems in search of the meaning of it all."

"At SFC we call that the professorial tenure syndrome."

She taught at San Francisco College because the uni-
versities had regulations against husband and wife serv-

ing as tenured professors on the same faculty. Privately he felt it was a wise regulation.

"I told Elderslee I'm testifying against Mrs. Boley. He delivered himself of the usual harangue. For some reason I listened this time. And you know he's got a point—a toss of the coin and I could just as easily be testifying for the other side."

"So?"

"The rest of the woman's life could hang on my whim. Maybe I chose to disbelieve her because I had something sour for breakfast. She could be committed on my error. I worry about it. . . . Did you hear, Calvin Duggai broke out?"

"Come on, Jay, nobody expects omniscience—all they want is our best judgment." She downed the last of the drink and stood up. "Getting chilly out here." Then, turning, she said in a musing voice. "Yes, I heard about Duggai. Maybe that's why I feel cold. I hope they catch him quickly."

In the house he stripped off his jacket and tie and watched her get into slacks and an old blouse. The swim had left her tight in her skin.

She gave him a sudden look. "Do you want to?"

"Later."

She buttoned the blouse. "Should we have wine with dinner?"

"Sure."

She went out of the room ahead of him and he followed her toward the living room. He banged into her when she stopped abruptly.

He looked over her shoulder.

In the center of the room loomed Calvin Duggai, his eyes cold as death.

Sight of the man stunned Jay to silence. Shirley's shoulders lifted defensively. She backed into him; he gripped her arms.

39

Duggai stood absolutely still for such a long time that his very motionlessness became menacing. It was a while before Jay noticed the huge revolver in Duggai's fist.

The silence nearly cracked his nerves before Duggai spoke.

"Come over here."

The chilly precision of the Navajo's voice was a terrifying thing.

4

Mackenzie's mouth was painfully dry and he was having trouble breathing with the rag stuffed against his tongue. His hands behind him felt heavy and dead; he could picture them thickened and darkened with blood. In fact he knew the wires were not that tight but everything was cause for terror and he was sensitive to every nuance of pain in his cramped bruised body.

He heard the key in the lock and soon the door swung open and admitted light into the camper from a streetlamp fifty feet distant. He expected Duggai's silhouette; he was taken by surprise when three shapes appeared, one of them a woman.

Then he recognized them.

At first they didn't see him in the shadows. Then as Jay Painter climbed awkwardly inside, his hands wired behind him, Mackenzie saw his eyes change with recognition.

Jay stopped bolt still for a moment. Duggai prodded him.

Their faces were half masked by clothesline gags. Duggai's scheme left no possibility of outcry or rebellion. Duggai wigwagged the Magnum and Jay obediently sat beside Mackenzie on the cot. After the initial contact Jay refused to look at him again; he averted his head. Duggai performed his noose-on-the-floor trick to prevent being kicked while tying Jay's feet. Then he shoved Shirley inside. She tripped and fell past Mackenzie against the provisions on the bench seat. Bent nearly double under the low roof, Duggai fastened Mackenzie's hands to a metal support behind him and wired Jay's hands to the adjacent support. It was to prevent them from untying one another's hands.

Duggai dragged Shirley to the back of the truck and sat her down roughly beside Jay and tied her up in the same way. It put Jay in the middle.

Duggai went. When the door slammed it took the light with it; only a vague illumination penetrated the checkerboard curtains. It was enough to see Jay's silhouette.

He felt it when Duggai climbed into the driver's seat. The engine started. Mackenzie saw a refracted red glow in the rear window when the taillight came on. The shift went into gear. He touched Jay with an elbow, leaning back at the same time, trying to tell Jay that he should brace himself. Jay didn't understand the message; he sat stiffly upright exuding anger and indignity and fear until the truck lurched away from the curb—Duggai was not a smooth driver. It caught Jay off balance and he nearly went off the seat. After that he leaned hard back against the wall and Mackenzie saw him hold his elbow out protectively in front of Shirley.

It was an eerie time. The three of them sat side by side in silent darkness in a tangle of unspoken emotions. Memories grenaded into Mackenzie's mind so powerfully they all but obliterated the agonies of the present moment. He was drawn back into recriminative bitterness: the mingled sordid complex relationships of the past.

He imagined he felt waves of similar feeling coming off his companions.

The truck pitched through back streets. It kept stopping and starting up again; he knew it could be no thor-

42

oughfare. Possibly Duggai had a road map on the seat beside him and was avoiding main-traveled highways because he feared roadblocks.

It had been easy enough during the morning to follow the truck's progress even though his imprisonment in the curtained camper had rendered him effectively blind. There'd been no mistaking it when the truck had gone out onto the blacktop county road, or when it had dropped through the foothills and gone onto the freeway. But at that point he'd lost his sense of bearings; he'd been uncertain whether they were traveling east or west until now. This of course had to be Palo Alto because that was where Jay and Shirley lived. He remembered their white stucco house, the red tile roof, the swimming pool, the sliding glass doors to the crisp modern living room.

The truck growled slowly through the streets: not hurrying. Hurrying might have attracted the attention of a prowling police car.

The pickup turned a corner, pressing Mackenzie back against the wall. He heard the folded transparent plastic raincoat skid lightly across the floor; he even felt it, light as it was, when it struck the side of his shoe. For some perverse reason he lifted his foot and stamped down on the little bundle, pinning it under the sole of his shoe. It was a bit softer than the truck floor. He held it there with the weight of his foot.

Mackenzie had a clear idea where Duggai would stop next. There had been four psychiatric witnesses at Duggai's trial.

5

Earle Dana watched himself on television, observing the performance critically.

He had switched off the lights in the apartment and he sat in the armchair facing the color set.

The interview had been taped yesterday morning. Certain things about the televised image disturbed him. The brown slacks and pale yellow turtleneck looked proper for the tone of casual informality he'd intended to set but the turtleneck betrayed his paunch. His pale hair, cropped close to the skull like fuzz on a tennis ball, gave him the look of a man of forty-five trying to emulate a collegian. I must take off weight and let the hair grow out a bit, he told himself.

The face was not quite as it looked in his shaving mirror each morning. He was distressed. The mouth had a way of folding primly at the conclusion of each statement. At other times as he listened to the interviewer's questions the mouth seemed too small and as rigid as a coin slot. He had extraordinarily thin lips.

He did not listen to the dialogue; he remembered clearly what had been asked and answered; he had comported himself well. But television was not a vehicle for words. He watched the mobile face as though he were a patient being counseled: would I have confidence in this practitioner?

He decided that he probably would. But there was something about that mouth that troubled him.

When the program ended he switched on the light above his chair, extinguished the television set and walked back into the bathroom. He faced the mirror and spoke loudly to himself and watched his mouth move: he tried to do it without punctuating each phrase with that prim grimace.

Quickly he realized that it was going to be a very hard habit to break.

A shadow loomed behind him in the mirror.

My dear sweet God. *Duggai!*

6

There wasn't room for a fourth on the bunk. Mackenzie watched Duggai bundle the trembling Dana into the truck and heard the swift intake of Shirley Painter's breath. Beside him Jay Painter had gone absolutely still and was watching Duggai surreptitiously out of the corners of his vision—as one might watch a poisonous reptile poised above one's chest.

Now he'll be having his fun with us, Mackenzie thought; bleakly he wondered just what form it would take.

Earle Dana sat down on the floor at Duggai's bidding. Mackenzie watched their captor pull the noose tight around Dana's ankles. Dana's wrists like the others' were wired behind his back and now Duggai fastened them to a leg of the cookstove; the gag in his mouth and the clothesline were identical to theirs.

San Jose, Mackenzie thought. Now where?

The truck started up and he heard Earle Dana's sudden grunt; then there was an awkward scrabbling as Earle moved around trying to wedge himself into some position in which he wouldn't get battered.

Mackenzie was thinking: If Duggai only knew—confining the four of us together is punishment enough. . . .

Somewhere in the timeless run of the night the truck stopped and Duggai let them out one at a time, freeing their mouths, feeding them sandwiches, giving them a little water to drink, allowing them two minutes to relieve themselves. It was a roadside rest area—a back road deserted in the starlight, California hills heavy on the horizons. Mackenzie found it impossible to guess their location.

Within a quarter of an hour they were on their way again, four people confined in blind fear. Jay Painter kept banging against Mackenzie's shoulder as the truck pitched them around. Each time Jay would draw away quickly as if he were trying to avoid a contaminating contact. In his pain Mackenzie almost smiled.

The skill with which Duggai had worked it all out impressed him. Clearly Duggai had a very specific destination in mind for them. He could have told them where he was taking them; it would have made no difference to their helplessness. But by keeping them ignorant he was fueling their terrors. His refusal to explain was more hideously sinister than any specified threat.

The gags on their mouths, the tying of hands and feet, the closing of curtains in the camper—these were matters of elementary security, to be sure, but they were also instruments of psychic torment. It was not accident; it was part of a scheme that had been honed down to the least factor. Incarcerate four surprised people in darkness, bind them painfully, prevent them from communicating with one another—and you had gone a good part of the way toward driving them into madness.

He heard the sighing sobs of Earle Dana's hysteria; Earle was flinging himself about in a panic-stricken effort to get loose. Now and then some part of him would carom off Mackenzie's knee.

Finally in half-strangled exhaustion Earle gave it up. Mackenzie heard beside him Jay Painter's disgruntled snort.

Daylight penetrated the curtains. He was able to see their faces, distorted by the ropes and gags. Shirley watched him for a time; he couldn't make out her expression and when Jay realized she was locking glances with Mackenzie he scowled at her and Shirley looked away. On the floor at Mackenzie's feet Earle seemed only half conscious. There was a dried trickle of blood on his upper lip.

The truck was going at a good clip up a smooth highway; the tires howled. As the morning advanced the sun made an oven of the aluminum camper body. Sweat formed on Mackenzie's face, under his arms, in his crotch. His eyes were gritty.

He tried to occupy himself with vague mental exercises. Nothing did much good; the discomfort was too acute. He was sure his hands were damaged by now—except for a very brief unstrapping eight hours ago they had been wired together continuously nearly three times the clock around.

Thoughts of the dog crossed his mind.

The truck went off the interstate once; he guessed it to be around noon. The camper stopped. He heard the clank of a filler-hose nozzle going into the fuel funnel. Mackenzie desperately bounced up and down, jiggling the camper, until Duggai's voice growled at him through the aluminum: "Shut up in there. Ain't nobody can see it." So it was a self-service pump.

Finally they were moving again. The heat was intense. His clothing became sodden with sweat. The enclosed airless cabin began to stink; he worried about carbon monoxide poisoning but there was nothing they could do about it. Actually there were probably cracks in the camper's construction; concerned, he felt currents of air on his ankles; it was only the heat that made it seem sucked empty of oxygen.

His mind performed an idle calculation. Duggai had come down off the Sierra with Mackenzie alone in the

48

camper yesterday morning and they had stopped once to fuel the tank, probably at eleven o'clock or so. Then they had driven perhaps two and a half hours and stopped in Palo Alto. Most of that section of the drive had been on a freeway: assume a hundred miles.

Then they had waited through the afternoon and the waning evening. An hour or so before dark Duggai had left the truck parked on the street. During the ensuing hour Mackenzie had torn his wrists trying to free himself but had got nowhere against his shackles. Some time after dark Duggai had returned with the Painters and put them in the truck. Then they'd ridden for an hour or an hour and a half, a good part of it on freeways again, down to San Jose to collect Earle Dana. That hadn't taken long—Duggai had left the truck for no more than fifteen minutes and returned with the fourth prisoner.

They'd left San Jose not later than half past ten at night. They'd gone slowly for the next two hours or so—traveling back streets and country roads from the feel of it. Some time after midnight they'd entered a freeway; no telling which one—California was scarred everywhere with them.

And for the past twelve hours Duggai had been driving steadily except for the brief interval when he'd let them out of the truck one at a time.

Even assuming they'd been traveling no faster than fifty miles an hour on the freeways it meant Duggai had put at least 750 miles on the truck since he'd last refueled.

A three-quarter-ton truck of this kind couldn't make better than eighteen or twenty miles to the gallon. It would need a forty-gallon tank to have gone that long without refilling. Mackenzie hadn't heard of any pickup truck with a tank bigger than twenty-five gallons' capacity.

There must be a reserve tank, something added to the

truck's normal capacity. Mackenzie had known a few ranchers who'd had reserve tanks installed under the passenger seats of their pickups. It made the vehicle into a death trap if there were an accident—the driver and his passengers rode directly on top of the added fuel—but it extended the range of the truck to as much as a thousand miles.

It meant Duggai could be taking them anywhere.

It was after dark when the truck left the freeway. Mackenzie had been asleep; the lurching brought him awake. Against his shoulder Jay Painter's weight was tipped uncaringly; Jay was snoring softly against his gag; in his sleep his hatred had dissipated and he was leaning against Mackenzie as a welcome pillow. Mackenzie didn't wake him. Jay was welcome to his resentment but there'd be little point compounding it now.

Mackenzie heard the roar of a souped-up car. Shortly afterward the truck eased to a stop, waited briefly and started moving again. Probably a traffic light: they were in a town. He heard more traffic intermittently. Streetlights briefly lit up the curtains and then faded behind.

Then they were out in empty darkness running along an uneven paved surface; no longer a freeway but neither was it an urban street. A country road most likely; and from its lack of bends it could be in the desert.

He drowsed again, fighting his body's agonies, but he was aware of it when the truck left the paved surface and went bucking across the expressively musical grid of a cattle-guard. For a crazy moment he wondered if they'd gone full circle and returned to the Sierras.

It was a dirt road with a good graded surface. The choking stink of fine alkali dust filled the compartment but the truck ran along at a good clip without jouncing much.

Beside him Jay came awake with a start and recoiled

away from him. Mackenzie heard the sudden swift rush of Jay's fast breathing when recollection brought terror back into his consciousness.

At his feet Earle Dana stirred and groaned. Mackenzie kept his raw eyes shut and tried to ignore everything: there was nothing to do but wait stoically for this interval to pass; if he were still alive at the end of the journey he would think about things then.

Somewhere in the midst of the night Duggai stopped the truck and let them out again one by one. When it was Mackenzie's turn he stood abaft the tailgate rubbing his wrists gingerly and watching Duggai.

Duggai indicated the canteen with his revolver and stepped back two paces. Mackenzie had trouble lifting the canteen: there was no strength at all in his hands. Finally by using his elbows to prop it he got it to his lips and drank slowly, forcing himself not to gorge. The tissues of his mouth had been eroded by the gag and the water stung ferociously as he ingested it.

Duggai watched him relieve himself at the side of the road. Mackenzie took the opportunity to survey the horizons. It was desert country—rocks and brush, the occasional spindle tracery of cactus. They were ringed by barren hills and mountains. More likely Arizona or Utah than California.

Duggai fed him a sandwich and another drink, then did his hands up again and replaced the gag. This time Mackenzie knew it was a method of torment rather than security; in this open empty wilderness there was no practical reason to keep the prisoners gagged. Duggai shoved him back into the truck and hauled Earle Dana out, the last of them. When the gag was removed from Earle's mouth Mackenzie heard him try to speak; nothing came out but a dry wheezing cackle.

Finally Earle was back in place on the metal floor and the truck was moving again. Perhaps, Mackenzie

51

thought, perhaps I have died and am in Hell because surely this is what Hell is all about.

Either the road petered out or Duggai left it deliberately; in either case the effect was the same—the ride became more violent, the truck bucked and pitched at decreasing road speed until after a while it was lurching along at a walking pace, the transmission singing in low gear. When the pitch bent uphill Mackenzie felt and heard the slap and whine of the four-wheel engage. Jay Painter was flung against him more frequently now and several times Mackenzie couldn't prevent the back of his head from rapping the metal wall. Quite evidently Duggai was picking a path across rock-strewn country—certainly this was no road—and Mackenzie was certain Duggai was using starlight alone to see by; there wasn't the faint reflection of red taillights at the back window that he'd grown used to.

It went on without relief and almost without end: there had never been a longer night in Mackenzie's experience. But the mind's instinct for self-protection cloaked him in a kind of withdrawn indifference so that experience and pain were distanced: he was not unaware of them but his awareness was abstract, dreamlike. Partly he knew it was the effect of trauma to the psyche: a kind of medical shock. Partly it was the cumulative result of thirst and hunger and fatigue and terror. Abruptly for the first time he was able to comprehend the bovine indifference of the Jews who had let themselves be marched into the gas ovens. Protective withdrawal.

They were going over mountains of substantial proportion; he guessed that much from the strain of the truck's engine and the length of time during which they climbed. Then there was an even more painful hour or more of downslope maneuvering; Duggai was using the gears and perhaps occasionally the handbrake but never once did Mackenzie see the flash of the brakelights.

Abruptly and for no accountable reason he believed he saw the end intention of Duggai's plan.

If he was correct then this was not Hell; this was mere Purgatory on a route charted toward Hell by the brown Charon at the wheel of the pickup.

The truck stopped; it was still dark; Mackenzie was wide awake now, hollow-hearted with anticipatory fear. He felt the truck relax on its springs when Duggai stepped out. The rear door opened. Duggai was a heavy silhouette against the night. Fragments of starlight glinted briefly on the barrel of the Magnum. Duggai climbed up into the camper bed and untied their feet quickly—almost carelessly because he knew no one had the strength or circulation to kick him.

Having untied all their feet Duggai backed out and jumped down and took Shirley by the arm because she was closest to him. Mackenzie saw her feet give way under her when she tried to get up. Duggai dragged her out bodily by the shoulder; she fell off the tailgate and Mackenzie heard her muffled outcry.

His feet free, Mackenzie moved them experimentally. They had no feeling in them. His right foot slid to one side and he remembered the folded plastic raincoat. In the spiraling bleak chaos of his thoughts there was a pinprick of alertness to its potential importance.

Duggai was hauling Jay Painter off the bunk seat. Jay fell to his knees and crawled precariously toward the tailgate where Duggai reached up for his collar and dragged him out face down; Jay was rolling to one side when he fell out of Mackenzie's sight and there was a terrible loud thud when he hit the ground but Mackenzie suspected he had been able to take the fall on his shoulder rather than his face.

Earle Dana lay with his feet toward Duggai and Duggai simply took him by one ankle and dragged him sliding out of the truck.

Earle managed somehow to explode an angry roar around the gag in his mouth: Mackenzie saw him lash back with his free leg and strike out, kicking at Duggai with his heel.

Duggai whipped the Magnum down and Mackenzie heard it plainly, sickeningly, when the heavy revolver hit Earle's shin. There was no mistaking the crack of sound: it had broken Earle's shinbone.

Duggai heaved Earle bodily out of the truck and no gag could have silenced the shriek of pain.

It was a scream that Mackenzie used to cover the scrape of his own movement. Sliding his foot quickly toward the tailgate he kicked clumsily at the floor. His purpose was to hurl the plastic raincoat out of the truck. It was a small thing of no weight; he saw it flicker as it sailed out over the bumper of the pickup but he was sure Duggai hadn't noticed it—Duggai was stooped in rage above Earle, ready to strike again with his bludgeon.

Mackenzie eased his way along the seat toward the back. When Duggai grabbed his bicep he was ready for it and let himself go slack; Duggai yanked him out of the truck and Mackenzie took the fall harmlessly on his hip and shoulder.

The folded rectangle of plastic lay just beneath the left taillight. Starlight winked off its surface.

Duggai went back to examine Earle Dana. It was evident Earle had lost consciousness—shock, nothing more; he hadn't been hit on the head. Duggai was doing something with his hands behind Earle's back. After a moment Mackenzie realized what it was: Duggai was removing the wire manacles from Earle's hands.

The wire clattered when Duggai threw it into the back of the truck. Then Duggai put his Magnum away in his belt, snugging it down. He went into a pocket and

Mackenzie, sitting up slowly, watched him unfold a pocketknife.

Duggai came forward hefting the blade. "Belly down, Captain."

Mackenzie obeyed. His own awkwardness infuriated him.

He was expecting Duggai to remove the wire from his wrists or the gag from his mouth; he froze in twanging panic when he felt the cold prick of the knife against his spine.

"I wouldn't move," Duggai said.

Then there was a tugging, a snagging sound of rending cloth—and suddenly Duggai was tearing the clothes off him. In horrified paralysis Mackenzie lay perfectly still while the knife ravaged his clothing and Duggai pulled shreds of cloth away from his flesh. He felt the sharp blade tug his belt tight and saw its way outward through the leather until the belt parted; then the blade was whisking down his pant legs from waistline to ankles; the sleeves were parted like halved ripe melons and fell away from his arms; and nothing that had gone before was half so icily terrifying as the whisper of the keen blade in fast strokes within millimeters of his flesh.

The boot took him completely by surprise, snapping perfunctorily into his ribs: not a brutal blow, not hard enough to damage him—a tap for attention.

"Roll over, Captain. Roll off the rags."

He rolled onto his back and lay stark naked in the night, his hands still wired behind him, his mouth still gagged. The hulking silhouette above him moved: Duggai picked up the shreds of Mackenzie's clothes and threw them into the camper.

Mackenzie lay stunned with disbelief and watched Duggai move toward Shirley Painter. Starlight raced along the knife blade.

Duggai destroyed their clothes methodically. He took their wristwatches and rings and shoes and pulled their socks off. He threw everything into the truck. Then he dragged them naked, one by one, about twenty feet from the truck. Mackenzie's hands were still wired together and took a great deal of punishment as Duggai dragged him across the rocky ground by one foot.

Matter-of-fact and without much show of feeling Duggai stood above them. He folded the knife and put it away in his pocket and walked back to the truck. Mackenzie heard the door open; he didn't hear it shut. A moment later Duggai came in sight unzipping the long rifle case. He tossed the case into the truck and walked toward them working the bolt of the rifle. It was a big-game weapon with a large telescope screwed on top of it.

Duggai balanced the rifle in his left hand while he used his right hand to untwist the wire that bound Mackenzie's hands together. Duggai left him and crouched by Shirley. Mackenzie rolled up on one elbow and gently rubbed his wrists. His hands had no feeling in them.

Duggai removed the wire from Shirley's wrists and then from Jay's; he stepped back and leveled the rifle.

Mackenzie kept trying to clear his throat.

At last Duggai spoke. "Now maybe you find out how much of a crime it is. Maybe you find out how crazy you got to be to want to live. I tell you one thing—whatever happens to you out here ain't half as bad as what they do to a man in them hospitals. You remember this—at least I'm gonna let you die in dignity. But I'm gonna watch it happen."

Mackenzie saw Jay try to speak. Nothing came out of his mouth.

Duggai's rifle pivoted toward Mackenzie and he watched it bleakly. "You're half Innun. I lived out there that time because I was Innun. Maybe you can live a while too. If you make it I'll be waiting for you, Captain."

It was all Duggai had to say. He walked back to the

pickup. Mackenzie saw him toss the twisted pieces of wire inside and close the back of the pickup. Then Duggai got behind the wheel and the camper lurched away. It was still running without lights and the night quickly absorbed it. Sound carried back for a while but then that was gone too.

A low wind soughed in Mackenzie's ears; there was no other sound.

He was thinking, by two in the afternoon it'll be a hundred and thirty degrees out here.

7

For an endless lethargic time Mackenzie sat shifting his naked buttocks on the hard ground and listening to the dwindling growl and rattle of the truck until finally the night absorbed it and there was nothing.

He looked slowly at the others.

Jay Painter was sitting up. A muscle worked at the back of his jaw. His thin body was a patchwork of tangled hair.

A gust of dry air spun Shirley's long hair around her face. She combed it away with her fingers and tossed it back with a shake of her head, an unconsciously impatient gesture. She was watching the darkness where the truck had disappeared.

Earle Dana writhed slowly, chrysalis-like, not really conscious.

Mackenzie slowly picked his way across the earth. Sharp stones made him hobble. He crouched by Earle. The man's face, drawn with pain, was swollen on the left cheek where he'd fallen. The eye was puffy and closed, the flesh sickly dark. The leg—well, at least it wasn't a compound fracture. No bone showed.

Jay Painter began to cough. When the coughing subsided the silence became so intense that Mackenzie heard the crack of his own knee joint as he stirred. He stood up, feeling lances of pain here and there.

Shirley spoke, her voice husky and cracked, hardly a voice at all. "He broke his leg."

"I know." Speaking the words made him cough.

Jay stared out into the night, brows lowered as if he were peering into strong light: with his head down and his eyes narrowed. Refusing to look at any of them. In a strange way it amused Mackenzie: they sat in deadly peril and they were reluctant to look directly at one another because of the embarrassment of nakedness. He fought down the impulse to laugh because if he began it could tip him over the edge of hysteria.

He coughed again; he felt along the ground and found a pebble. When he straightened up he put the pebble in his mouth and sucked on it in an attempt to get the saliva flowing. He kept rolling it around with his tongue.

Shirley said, "Shouldn't we make a splint?"

Jay's head came up. "What's the use?" The painful grating of his voice set Mackenzie's teeth on edge. Jay went into a fit of coughing, recovered and finally spoke again: "What does he want from us?"

"I guess he wants us dead," Mackenzie said. He peered at the landscape, trying to decipher the dark terrain. Scrub sloped up along a series of eroded cuts toward higher ground. There was scattered vegetation: greasewood, catclaw, tufts of brittle grass, cactus in various configurations. Each bit of growth stood in lonely isolation, ten or thirty feet from its neighbors. For the most part the ground was hardpan and stones, cracked clay, alkali.

"Sam." Jay Painter's voice hit him like the flat of a hand. He turned.

Little pale patches of hate glowed around Jay's nostrils. "You know a little about the desert, right? How long have we got?"

"I don't know, Jay. I guess it depends."

"That's a crock." Jay's chin crept forward, querulous

like an old man's. Naked he looked a bit spavined. His torso was long and too narrow—like that of a fast-growing teenager who hadn't filled out yet. Wiry hairs coiled on his shoulders and chest and belly and legs.

Mackenzie thought, *We've got to keep control*. He moved closer to Jay because it was more difficult to appear calm when you had to raise your voice across a distance. Fragments of stone chewed at his soles. "We're not carrion yet," he said. "Take it easy."

Jay pushed a boyish lock of hair back from his eyes. He stared at his wife for a moment. Mackenzie followed the line of Jay's glance. Shirley was brooding toward the earth ten feet ahead of her: she was standing upright now, fists clenched at her sides. Mackenzie thought how many times he'd coveted that body. Even now—cutting right through his terror—she had the power to excite him; he looked away, ashamed.

Jay said, "How long can we last? Come on, Sam, what's the point of lying? Twenty-four hours? Forty-eight?"

Mackenzie's scalp contracted. In a bitter part of him he felt contempt for Jay's despair. He regarded the desert disdainfully until Jay stumbled to his feet hefting a small rock in his fist.

Mackenzie stepped back. "Easy. Easy. Gentle down, Jay, this may not be your last chance to die."

Shirley's voice struck into it, small and crisp like a spark falling into gunpowder. "Put it down. You look ridiculous."

Jay's face crumpled. He dropped the stone. Shirley was down on her knees now; she pressed her hands to her temples.

Mackenzie turned away. For a moment he thought perhaps it was because he saw himself reflected too closely in Jay's weakness. Then he realized that was no cause for shame. They were all human.

Shirley kept looking at him—staring, he was sure, at

60

his gnarled stomach muscles. After a moment her fiery eyes shifted toward her husband's narrow caved-in body, hunched as he sat with his arms wrapped around his knees, genitals dragging ludicrously. He had sat down like that; now he stood up again. Every flicker of emotion was mirrored transparently on his long face. Something—an anguish of memory?—drove him striding away in inarticulate rage until he stamped on a sharp edge and fell, breaking the fall with the flat of a hand, sitting down hard, turning his head balefully to stare over his shoulder at Mackenzie and Shirley. "Why did he do this to us?"

Mackenzie said, "We've always got reasons for killing each other, haven't we?"

Shirley went from her knees back onto her buttocks and sat up in unintentional imitation of Jay's previous pose: she folded her arms around her upraised knees until her breasts flattened against her thighs. She had a long supple body, a fine waist, fashion-model legs. "Four years, five—how long, now? He must have been nursing a fixation about us. It's long enough for casual hate to turn into an obsession." She glanced at Jay— wry. "At least we know we didn't make a mistake calling for his commitment. He's proving his insanity right now."

Jay was offended. "Insanity's a legal term. It means nothing. You know better." He was barking at her unreasonably.

"Well then, shall we sit and discuss him clinically?"

Mackenzie said, "I don't think we need to worry about his motives. We need to worry about his intentions. He intends to murder us—or let the desert do it for him, if you want it spelled out. He said he'd be watching and waiting. It's a Navajo torture—all wrapped up in medicine and witchcraft and I guess some twisted ideas of the heritage that he's clung to in distorted ways. His uncle was a shaman, remember?

61

He's got his head full of bits and pieces of the old medicine. Exorcising his own demons by destroying our ours. It's too mystical to make psychiatric sense. What's the use talking about it? He put us here to die. That's what we need to worry about."

Shirley said, "All right, he wants us to die. It doesn't mean we have to accommodate him."

Jay laughed—a sour noise of bile. "Looks to me like he hasn't left us a whole lot of choice."

Mackenzie half heard them. Their voices trailed off and they were both looking at him, waiting for his verdict, putting the responsibility on him: in a way they trusted him. And, in a way, he resented their trust. He doubted he could reward it.

His words tried to plot the erratic course along which his thoughts moved. "We left the road about six hours ago, I guess. We could be fifty, a hundred miles from the nearest highway."

Jay kept rubbing his thumb across the pads of his fingers. "So?"

"I guess it doesn't matter. All it means is we can't walk out of here."

Shirley said, "He wouldn't let us anyway."

Jay nodded his head up and down like a puppet's. "It's hopeless. That's what I've been saying. What's the use of talking about it?" He threw his head back. "Nice and cool now. Too cold, really. The sun's going to come up and then we'll just curl up like strips of frying bacon. Anybody know any prayers? Our Father Who art in Heaven, hallowed be Thy name. . . ."

Jay's voice droned on.

Shirley began silently to weep; her shoulders shook. Mackenzie felt powerless to move. He listened to Jay: ". . . Thy will be done . . ."

Silence ran on for a bit afterwards and then with a dry chuckle Jay said, "Dust to dust."

Shirley shouted at him. "Shut up. You're no help."

"Yes, my love."

"Oh Jay, I'm sorry."

"Yeah. So am I."

Then—it seemed belated to Mackenzie—Jay hobbled over to her and sat with her and they cradled each other. Mackenzie looked away, his throat hollow, stricken by loneliness. At least they had comfort in each other. Mackenzie thought, I was happy to live alone but how terrible to die alone.

That was the ultimate fear and it kindled inside him a rage that took fire and seared its way into his mind until he bolted to his feet. His voice emerged, constricted, thin against the faint dry wind: "Barefoot creatures of the Stone Age. That's what he's reduced us to." He filled his chest, arched his back, defied the sky. "Well God damn it they survived in the Stone Age."

Jay heard him and muttered a reply: "In a desert like this?"

"What?"

"Sam, for God's sake we don't even know where we are. We don't know if we're in Nevada or Utah or Mexico or Arizona or what."

"We can find out where the hell we are. It's hardly the pressing problem at the moment."

"All right. I stand corrected. If it's any comfort to you."

"We can live," Mackenzie roared. "If we want to. We can."

Jay averted his face. "Sure. For a few hours. A day maybe. How much *time* have we got?" His voice was muffled against Shirley's shoulder. "False hopes. You're a sadistic bastard, Sam Mackenzie."

Shirley said, "At least listen to him. Don't you want to know?"

"No," Jay said. "Yes."

"We can live."

Because Mackenzie said it quietly his words had force.

He wished he believed them himself.

"By ten o'clock if you lie naked in this sun you'll fry."

Jay straightened. "There's bushes all around. Creosote, whatever. There's shade."

"Not enough to do any good. One day and we'd have third-degree burns."

"You're the Indian. You tell us."

Mackenzie drew a long breath deep into his chest. It shuddered going in; he made fists to conceal the tremor in his fingers. "I don't know why I should make much effort to help you if you don't want to listen to me." The words seemed inadequate, so lame he immediately regretted having said anything at all.

Jay brooded at him. "Tell us."

Mackenzie pretended to take his time as if thinking it out. His mind raced as if it were a motor that had been turned loose to freewheel: straining at such speed that it felt sure to burn itself out. Thoughts exploded one on top of the other. It was panic, he told himself, and panic was the one thing he had to push away: panic was the one thing he couldn't show them.

The infection of Jay's weakness kept unbalancing him. What's the point after all? We're naked in a waterless plain, nothing but scrub and rocks and hardpan, no water in forty or a hundred miles; by afternoon it'll be an oven and two days from now we'll be clean white bones. . . .

A chill ravaged him. To cover it he stood straight up and turned a full circle as though absorbing information through his senses and coming to decisions.

Finally he had his voice under control. "First thing's to put priorities in order. One, counter the heat. Two, water. Three, take care of Earle's broken leg. Four,

64

food. There's a lot more but if we can't handle these four we'll never have time to worry about any of the others because we'll be dead. The thing to do is solve one problem at a time. Solve each problem and give ourselves time to solve the next one."

"He makes it sound so easy. Any child could do it."

"Any Navajo child probably could," Shirley said.

Mackenzie said, "Duggai could."

"Duggai had a truck," Jay said, "and he had his clothes on. And you're not an Indian the way Duggai's an Indian."

"*I can try,* at least."

Shirley said, "Sam spent summers on the reservation with his father when he was a boy."

Jay talked through his teeth: "Maybe—maybe, sure, but *Sam's* still forgetting one thing. *Sam's* forgetting how pointless it is. Seems to have slipped his mind that Calvin Duggai's waiting right out there with that elephant gun just in case we manage not to die of thirst or heat or snakebite or exposure. So what's the point—*Sam?*"

Shirley said, "You're really asking for it, Jay."

"Why shouldn't I go out now, standing up? At least I'd enjoy trying to beat his head in. It looks pretty attractive when I think about the alternatives. Shriveling in the sun waiting for the buzzards to eat my eyes. Or crawling out of here somehow after God knows how much suffering only to find Duggai standing there just this side of the water. Watch old Duggai pick us to pieces one bullet at a time until he gets tired of playing cat games and takes pity on us and finishes us off with a hive of ants or a scalping knife or whatever he's got in his twisted mind."

Mackenzie's temper bubbled. "It doesn't have to go according to Duggai's scenario. We don't have to play his game."

"Out here in this place without a stitch of clothes or a

drop of water—if we're not playing Duggai's game then whose the hell game are we playing?"

"Mine."

"What?"

He was faced away from them. His eyes were squeezed shut against the flood of fear and anger. He had to wait a bit before he could answer. But he needed the rage, needed to nurse it and encourage it because it could provoke him to survive.

"We'll settle up with Duggai. We'll do it our way, not his."

"And somehow that doesn't entail our scrabbling in this dirt in some misbegotten attempt to survive?"

"We'll scrabble," Mackenzie said. *"We'll survive."* His fingernails cut into his palms.

"That's exactly what Duggai wants."

"He wants to win," Mackenzie said. "He doesn't want to lose." He wiped his face and turned, looked at them. "In my game he loses."

"Mackenzie, all right—all right. What the hell is your game?"

"We start by solving one problem at a time. We dig."

"Dig what?"

"Our graves."

"Listen to him, Shirley, he's cracked."

"I'm listening to him."

Mackenzie said, "I'll keep you alive if I can. But it's my game now. We'll play it by my rules. I'm the captain of the team—I don't put decisions to a vote. Understood?"

It brought Jay halfway to his feet. "Just who do you think you—"

Mackenzie's voice climbed to an unreasonable pitch: he fought it down. "I'm the one who's going to keep you *alive.*"

He saw Jay's teeth: a rictus grimace or a bitter smile; he couldn't tell which.

"From this point on talk only when you have to. Talking dries the tissues, makes you thirsty."

He glanced at the sky. "We've got maybe half an hour to first light, less than an hour to sunrise, less than four hours before it's too hot to move. That's our deadline. We've got to be dug in by four hours from now."

"Dug in." Jay parroted it hollowly as if trying to absorb the information through an opaque screen.

"The objective is to keep cool and keep quiet through the heat of the day. We've got to conserve body fluids. We'll dig pits. Three feet deep. A trench for each of us—running from east to west."

He waited for protest. Shirley only met his stare and in the poor light he couldn't make out her expression. Jay picked at a toenail. Mackenzie said, "If it's aligned due east and west the sun will never reach the bottom of the trench. We'll be in shade all day long. Avoid sunburn and heat dehydration. Three feet below ground level the temperature can remain as much as sixty degrees cooler than it is on the surface."

"Who told you all this?"

He'd read it somewhere in a book. He didn't admit it. "It's something all Navajo daddies teach their children before puberty."

"What do we use for tools?"

"Rocks. Sticks. Your hands."

"Straight down? This stuff's like concrete."

"Dig." Mackenzie said it without force.

"Why not start walking? We could head for the mountains. If we've got four hours surely we can find good shade. A cliff facing north or a clump of trees or something. . . ."

"How far could you walk on bare feet, Jay? How much fluid have you got in your body that you could afford to burn up getting there? That's what kills faster than anything else in this desert."

"And digging like beavers won't burn it up?"

67

"Dig slowly. Don't work up a sweat." Mackenzie's hand described an impatient arc. "Which way would you walk? Forget it. It's better to dig here—those mountains are solid rock."

Jay studied him, full of resistance. "How do we know which way to align the trenches?"

Mackenzie found the Dipper, traced it toward Polaris. "That's the North Star. Guide on that."

"What about Earle?"

"We dig four trenches."

"Why not one long one?"

"Body heat. And it's bad enough to breathe the stink of your own sweat. . . ." He couldn't face lying in the same hole with the rest of them.

There was a beat of silence. Jay said, "All right. We'll dig. But what about water?"

"One thing at a time."

8

While they still had the stars for a guide they scratched outlines in the earth. Mackenzie found an oblong rock that came to something like a point. He gave it to Shirley and hunted for more; finally they began to dig.

The top layer crumbled easily and took them down three or four inches but after that it was rocks and clay; it was like trying to dig through an adobe wall. He had to force himself not to slam and whack away at it. He used the rock as a pickax, breaking up the surface and then carrying away the loosened clots with his hands.

"Make the pile on the south side of each trench. It'll help shade us."

Eight inches down he came on the face of a boulder and wanted to shriek out his frustration. He tried to dig around it but it seemed to have no end. He had to move ten feet away and start again.

The crumpled folds of the mountains that ringed the horizons began to turn blue with shadow. A drop of sweat dripped from his nose onto the back of his hand. He forced himself to relax, slow down, dig with less effort. He remembered a time when he had been lost in the mountains and happy to be lost: he'd had a backpack and a canteen of water and no place in particular to go.

The earnest task occupied his attention and freed him

69

from the obligation to think ahead. It took all his concentration to shape the trench. Keep the walls vertical. Dig carefully around each rock—some of them were the size of a man's head and weighed seventy-five pounds—and lift it out and place it on the rim of the dig to absorb and deflect the sun.

He worked slowly, on his knees, right hand steadily lifting and falling like the arm of a steam hammer. Break up a layer of clay and lift it out a cupped double-handful at a time. Pack it down on the rim. Lift another. He made rakes of his fingers.

But the thought of water came relentlessly into his mind. What good was it to postpone death a few hours if there were no solution to the second question?

There was a little cactus. Staghorn cholla mostly. No water in that; it was as spindly as rib bones. In the late afternoon when the heat waned they would have to make an expedition in search of fat varieties of cactus: the barrel, the jumper, even the prickly pear could be mashed to pulp for liquid. But he doubted there'd be enough to sustain them for more than a day before they'd cleared this area of moisture-bearing cactus: he doubted there was more than one clump in each quarter acre.

Underground water? No—not within reach of the surface; otherwise there'd have been deciduous trees. He tried to remember the signs: obviously a cottonwood or sycamore meant water close to the surface; but he'd seen none.

The light strengthened. He examined the country.

It was a surrealist landscape. Spotted scrub writhed on the bare tan-yellow plain. The ground was desolated by drought, naked and barren. A few miles away in any direction lilac hills undulated toward mountains that loomed in tilted tiers of gray and blue and cayenne red.

The most common growth he saw was creosote:

greasewood bushes with their leaves dark oily green. He remembered desert horseback trips, his father taking him out of Chinle for camping and hunting weekends. A horse wouldn't eat greasewood. It suggested poison.

Keep it in mind.

He saw tall spindly fans of ocotillo. Nothing there but solid dry stalks of brittle wood clothed in spines.

The little hat-sized clumps looked like sagebrush but they weren't. Saltbush, he recalled; you could tell by the yellowish-green color—it didn't have the pastel blue hue of sage.

Twenty yards down the slope he could make out a manzanita shrub by its gnarled red bark. More of them farther out along the desert. No help there either.

Catclaw everywhere: the weed of the desert. A bush in size and shape. No nourishment or moisture in it.

Grass in odd spotted clumps: sometimes a single blade of it, sometimes a bouquet. The tips had gone to tufted wheatlike seed pods. Yellow and dry.

Maguey—the century plant. Tall stalk, sunflower top. Blades around its base like a palm tree. The Mexicans made beer and liquor out of the maguey. Might get moisture by pulping it. Worth a try anyway. He saw six of them within walking distance.

He counted nine jumping-cholla clumps in a hundred-yard circle. There was one barrel cactus higher along the hill; it looked skinny—they only fattened after a heavy rain—but it was the nearest thing to a life-saving supply of water he could see within reach. That would be the first target.

The Senita would be next. It was an organ-pipe cactus only about two feet tall but fleshier than most varieties.

It meant they were definitely in Arizona; the Senita grew throughout northern Mexico but in the United States it was found only in Arizona near the border.

They weren't in Mexico; they'd neither crossed at a border station nor cut their way through a fence.

All the while he kept digging. The sun appeared.

A breeze, much hotter than before, raked him with its sinister caress. He began digging the second trench. Jay was helping Shirley at the fourth dig. Mackenzie scraped the chalky topsoil away and began to cut into the earth with his stone. His fingernails were cracked; blood had congealed on one thumb.

The sun began to flush him; it drew the sweat out of him. A sense of urgency quickened his breath. He had to fight it down.

Toward the east the earth glittered as if perspiring: mica particles, pyrites, quartz in the rocks picking up the sun's reflection. A small lizard darted toward shade.

Under his hair the scalp prickled with sweat. He stopped work and returned to his first trench and lay in it to cool off. The earth around him was damp and thick with a musty redolence. He watched the sky—cloudless, pale. A bird passed high overhead with a steady slow wingbeat.

After a few minutes he crossed the twenty feet to the slope where Jay and Shirley were digging. The hole was more than two feet deep. All he could see was their heads and shoulders until he was up close: they'd built up the parapet.

He interrupted. "Jay can finish this. Have a look at Earle's leg, will you?"

He saw she was trembling. Exhaustion, fear, hopelessness. He gave her a hand up. Jay looked up at him, wearing an expression of black fury.

Mackenzie watched Shirley pick her way toward Earle Dana, who had not moved in the past hour.

Jay grunted with the effort of lifting a stone out of the pit. "I don't know what good it'll do her looking at his leg."

"She's the only one among us who's used her M.D."

"He needs splinting, right? We haven't even got the equipment to splint him. Sticks, sure, we can break off sticks—but what do we tie them with?"

"Shirley's hair."

Jay gaped at him. "My God."

"You'd better lay off down there—that looks deep enough."

Jay sat back weakly against the wall of the pit. The sun only reached his face. His hairy legs were as spindly as a colt's: you could see every bone. He had no fat to live on.

Something glittered in the corner of Mackenzie's vision. At first he disregarded it, taking it for another bit of desert glare. Then he turned and had a better look. He moved off.

"Where are you going?"

"Brass collecting."

"*What?*"

He walked slowly, picking spots for his feet. What time was it anyway? Six? Half past six? The sun was three diameters above the horizon. This early it wouldn't burn the skin badly. He kept walking toward the dazzling yellow reflection, searching to either side of it for more metal.

They'd come tumbling out of the sky, falling ten thousand feet or more, and they'd spread themselves out in an uneven row across the desert—two shells quite close together, then forty yards away another and far beyond that he saw the glimmer of yet another.

He picked up the two at his feet. They'd be enough for the time being; he didn't use the energy to walk farther. He turned and went back up the slope.

Thirty-caliber aerial machine-gun shells. No telling how long they'd been out here. Everything was metric nowadays: millimeters.

"What the hell good are those supposed to do us?"

73

"We've just moved from the Stone Age into the Bronze Age."

He kept the shells in his hand and walked right past Jay across the slope to where Earle lay asprawl with his mouth open and his eyes shut. Shirley looked up. "It's shock. I think. He's still chilled—you can see the goose bumps."

"Can we move him into one of the holes without torturing him?"

"Maybe if all three of us carry him. One of us on the broken leg."

"We'll splint it tonight."

"Sam—is there any point? Can he possibly live long enough to care whether it heals?"

"There aren't any guarantees but we all took the Hippocratic Oath."

"Earle was never an M.D."

"Well he hasn't got a vote anyway, has he."

She said, "I didn't think you were putting things to a vote."

"I had to sound tough. We'd never get anywhere if Jay felt duty bound to dispute every instruction I gave."

"We almost made it," she said. He couldn't tell if there was bitterness in her solemnity. "We were almost finding out how to be content together."

"I didn't come back by choice, did I." He wheeled from her.

He heard her say, "What a grisly waste." He went a few paces away and put the two brass shells down and beckoned to Jay, who came reluctantly out of the pit and walked forward with his eyes on the ground, toes curled protectively, avoiding stones and stickers.

"We'll pick him up very carefully and put him in that nearest trench. Shirley takes the bad leg. Jay takes the good leg. I take the head and shoulders."

"It'll wake him up," Jay warned.

"He can't stay here."

Even in his unconsciousness Earle Dana's mouth was pinched into a prim pout. Very gently Mackenzie crouched down and got his hands under the shoulders. "Ready?"

"Wait." Shirley was testing the leg, trying to find exactly where the break was without disturbing it. He watched her make her decision: she slid one hand in under the calf just below the knee and gripped the ankle with the other hand. "Now I'm only going to hold this leg. I'm not going to support any of his weight."

"Understood," Mackenzie said. "You give the word."

"All right. Slowly—now. Lift."

Ever so slowly he pulled Earle's shoulders up off the ground. Earle's arms swung wide and flopped like dead wings. Jay had him under the small of the back with his left forearm; Jay's right hand gripped the underside of Earle's knee. In that manner they picked him up. Shirley's face pinched with concentration as she held the two sections of the broken leg, trying to maintain the separation and distance of the break so that the jagged bone ends wouldn't grate or penetrate the flesh. Internal bleeding had already taken place; the injured leg was bruise-black from knee to heel and swollen half again the thickness of the right leg.

A sharp stone jabbed Mackenzie's heel when he put his foot down but he couldn't shift it without breaking the rhythm of their walk. He put his weight on it and went on.

They lowered him with infinite patience into the trench, climbing down one at a time with him.

It was when they put him down that something happened, a twist or pull that shot pain through Earle explosively: he cried out in a bellow that climbed to a scream.

There was instantly the stink of excrement.

Earle blinked at them, heat-flushed, panting with ag-

75

ony and weakness and disoriented terror. "What—?"

Shirley touched his forehead with her palm. "Take it easy, Earle. Try not to move. Try to relax."

"You're burying me!"

"It's to keep the sun off. Keep you cool."

"Duggai—"

She said, "You two go on. I'll talk to him."

Mackenzie climbed out of the hole. He stood facing Jay across the open grave. Two grown men standing bare-ass naked with their privates dangling ludicrously. "Get under cover, Jay. Stay there until late afternoon. Sleep if you can."

"And then?"

"Then we'll find something to drink."

"I'm already parched beyond belief."

"You'll make it."

Jay's mouth twisted. "Sure. Hang in there. Keep on truckin'. Stiff upper lip. Act like a man. Mackenzie, aren't you even just a little bit terrified?"

Mackenzie walked back to pick up the machine-gun shells. He took them to the farthest trench. He hadn't finished scooping it out; he picked up his digging stone. The sun, early yet, prickled against his back.

He made himself dig with slow measured movements until it was deep enough. He had husbanded his energy; all the same he was panting in short bursts and oiled with sweat.

He lay down in the pit with the brass cartridge cases and the digging stone. He dug a plate-sized rock out of the wall: it would do for an anvil. He had no idea if it was going to work but it had to be tried because otherwise they'd be trying to chop open spiny cactus with bare hands and pulling Shirley's hair out by the roots.

Lying back in the trench he squinted at the blazing sky. His tongue and eyelids were gritty. They had at best the chance of a snowball in hell, he thought, but he was a prisoner of his morality. Wonder stabbed him: his

76

grandfather had taught him too well. *I guess I'm a good man in spite of myself.* A fine discovery now that it was too late to matter. He felt himself smile at the irony.

Leaning up on one elbow he began to work the brass.

9

He had only read about such things and the pit amazed him as the sun climbed. If anything, he felt chilled against the dark moist clay.

He knew it would be best to lie quiet until evening but there was too much that had to be done.

The brass was something he could do without leaving the trench.

The large rock served as his anvil. He stood one .30-caliber shell upright on its base. He upended the second shell and held it on top of the first one with the necks overlapping, slightly askew. He lifted the second rock and pounded it down.

The brass lips crumpled a bit. He hadn't hit very hard; hadn't wanted to chance ruining it.

He struck again. The lower rim crumpled more, bending in on itself, but the upper shell began to split and that was what he was after.

He pulled at the split with his fingernails but the metal was too hard for him. He placed the shells muzzle-to-muzzle again and hammered away, stopping after each blow to inspect the work. The split worked its way up the length of the shell, the second shell acting as a wedge driving deeper with each blow.

Each shell was about four inches long. When the split had traveled two-thirds the length of its casing he stopped hammering and tried to pull the two casings apart but they were wedged together and he had to think about that for a long sluggish time before he saw that he was going to need a third shell to finish the job.

He sat up slowly. The molten sun exploded in his face. What time? Nine o'clock? Couldn't be much later than nine yet. Possibly only half past nine; hard to tell by the angle of the sun—his celestial navigation was rudimentary.

Worth a few minutes' risk, he decided. He left the hole and went down the slope, remembering where he'd seen the other casings. He gathered three of them before he made his ginger way back onto the slope. In these few minutes the skin of his back had already begun to cook.

Approaching the trench he heard a groan higher along the slope. Earle.

Mackenzie went that way and crouched at the rim of Earle's pit. The stench of excrement came up out of the hole. Earle was revolted by the fact that he had fouled himself; he wouldn't look Mackenzie in the face.

Mackenzie climbed down, wedging himself into the narrow trench. "Roll over on your left side just a little, can you? I'll get this out of here."

Wordlessly Earle lifted himself on his right elbow until a wince of pain crossed his face.

"That's high enough. Just hold it there a minute."

He used the handful of shells as a digging tool to scrape around the moist pool of human manure. He dug in an arc and lifted the crumbling half-ball of earth, sliding it out from under Earle's upraised knee, lifting it to the rim of the trench and setting it down there. It had taken several minutes and Earle sagged back in exhaustion.

"Take it easy now. We'll get you splinted up tonight when it's cool enough to move around. You're going to be all right."

"Any damn fool knows a man needs water to survive." The clarity of Dana's voice surprised him.

"We'll get water. Where things grow there's always water. Get some sleep." And he left because he couldn't stand talking to the man. He carried the earthen tray of excrement away and threw it up the slope and limped back to his trench and lay absolutely still until his pulse slowed and his breathing lengthened and the sweat cooled on his body.

He used one of the new shells to pry the split cartridge apart far enough to remove the case that had been wedged into it. Then he began to work with the split case. He hooked a new shell over it and worked it slowly back and forth. He lay back to do this work and expended his effort with miserly sloth. After a long time metal fatigue set in and the bent side broke off.

He laid the split shell on the anvil rock and began to hammer, using the second shell as a punch, flattening the long side of the split shell. He kept working until he was satisfied, not hurrying. In the end he had a knife.

Now he began to hone the blade against the rock.

He made three knives before he ran out of material—the fourth and fifth shells had been crumpled beyond repair in the workings. When he was satisfied with their sharpness he put them aside and looked up over the edge of the pit.

Far away to the north he saw the thin streamer of a high jet contrail. A small cactus wren flitted from shrub to shrub down on the flats. They would have to set out some sort of signals to attract aircraft. They could watch what the birds ate and eat it too; he knew of nothing in the desert that a bird could digest that would harm a man.

And the bird itself was food if you could catch it.

By the sun it was early afternoon. He lay back in his cool shelter and closed his eyes against the brightness of the sky; he tried to blank his mind because he needed to sleep but anxiety overcame him and he went pawing frantically around in his memories trying to find clues to survival.

He had camped out numerous times with his father on the reservation but it was nonsense to rely on atavistic mythology. He was no more a primitive wilderness-dweller than any of them. His last camping trip on the reservation had taken place thirty-six years ago when he was twelve years old; after that his father had gone into the army and two years after that had been killed by a Stuka in North Africa. His mother, the daughter of a Presbyterian missionary from Scotland who had run the church at Window Rock, had moved with Sam to Denver after the war and he had been back to the reservation only three or four times in all the years since, never for more than a day or two.

For all he knew there could be more survival knowledge in any of their heads than there was in his. Jay had done three years in the army in Korea; Earle Dana had been an air force chaplain; either of them might have been a Boy Scout. Even Shirley was something of an outdoor girl: her father had been a fanatical trout fisherman and the family had gone off far into Canada on angling expeditions that lasted weeks.

But I'm half Navajo by blood and I work in the forest nowadays and that's supposed to endow me somehow with the powers of a Moses to lead them through this wilderness.

It was farce. The fall of a coin. He must have made some snappish remark, forgotten now, that had caught all of them—himself included in that crazy first moment—in the grip of the notion that Mackenzie had the answers. Mackenzie had the blood and the instincts. Mackenzie had been born in the desert. Mackenzie was invincible. Mackenzie would save their lives.

I'm older than any of them—a good twelve or thirteen years on Shirley, for God's sake—it ought to be up to them to look after me, not the other way around.

But they'd abdicated. They'd embraced despair: it had been their first thought. Hopelessness. Surrender and die. He'd been the only one to fight it and that made him the leader.

For better or for worse until death do us part.

But what the hell do we do now?

10

He didn't hallucinate but his mind jumped the straight track and he frittered hours away on meaningless calculations.

A hundred and thirty degrees Fahrenheit was what, fifty-one degrees centigrade?

They were in Arizona certainly—but where in Arizona? The state was nearly as big as all of New England.

Brass shells meant aerial gunnery practice but there'd been innumerable training bases in the desert during the Second World War and after. Davis Monthan outside Tucson. Fort Huachuca test range near Tombstone. Another one outside Phoenix—he kept trying to recall the name. A marine air station near Yuma. Another air force thing of some kind near Kingman. Another at Marana. Luke Air Force Gunnery Range. The Kofa Proving Ground. Florence Military Reservation. The Army Proving Ground at Yuma. Williams—that was it, the one near Phoenix: Williams Air Force Base.

Quit wasting time now—you haven't got it to spare.

There was no saliva in his mouth to be drawn by the rolling pebble. He took it off his tongue and lay back breathing through his nose and tried to push away the tentacles of panic.

Time was so short. It was possible to die very quickly in the desert. The ancient rule of thumb was that a man could live at least three days without water but that was not true in the desert, where the sun and the sand-dry air and the furnace plains leached the body of its moisture. You could die in twenty-four hours. Duggai's companions five years ago had died in less time than that. Because they'd been overcome by panic: they'd tried to hike, perhaps even tried to run. The desert had consumed them as fire consumes kindling. But even without exertion they'd have died by the second morning.

The ground pit might add an additional twenty-four hours to their lives now but the clock had started running early last evening when Duggai had given them their last drink from the canteen.

We'll make it through tonight. But if we don't get water we'll die tomorrow before the sun goes down.

An early effect of fasting was urinary cleansing. That was a medical fact with which he was familiar. During the day he'd left the trench at least half a dozen times to urinate. He'd heard the others doing the same. By now Earle Dana's trench probably stank of ammonia because Earle didn't have the luxury of mobility.

It was tempting to hold it in as long as possible under the delusion that by retaining fluid the body held its grip on life that much longer but he knew that wasn't the case at all—once the fluid had gone through the organs it was of no further use and the body only damaged itself by locking acid into the tract. So when the impulse overcame him he obeyed it.

But it would strike with ever increasing frequency until in the strong-stinking trickle of their final discharges there would be gritty little green crystals of pure uric acid.

By that time they would be too dehydrated to notice the pain.

If we get that far we'll never come back from it.

He suspected it was self-delusion to hope they could sustain themselves for more than a few hours on cactus. It contained moisture to be sure. But not much. And it would contain enzymes and bacteria that could produce dysentery—cathartic and dehydrating reactions. Cactus might prolong life but certainly couldn't improve it. To cheat Duggai's hell they needed more than survival: they needed strength.

There was something. It caromed through shadows in his mind. Elusive. Maddeningly it shied from the light.

There was something and if he could remember it they might have water, they might live, they might win.

And he couldn't remember it.

Reviewing the recalcitrance of Jay Painter's despair, he fanned himself into new anger. Mackenzie had a terrible strong temper which he held under tight control whenever he could and as long as he could: once lost it was hard to regain. He had always envied Shirley the ability to get hot and quickly get over it. She and Jay squabbled all the time.

Audrey had been a woman of moods. In depressed hours she might snap at Mackenzie but it was a keep-away snap, not a preamble to a fight.

Sudden memory kicked in him. The five of them—and Duggai.

Audrey had not always been a somber girl but there'd been shadows here and there. They'd been married nearly ten years by the time he first met Shirley and Jay. By then it had led to the inevitable disenchantment but not beyond it—they'd still liked each other.

Audrey thought she had some Indian blood too: a great-great-grandfather or something. Once they'd gone to a cowboys and Indians movie and she'd winked at him afterward: *Well we pret' near won that one.* She'd had a job then as factotum to a producer of TV commercials in San Francisco; Mackenzie had been stationed at Fort Ord. A base chaplain had married them and six months later he'd been transferred to West Germany and she'd had to quit the job. That had been the first obvious wedge.

After that he'd done tours in all parts of the world: Walter Reed and Fitzsimmons; the racketing madness of Tokyo; the shabby drear of Fort Bliss. By the time he came back from Indochina to the Presidio in San Francisco—1970—they weren't yet estranged but they were like old friends who hadn't seen each other in a while and had lost touch. It wasn't so much that they inhabited different worlds—they inhabited the same world but different aspects of it. The view from beneath was a view in the dark: his last tour in Saigon had been an exercise in hopeless idiocy and he'd lost some of his capacity to enjoy things. They'd gone on trying to behave as if nothing had happened but there was a constraint between them that hadn't been there before. Mackenzie had changed: his soul viewed things with repugnance, the laughter had gone out of him.

Then they'd assigned Duggai to him.

The army had taken Duggai out of his freshman university year because he was failing most of his courses and couldn't sustain his draft deferment. To the extent that Mackenzie came to know him—it was never very far—it appeared Duggai must have been an amiable indifferent youth, a kind of red-skinned plowboy whose aspirations tended toward hunting, casual sex and the consumption of beer. A counselor in the reservation high school had inflamed Duggai's parents with ambitions for the boy—lift him out of the reservation rut, give him a chance to make something of himself in the modern world; Duggai had packed off to Tucson and found himself lost in the academic grind.

Duggai was a born marksman, lifelong hunter, and

when he scored at the top of his basic-training rifle class the army put him through a series of combat specialist schools designed to make a wizard killer of him. Race mythology to the contrary Duggai didn't seem to have any particular warrior instincts; all he had was docile pliability—that and his uncanny skill with a rifle. He was indifferent to the power of authority but tended toward mindless obedience as the line of least resistance.

He had been shipped to Vietnam with a special combat team of saboteurs and snipers. He never exceeded the rank of private first class. He was equipped with a backbreaking assortment of telescopic and infrared accoutrements; his job was to kill people at incredibly long ranges or at night or in monsoons. In one of their sessions he mentioned offhandedly to Mackenzie that he'd assassinated one Cong officer in a fine drizzle at a distance they later stepped off to confirm it: "Eight hundred seventy-five yards. That's over half a mile, Captain."

Certain villages in the boonies tended to be friendly during the day and unfriendly at night when the Cong would infiltrate and receive the clandestine embrace of the villagers, sack and pillage whatever supplies the village had conned out of the Americans, then drain away into the jungle before daybreak. To pacify such villages the army assigned mechanics like Duggai to lie in ambush with infrared scope and silenced rifle—to pick off everything that moved in the village after midnight.

In therapy Duggai always skirted the details but Mackenzie forced him to go over the ground innumerable times in the course of several months. He judged that Duggai must have murdered more than a hundred Vietnamese from the night. Vietnamese people were very small to the eyes of a hulk like Duggai; women and men wore the same loose pajamas in the rural areas. Duggai was aware of the fact that a good number of his victims had been women and children and very old people: the heat image on an infrared scope seldom reveals the sex or age of the target.

Duggai had done his work with unquestioning obedience but nothing in his upbringing had steeled him to it cinated. As the subconscious rebelled, so the efficiency on even so rudimentary a psyche as Duggai's. He began to disturb his tentmates with his nightmares. The nightmares trickled across into his waking hours: he hallucinated. As the subconscious rebelled, so the efficiency deteriorated. Finally Duggai was put into a base hospital for observation. The case had been kicked back up the line until finally he had been rotated back to San Francisco for major psychiatric overhaul. The department had implanted him in Mackenzie's care because all Indian patients were assigned to him: something about empathy.

Duggai had a peculiar intellect. His aptitude tests showed extremely high scores on anything to do with simple logic, practical things, mechanics. Mackenzie tried to teach him chess—he seemed to have the attributes for it—and Duggai learned the game quickly but he played only when Mackenzie badgered him into it. Left to himself Duggai chose isolation. In the ward he could sit in a chair and stare at a point on the wall for hours.

School and army records indicated he had formed no friendships and few acquaintanceships. He was not paranoid; he didn't give a damn what anyone thought of him. He did not relate to other people at all; he seldom seemed to care what they thought or felt. It was as if they didn't exist. To an extent he was a textbook psychopath isolated in solipsism. This was the most difficult syndrome to treat because the patient left no bridge open across which the therapist could approach him. There was no inner demand to make contact with another human. Duggai usually seemed aware of the existence of other people only to the extent that they annoyed or offended him or got in his way. He'd been reasonably polite to Mackenzie because he'd seen Mackenzie as his ticket out of the place but that was all.

Such patients had no curiosity about other people; it followed they also lacked any curiosity about themselves. The army's psychiatric services packed in a great many Duggais—some of them suicidal, some incoherent; you couldn't brainwash a farm boy into committing atrocities and expect it to have no effect on him afterward. But with a Duggai there was no possibility of goading the patient into insight. Feelings were to be obeyed and indulged but never examined.

There'd been no reaching Duggai. Because of the twitch of a government digit somewhere he'd been discharged—from the hospital and from the army—and Mackenzie had been relieved to see the last of him.

But then Duggai had gone brass-scavenging in the Mohave Desert; men had died; the change of venue brought the trial to San Francisco; and a bored defense attorney, court-appointed, went through the motions by seeking out psychiatric buttresses for his "not guilty by reason of insanity" defense. Mackenzie came forward willingly enough; testified as truthfully as he knew how; again that should have been the end of it.

Duggai—and the appearance at the trial of Earle Dana as an expert witness—had brought the rest of them together. Jay Painter initially came into it as a witness for the prosecution but his examination of Duggai bore out the results of Mackenzie's and the prosecution declined to call Jay to the stand. When Duggai's attorney learned of this he brought Jay over to the defense team.

Mackenzie met Jay for the first time in the courtroom.

Jay had asked Shirley to interview Duggai because it

had occurred to him that Duggai might open up more with an attractive woman. Duggai hadn't but the defense attorney, eager for all the help he could get, persuaded her to testify. The three of them were in court that day and afterward they went out to dinner. There was some speculation around the restaurant table about the fourth defense witness—a psychotherapist they'd all heard of, Earle Dana, regarded generally as a publicity hound and a quack. Their own testimony was concluded but they agreed to meet next morning in the courtroom to listen to Earle Dana.

Dana had written six self-help books—*How to Get the Most Out of Sex* was the one that made them titter the most—and wrote a newspaper column of mental-health advice that was syndicated to several West Coast newspapers. He was not a doctor; apparently he was self-taught. He'd been a minister of some persuasion and had served as an air force chaplain for some years before resigning both his commission and the ministry to join a consciousness-raising cult in Southern California. Then apparently he'd begun to read books for the first time in his life and had been smitten by the relentless reasoning of some of the neo-behaviorists with their Skinner Boxes and conditioned-reflex therapy techniques.

The defense attorney had asked Earle to testify because of his notoriety; Earle had agreed because of the publicity. Most of Earle's testimony had little to do with Duggai; it was a simpleminded advertisement for his brand of behavior therapy. "In many cases, the point is, other methods fail and our methods work." And Shirley had whispered in Mackenzie's ear: "So does torture."

Then to their horror Earle had buttonholed the three of them on his way out of the courtroom and insisted on standing them to lunch. They'd had to listen to his nonsense for hours before they'd been able to break away.

Audrey met them after work at the St. Francis and

90

the four of them had giggled over recollections of Earle Dana's prim pomposities. On any psychiatric subject Earle was prepared to rush in where the best minds in medicine feared to tread. His brief appearance in their lives gave fuel for uproarious amusement. And because they laughed together they decided they loved one another; the foursome became an institution for a brief while: Jayandshirley, Samandaudrey.

For Mackenzie it had gone beyond that. Perhaps it was inevitable. Not Audrey's fault but she'd failed to share too many of the experiences that had changed Mackenzie. Around the Painters' swimming pool or isolated by crowds at parties, Mackenzie and Shirley had discovered each other. She too was lonely in her marriage; her loneliness followed her into Mackenzie's life. A few drinks, outpourings of confidences. Jay's indifference. Audrey's withdrawn distance. Noncommunication in both marriages.

Mackenzie's adulterous love for Shirley came to dominate him: a big deep thing that sometimes for no reason made tears well up in him. Even in Jay's presence he became capable of enjoying his happiness in nothing more than sitting for great lengths of time watching her do little things—drying her hair, dusting a room, climbing out of the pool—just witnessing the grace of her face and body.

It never became an affair. They were both prisoners of honor—on occasion they teased one another abrasively about their old-fashioned principles. Mackenzie never allowed them opportunities for clandestine meetings. He wasn't gaited that way. It would be a complication he wouldn't be able to handle; he knew that. The love between them was real but physically unconsummated. That was unnatural; inevitably things had to come unraveled.

Jay had been badgering her: he wanted a baby. She was sure they'd be divorced; she didn't want to inflict that on a child. She kept taking the pill. Jay's anger took the form of cold-shouldering her. It compounded the frustrations—hers and Sam's.

The we-can't-go-on-like-this hour arrived the day before an explosive evening: Earle Dana again the catalyst. Every few weeks Earle found some excuse to gather them around him. He was an expansive host; there was always a vacuous large-breasted blonde or redhead on his arm—sometimes Mackenzie suspected Earle hired them—and the soirees provided fuel for the next month's cruel laughter, so they always went.

It had been nearly a year by then. Mackenzie never learned what triggered things but it all blew apart at that last party of Earle's.

He'd seen Jay and Shirley through a gap in the crowd. Hissing at each other. Their bodies twang-taut, every tendon standing out, faces livid. It wasn't one of their normal spats. Those came and went with metronomic regularity; they were loud and only mock-violent and they passed quickly. This was not anger; this was hate.

Audrey beside him saw the direction and alarm of Mackenzie's glance. She looked that way; moved closer and gripped his arm. "What on earth?"

People around the Painters were backing away as if from something that frothed with rabies.

Jay spat something at Shirley—a sibilant awful whisper. She rocked back on her heels, went stone-silent and still. Abruptly she wheeled. Her little fists rose and fell with inarticulate rage. She stormed toward the door.

Mackenzie was right in her path.

She touched his hand. "I'm sorry. I blew it. He just got me so mad. . . . Forgive me." Then she was gone. The door slammed with a shuddering crash.

And Jay Painter was stalking toward Mackenzie with murderous eyes.

Audrey clutched at his arm. "Sam—"

He tried to get her out of there but all the while Jay was railing at him with a "Keep me away from him I'll kill him" performance and by the time Mackenzie got Audrey out of the place she'd heard more than enough to fit things together and she'd jumped to the conclusion that was natural if not correct.

She refused to hear his protestation. She didn't talk to him at all. She locked herself in the bedroom.

The next afternoon when he came home she was slumped in the car inside the closed garage. The engine was still running. She'd been dead for several hours.

A week later Mackenzie left the army and put his M.D. and his psychiatric shingle away in storage. Nothing had forewarned him that Audrey might be that close to the ultimate breakdown. When he looked back he could count off all the classic symptoms as they'd appeared one by one—the shock of his presumed physical betrayal had been only the trigger, not the cause—but the horrible fact was that he hadn't seen any of it coming.

If I'd been any kind of a shrink at all I'd have been able to head it off.

He was forced to recognize himself as a third-rate shaman, incompetent psychiatrist. If there'd been any real talent he wouldn't have stayed protectively in the army. The facts had always been there; only the insights had been lacking. And a psychiatrist without insights was like a toxic agent turned loose in a water supply: incalculable the damage it could do.

After a while he realized that sort of thinking was extreme—guilty overreaction—but he never had the impulse to go back to the profession. And until now he'd never had further contact with any of them. They'd had key roles in the disintegration of his life, the destruction of Audrey's: they were the instruments of his guilt.

And clearly they hated him. Earle rankled still from the things Mackenzie had shouted at him when Earle innocently phoned to offer condolences. Shirley couldn't help hating him for what she'd done to herself: he'd been her willing accomplice. Jay owned the cuckold's rage. Duggai—he was the ultimate victim.

In time he had found something new to justify his existence. A love of the forest. He'd been happy. But now Calvin Duggai and the past had returned to deform the present.

He rubbed his forehead fiercely as if that could expunge his memories. He watched the line of sun-shadow move across the north wall of the pit. Its angle grew flatter but when he lifted his head to scent the air he discerned no reduction yet in its stifling heat. He sagged back into the grave to wait it out.

During the morning at intervals he'd heard Jay and Shirley calling across the island between their trenches but since the descent of the day's heat he hadn't heard any more of that.

It took no imagination to chart their symptoms; Mackenzie shared them. The tongue had begun to swell: it cleaved to the flesh of his mouth. His eyes had gone dry and it was painful to open them, even to slits. His lips were cracked. His belly had begun to knot. Soon he suspected there would be cramps. Lying still he could feel the solemn stubborn thud of a pulse in his ears: it made a rhythm against the high-frequency whistle there. His head ached.

All that would get worse. But it would be a while before it became incapacitating.

A buzzard drifted overhead, circling lower for a better look; it cruised in and out of the frame of his vision.

Finally it skimmed so low over his trench that he felt the breeze of its passage. He sat up. The blood rushed from his head and he felt consciousness flood away; he tightened the band of his stomach muscles against it and through the gray haze on his vision watched the buzzard flap away, startled by his movement. It planed along the flats until it caught an updraft; he watched it swing aloft. For the next half hour it hovered in vast lazy circles far overhead. After a while several others joined it.

The color of the sky began to change. He drowsed fitfully, rousing himself at intervals to have a look at the buzzards; if they came low again he'd throw something at them to warn them off. He didn't want to be awakened by a beak drilling into his eye.

It was too easy to envy the buzzards their freedom. With their cambered wings they could slide effortlessly—a hundred miles in a few hours if they wished—to water or to a safe nest.

It made him think of Calvin Duggai. Somewhere on the surrounding heights Duggai was sure to be camped. Every now and then he'd be taking out his field glasses to find out how his victims were getting along.

He went half asleep and didn't realize it until a sound startled him and he split his eyes open and saw Jay Painter's silhouette against the sky foreshortened by perspective.

Jay didn't speak at once. Mackenzie got up slowly, giving the circulation time to adjust. He stood in the hip-deep hole and scanned the desert. The sun, not nearly so strong now, slanted down from a flat angle near the horizon. Dust devils funneled erratically along the flats some distance away, a yellow wheeling of sand and twigs and leaves.

The buzzards were no longer in the sky. Perhaps Jay's perambulation had discouraged them.

"What now?" Jay's voice was painfully hoarse.

Mackenzie picked up the brass knives. "We cut open a cactus."

11

Jay and Shirley watched his work with dubious expectation, reserving hope. Resentment deformed their features.

The barrel cactus had heavy fishhook spines and he had to cut them out one by one with the clumsy short-bladed tool. He heard Jay's mutter: "Come on, come *on*," and ignored it. It would have been faster to smash the cactus with a rock but that would have wasted half its precious juice. He denuded a collar band around the plant and sawed through it and lifted the lid neatly off the cactus. Then he dug inside with his fingers, scooping out pulp.

He turned, proffering. Shirley took the handful of moist dark substance from him like an addict snatching an overdue fix.

Mackenzie could have let them dig for themselves but by bestowing water upon them with his hands he maintained his fragile leadership. He withheld his thirst; he drank last—because anarchy would kill them faster than anything else. The one-eyed man in the kingdom of the blind: fuehrer of the dung heap.

Jay shoveled the stuff out of his cupped hands: lips peeled back in a simian grimace, jaws working.

"God," Shirley croaked. "It's horrible."

"It's wet." Mackenzie cut out a section of pulp and

sucked on it. His throat and tongue absorbed the bitter liquid greedily. The spasmodic constrictions of his swallowings were ferocious and painful. And all for a few drops of moisture the taste of which was as tart as the smell of new-mown grass.

He scooped out more of the plant's innards. "Take it to Earle." Jay held his hands out and looked at it greedily: a dark soggy fibrous substance as unappetizing as compost. Mackenzie swung away.

Jay spat something out. "Where you going?" His suspicion had the querulousness of incipient panic.

"Splints. Go on, Jay."

Only the manzanita had any approximation of solid wood—gnarled, stunted, its bark the color of ripe cherries. He found a suitable branch and put his entire weight on it to split it loose from the twisted trunk; the limb broke but the bark refused to let go: it resisted him with ropy tenacity. He twisted and pulled and cursed, dragged the branch all the way around the tree, finally broke it free, taking a long curling strap of bark with it. He tried to slice this off with the cartridge knife but the metal was neither strong nor sharp enough; it hardly scored the bark. Finally he held it down under the ball of his foot and pulled up, tearing off most of the length of the limb. He stripped the twigs off one by one until he had a pole a few feet long.

It took half an hour's hobbling about the slope before he found and stripped four branches of suitable size: two on each side of the leg ought to be sufficient. He carried them back toward what he had begun to think of as the cemetery.

The sun fell; the plain filled with twilight.

The gravity of Shirley's glance disturbed him. He had the feeling Jay had told her he meant to use her hair to bind Earle's splints and he had a fair idea of the tone and choice of words Jay must have used.

98

They sat on the rim above Earle. He looked up at them, his mouth pinched into a small line. When Mackenzie came up he was assaulted by the stink of urine.

Earle said, "Why don't you just fill the hole in. With me in it."

"You'll make it, Earle."

"I don't mind. I've made my peace with God."

Mackenzie glanced at Jay. They got down in the hole and Mackenzie laid the poles out beside Earle. "First we'll splint you up. Then we'll get you out of here."

"I'm cold."

"It's warmer topside. The sun's had a chance at the ground."

"That won't last. Going to be a cold night."

"We made it through last night, didn't we?"

Earle licked a shred of cactus pulp off his chapped lower lip. "You're the doctors. I'm not a doctor, you know."

"That's all right. There's enough doctors here."

"Well if you insist on trying to make repairs I don't mind. Get on with it."

Mackenzie looked up. Shirley sat crosslegged at the rim, the small tight breasts shadowing her rib cage. Her shoulders were beet-red. Bits of earth clung to her skin.

"Jay told you what we're going to do?"

"I'd just about decided to cut off all my hair anyway. A week ago." She lied listlessly.

Mackenzie tested the knives and selected one. "I honed this one as sharp as I could." He offered it to Jay. "You want to do it?"

"No. But I suppose we've got to."

"Nothing else we can use out here. The plants are too brittle."

Shirley said, "For God's sake stop talking about it. Do it."

It took several hands. Mackenzie had to help. Jay

kept scowling at him, the air whistling expressively through his nose.

They sawed through Shirley's hair, plaited the strands and made their twine. It took a great deal of time; it left Shirley with a ragamuffin thatch.

She ran her hands experimentally through the tomboy remains that tufted her scalp. Then she turned her face away from them. *"For Whom the Bell Tolls."*

Mackenzie doubted it would be given time ever to grow back.

Jay said, "I guess we'll have to palpate Earle's leg."

It had to be pulled and twisted to set the bone in place. Mackenzie was the heaviest of them and practicality required that he be the one to hold Earle down.

He crouched above Earle's head and pinned down both biceps. Then the high ring of Earle's scream stabbed through his skull and he almost lost his grip when Earle convulsed.

"Okay Earle. Gentle down. It's over."

"Dear sweet Jesus help me." Earle's voice broke.

With braided ropes of human hair they tied the splints in place. If the swelling began to go down they'd have to retie it; Mackenzie cautioned them to tie bow knots.

Finally Shirley collapsed back against the wall of the pit. "It'll have to do."

Sweat stood beaded on Earle's flaccid skin. The last twinge of acute pain faded across his face. His earsplitting outcry still seemed to echo.

Jay removed something from his ear and examined it. "All this high-priced medical talent and that's the best we can do."

"It should heal as straight as it ever was," Shirley said.

They lifted Earle from the pit and took him down the slope and scooped an earth bed for him in the lee of one of the manzanitas. At least it would cut some of the wind.

Dusk waned; darkness condensed. Decisions needed taking. A score of things needed doing. But Mackenzie had sunk into a constraining ennui and he stood listless.

Shirley's furious scowl: with her hair cropped she had a pouting-child look: she gave both of them sour up-from-under looks. Jay crabbed his way closer to her as if her public nakedness still embarrassed him. Parched and famished and abraded to raw sores, Mackenzie had no carnal drives left and would have been astonished if Shirley had indicated anything like passion toward him but Jay was going through reflex motions and possibly that was because it was a peg of reality to cling to.

Mackenzie roused himself fretfully. "I hope you had some sleep during the day. We've got a lot to do. We don't need to have me deliver a theatrical harangue, do we?"

"What's on your mind?"

"We can't keep thinking in stopgap terms an hour at a time. We're going to be here a while—we've got to plan it out."

"How long can we stay here and live, Mackenzie?"

"Earle can't be moved any distance."

Earle spoke with drunken thickness. "Leave me. If there's a chance you can get out—"

"Shut up, Earle." He wished there were some way to avert Earle from feeding in the trough of his guilt: things were bad enough without having to dissuade Earle from martyrdom at every turning.

"We'll get out in time," Mackenzie said. "We'll need clothes on our backs—shoes on our feet."

There was a burst of inverted laughter from Jay. "Where's the department store out here? I must have missed it on the way in."

"You've got to stop fighting me." Mackenzie's head ached. He fought to concentrate. "This isn't dead ground. Things live in it. Animals, birds, plants. We've got to be predators, that's all."

"We're plastic people from a transistorized civilization two thousand years removed from all this," Jay said with stubborn cynicism. "I don't see how we can wipe that out overnight."

Shirley began to speak but Mackenzie held up a restraining hand. Jay's last words rattled around in his head—something vitally important: he reached for it, chased it around his mind. An answer was there—he had to find it. The same answer that had eluded him all through the day. *What?*

Plastic. . . . Then he had it and he bolted to his feet.

Jay's head rocked back. He stared at Mackenzie in sudden terror.

Mackenzie was turning, searching the slope, reconstructing last night's scene. The truck had been—*there*. He walked toward it as swiftly as he could. Something jabbed his heel and he almost turned his ankle; it made him stop and proceed more cautiously—all they needed was another cripple.

Jay limped after him. "What is it, man?"

"That blessed beautiful plastic God damn raincoat."

12

It wasn't where he remembered it falling. Something heavy sank through his throat — a hollow sensation of abject fright.

He went down on his knees and searched. "Help me find it—it's got to be right around here."

"What are we looking for?"

"Little rectangle of clear plastic. Folded up. Maybe eight inches by four inches."

"What good would that do us?"

He made no answer; he swiveled desperately on his knees, pawed at the ground, searched the pale silver earth in starlight. So clearly last night he'd seen Duggai's scheme; he'd kicked the raincoat out of the truck knowing it could make the vital difference—then forgotten it perversely in the tangle of fears.

He groped, widening the furious search. Had Duggai found it, tossed it back into the truck? But Mackenzie had been watching him for just that—hadn't seen Duggai stoop to pick anything up. Then where had the God damn thing gone?

"This what we're looking for?"

Jay was thirty feet away. Mackenzie gawked at him, got his feet under him, crossed the slope lifting his feet as if from a white-hot surface. "Wind must have blown it around."

"I don't see what good it'll do—it won't even keep the sun off anybody."

Mackenzie unfolded the packet. The plastic smelled musty. He stretched it out. Through it he could see the stars.

"Thank God."

"Mackenzie, I swear to God I'm going to—"

"Come on." He moved away muttering: "Duggai's watching us of course. We've got to pick a spot he can't see. If he knew what we were up to he'd come down here one fine noon and cut it to ribbons. We need a hollow—maybe some brush to screen it from him."

Jay stopped behind him. "You're going around the bend, Mackenzie. You're babbling. Incipient paranoia."

"Come on, damn you—over here, this'll do."

It was a dry ravine with irregular V sides not more than three feet deep at the center but it made an S-bend here and clumps of catclaw stood on either bank. You couldn't see the bottom if you weren't standing directly above it.

Jay approached with wary stealth. Mackenzie climbed down into the ravine. "Give me a hand. We've got to dig."

"Again?" But Jay came painfully down the sloping bank and waited for instruction.

They scooped a bowl in the bottom of the ravine. Mackenzie used the unfolded raincoat as a pattern: they made the bowl a few inches smaller in diameter than the plastic.

The bowl sloped down to a bottom about two feet deep where Mackenzie carefully built up a large cup of earth, molding it like a piece of pottery. He cut half a sleeve off the raincoat, slit it open and used it for a liner in the cup. It had a capacity of perhaps three quarts—more than enough. The plastic liner ought to prevent anything from seeping into the ground.

The cool subsoil was slightly damp to the touch. That

104

would be enough moisture to start the action; later it would have to be fed with earth and succulents.

Jay followed his instructions as if mesmerized. His initiative was pretty much gone. He didn't ask questions and Mackenzie perversely volunteered nothing, withholding knowledge because mystery cemented his power. There was still the possibility of mutiny—Jay's tractability of the moment might not last.

Mackenzie laid the raincoat carefully across the top of the open bowl of earth. He made gestures and Jay imitated his actions: they anchored it down all the way around with heaped earth and stones until the thin plastic was stretched like a drumhead across the top of the hole in the ground. Then Mackenzie placed a small stone in the center of the plastic to make it sag, the stone hanging directly above the plastic-lined cup beneath.

He knew it would work in theory.

But I'll believe it when I see it.

The spines of the Senita scraped off easily with the knife—like rows of kernels slicing off a corncob. They sucked thin watery sap out of the cactus pulp until their throats no longer constricted in spasms. Mackenzie cut up the rest of it in chunks and dropped them into the hole under the taut plastic.

Jay was dubious. "It's bone dry in there, Mackenzie."

"Wait for the sun."

Mackenzie tested the knife blade with his thumb. When the three of them went back across the hill toward Earle they hobbled like cripples. His feet felt twice their normal size. He limped painfully back into the bushes, impelled by rumbling volcanic pressures inside him. The beginnings of dysenteric diarrhea— unavoidable but frightening: if it got bad enough it would sap every vestige of strength. It ran through him painfully; he cleaned up as best he could with grease-wood fronds; then he made his way as far as Earle's bush and sat down, taking his weight on one palm to lower himself and sitting awkwardly on the side of one buttock to twist the soles of his tortured feet toward the air.

Shirley said, "Not to be gruesome, Sam, but how long has it been since you had a tetanus shot?"

"We get one every spring. Forest Service manual."

"Then that's all right. The rest of us could be in a bad way if you went lockjaw on us."

Jay said, "A bad way compared to what?"

A sheaf of Shirley's cutoff hair—the strands they hadn't used up on Earle's splints—lay weighted with a rock. Mackenzie considered it and leaned back on his elbow and propped his cheek against his palm. An ant climbed his arm and he flicked it away.

"Earle's probably going to have chills tonight. We'll need wood and dry tinder. Shave off some parings of that manzanita bark. Bust up ocotillo and catclaw—it should make good kindling. Any of this brush around here will burn."

Jay cackled. "What do we start it with? Rub two Boy Scouts together?"

Now just use your head before you go charging off in all directions.

You're not going to catch anything in your bare hands. Not even a lizard—they move like hell.

Now think.

He listened to Shirley and Jay snapping off branches—the sounds seemed curiously far away. Earle's breathing was deep and slow: the exhausted sleep of invalid weakness.

Mackenzie salivated over memories of desert cook-fires on the Window Rock Reservation—his father roasting coatimundi on a spit.

The thing to keep in mind before panic set in was that the desert teemed with an astonishing amount of life. In the past twenty-four hours he had seen only a few buzzards, a cactus wren, some other high-flying birds and one lizard; but desert animals were mainly nocturnal. This far from water the available species would be limited to those whose metabolism made it unnecessary for them to drink—they absorbed moisture from the vegetation they ate—but that still left room for peccaries, owls, mice, kangaroo and pack rats, jackrabbits, kit foxes and probably scores more. Of one species he was certain: he'd seen the run several times as he'd made his way back and forth along the slope. It was a well-worn jackrabbit trail and he'd known it all the time but the knowledge hadn't registered until now. Forty years was a long time; it was damn near impossible to resurrect specific memories that old. But he had to milk the memory cells of every drop now.

In the cool night breeze it was possible to think calmly and without urgency. Mackenzie had to do his best thinking right now because if he went much longer without food the brain would begin to starve for nourishment and the ability to reason and recall would be the first to deteriorate. Right now the initial adrenaline alarms had worn off, the stultifying furnace heat had dissipated, panic had receded: the organism was functioning as well as it was ever going to function. He had the next few hours and no more because after that protein starvation would make its effect and everything would begin to disintegrate unless they made fast improvements in their physical situation.

He heard a coyote's yapping, so far away it was barely audible. Sound carried here; that coyote might be five miles away or more. But it was vaguely encouraging: a coyote wouldn't stray too terribly far from some source of water. Sooner or later they were going to have to move out of this spot; the move must be toward higher ground; somewhere up there, the coyote told him, there was water. A natural water source would mean big game.

He turned his head slowly and waited for the coyote to speak again. When it yipped he turned his head quickly. The coyote's announcements broke off and the desert went silent again; but Mackenzie had time to narrow it to the northeastward quadrant.

When we go that's the way we'll go.

First they had to have shoes. They wouldn't be able to make more than a few miles each night because they'd have to carry Earle or drag him on a litter and they'd have to stop early enough to dig pits for themselves and dig a new hole under the plastic raincoat.

But it would be better than staying here.

Lying on his side, he let his mind range loosely; it was the best way to recover information from the subconscious.

He put himself back inside his child's skin, sat himself down beside his father's campfire. In their hunting days they'd gone out sometimes by pickup and sometimes horseback; they'd explored hundreds of miles of reservation desert. His father had been a silversmith; the ostensible purpose for their expeditions had been prospecting for turquoise and agate and obsidian and the petrified wood that tourists paid dearly for; but it had been excuse more than purpose.

"Mackenzie" had been the missionary's name. When the silversmith married the missionary's daughter he took her surname. He was a full Navajo born and raised at Chinle in Cañon de Chelly in the heart of the reservation; his tribal name was Tsosi Simalie but it was common for the Navajo to take a second name that would go easier on white men's palates. When Mackenzie was born his grandfather baptized him Samuel Simalie Mackenzie and his father Tsosi gave him the name

Kewanwyti, which had no particular translated meaning in English. His father called him by that name only when they were alone together.

His father felt that Sam's white blood entitled him to the fruits of Anglo civilization; Mackenzie silver was the best Navajo jewelry of the 1930s and even in the Depression there was money to give the boy the best possible education. Sam saw his father only during the summer holidays—the rest of the time he was a white boy—and now his memory picked its way through the sparse weeks when they'd crossed the desert together and his father had tried to reinforce that other half of Sam's heritage.

The legends of White Painted Woman and Coyote. The campfire stories of Navajo history—the wars with the rival Apaches and Hopi; the Kit Carson debacle at Cañon de Chelly that had forever destroyed the tribe's ability to make war; the Long March across New Mexico that had decimated the Navajo nation; the hunters and warriors and shamans and leaders who were the heroes of Navajo mythology.

His father showed him how to track bobcat, how to stalk the desert bighorn, how to keep downwind and move slowly so as to blend into the country. One year they ran a trapline along a stream but it snared only one old beaver. His father tried to teach him the ways of the Old People and the pleasures of the wilderness.

The silversmith was a contemplative man with a lyrical sense of awe. He would tell ancient stories about mesa formations and rock spires; he would speak poems about crows and snakes and mountains. He had a magic way of evoking in the small boy's mind a long-vanished world of fantasy. He taught the boy the happiness of solitude, the astonishing fascinations to be found in a handful of desert sand or a single pitted crag. When he spoke to the boy he became luminous and reverent and filled with sly humor.

Now he remembered those lazy campfires, the talk late into the night, the glowing eyes of creatures that sat outside the circle of light and stared into the fire. . . .

The discovery pleased him; reverie was paying off. Fire was the answer.

13

He plaited the fine strands of red hair into strings and made his way along the jackrabbit run to set his snares. They were beings of strange habit: for reasons that had no apparent connection to territorial urges or mating rituals or access to food they would run the same worn paths for years. The cause had never explained itself but from Saskatchewan to Sineloa the jackrabbit made his deep track across every patch and corner of desert as plain as signposted footpaths in a park.

The track ran in dogleg meanders from bush to bush. Wherever it ran under an overhanging limb of manzanita Mackenzie set his nooses—each snare an open oval loop a few inches above the ground anchored lightly to the earth with a forked twig hooked over it and the twig driven into the soil—to keep the snare from fouling in the wind.

By themselves the snares might do the job tonight or tomorrow night or sometime next week but Mackenzie couldn't wait for chance: the traps had to be baited and fire was the bait.

They built the fire up-trail from the snares and Mackenzie made a little tinder pool and built a thatch of twigs on it and set the ocotillo branches close at hand. Then he settled down to the tedium of rock chipping.

The desert was littered with quartz. It wasn't as sure as flint but it was hard enough to make sparks from the friction of collision. Mackenzie worked close against the tinder and shielded the work with his body against the steady southwesterly. The sparks were weak, ephemeral, mocking.

He blasted pale sparks into it for a long time and nothing caught. In the corner of his eye he saw Jay turn away with morose dejection. Mackenzie's arms grew tired and his fingers began to cramp. He kept slamming the rocks together. The metered clicking was like the rattle of some primitive instrument: he saw Shirley's head begin to sway. She was unaware of it.

He got down closer, shifted his alignment—perhaps it was the wind. "Move in here, Jay. Give me some shelter."

Jay came reluctantly beside him and they squatted together and the quartz clicked like bones. Shirley said, "You look like figures in a cave painting."

Finally a pinprick ember glowed in the tinder. Smoke began to curl. Mackenzie fanned it with his open hands. The ember went black.

Jay said, "Oh."

Mackenzie picked up the stones again.

Jay said, "It's no use, is it."

"If you've got something better to do with your time—" He snapped it waspishly and regretted it; there was no point feeding Jay's despondency with sarcasms.

Then it well and truly caught: he fanned it and watched the infant flame grow. And Shirley said, "Behold the invention of fire."

Once it caught it went high and ravenous: the consumption of brittle twigs was ferocious and Jay started heaving armloads of brush on it until Mackenzie stayed him. Mackenzie rammed four long manzanita branches

112

into it end-first so that they could be shoved steadily into the center and reduce the speed of consumption; they'd gathered a good supply but there was no point wasting it.

He'd had to position the fire on the rabbit trail rather than for Earle's convenience; it meant they had to move Earle and this aroused half-coherent mutterings. They set him down close to the fire and Earle smiled in childish gratitude and sank quickly back into sleep.

The light flickered against their pale bodies. Jay, his spine hunched, brooded bleakly into the flames; his thick pelt of body hair emphasized an aspect of the scene and caused Mackenzie to realize what had put the caveman image in Shirley's head.

She lay close by the fire half on her side, breasts askew, legs scissored; ruddy patches grew on her face. The fire brought the night closer around them and exacerbated the sense of malevolent isolation.

Then they heard the distant growl of the truck.

At first Mackenzie thought it was imagination. It was very far off—hardly audible. But he saw the others respond. He could hear the juddering whine of the transmission. After a few moments it stopped abruptly, switched off. Jay's face, at first expectant and hopeful, collapsed. "Duggai. He's coming for us. To finish us."

"Not yet," Mackenzie said. "He's not sick of the game yet."

It worked on their nerves. For a while no one spoke again. Shirley's eyes had a vacant glaze. Jay picked sunburnt skin shreds from his nose. Earle's breath began to raise frightened puffs of dust from the ground—like a fallen horse. Shirley put a hand to his forehead to gauge Earle's fever and Earle uttered a thin startled little cry. His eyes opened to the fire: he looked over his shoulder into the darkness and winced from it like a galley slave.

Shirley said, "Duggai did that on purpose. To remind us he's there."

At least it confirmed Duggai's presence; it was no longer a paranoid supposition.

Mackenzie saw something wink from the darkness—an animal attracted by the fire. Its motionless eyes gleamed. Mackenzie's hand gripped the knife. There was nothing out here big enough to attack a man—nothing but Duggai—but Mackenzie's hand grew slippery on the knife. *We'd make good targets for him against this fire.*

But he knew Duggai this well: Duggai couldn't kill them yet. There were reasons that would make no sense to anyone but a Navajo; but they were binding. Duggai would not attack—not yet.

Shirley ventured toward the fire; she began to hum a tune—her voice small but true. Perhaps she wasn't aware she was doing it. She used to do that, he remembered—she used to sing to herself when there was trouble she couldn't handle.

Jay watched, his chin tucked in with disapproval.

Mackenzie watched the disembodied glowing eyes out on the edge of the night. His father had taken such things as signs. His father's spirits and demons had not been the sort of gods Mackenzie had ever understood very well; they were vain, whimsical, crafty, corrupt, easily bored and frequently inconsistent. But his father had been comfortable with them.

Earle startled him—not by speaking but by what he said, because it lapped across the drift of Mackenzie's thoughts:

"Are you religious, any of you?"

None of them answered right away and Earle turned his plea on Shirley: "Are you?"

"I was," she said. "I don't know."

"We're still alive, aren't we? God's looking after us."

114

Jay snorted audibly.

"Jay, you may not believe in God but He believes in you. Yesterday I heard you praying. The Lord's Prayer."

"An aberration."

"You've got no faith?"

"Faith? Crap. Faith is accepting something without evidence. No. What good's that? You can't eat faith. You can't drink it."

"God is keeping us alive. I don't know why."

"If you want to talk let's talk about something else."

"There's nothing else to talk about."

"Then shut up."

Shirley said, "Jay," with quiet reproach. Mackenzie caught a sour whiff of Jay's sweat.

Jay said, "I've always resented living in a society that requires me to profess a belief in a nonexistent God in whose name people can justly any heinous crime they choose to commit. Now we're out here away from all that—a whisker away from dying and this idiot's trying to lay that crap on me. It's something I damn well don't need right now."

Earle withered a little.

Mackenzie discovered a second animal out along another vector from the fire—he saw the pink reflections of its eyes.

Shirley had seen them; now Jay turned to watch.

A kit fox came in plain sight and sat fascinated by the fire twenty yards from them.

Opposite the fox the pink-eyed one moved into view more cautiously, materializing tentatively: an antelope jackrabbit, huge ears erect, nose twitching. It sat up like a kangaroo and emitted a series of faint guttural barks. Its big feet drummed a fast tattoo: Mackenzie could feel the vibration.

It was talking: inviting others to come see the fire. Mackenzie began to smile.

"There are answers for everything." Jay kept his voice right down but it was harsh. "It happens we have very few of them but that's no reason to be an abject fool about it."

The fox sat still, no bigger than a squirrel, far too small to threaten the jackrabbit: the herbivore and the carnivore sat in the same circle of light and studied the mystery of fire.

Jay's monotone droned fitfully. "The thing that boggles the mind is how every religious fanaticism has to be so hostile to all the other fanaticisms. So you have endless atrocities committed by one fanaticism against another. Even if you were stupid enough to concede that one of them might be true—out of all those thousands of idiotic faiths not more than one could possibly be true. So all the others are false."

Shirley looked away as if Jay's maunderings embarrassed her: they seemed to reveal too much about Jay. He was reverting to banalities: attacking Earle, who was the most defenseless of them—and Mackenzie, when he felt a wave of anger against Earle, realized they were like a flock of mindless chickens who would suspend their pecking order just to hammer a sick member of the flock to death.

Mackenzie's square brick of a hand lifted against the fire and splayed, drawing their attention. "Quiet down, Jay."

The big jack thumped several times, patterns of sound. Something swept past over their heads—owl or bat. For a while it was a studied tableau: four naked humans, the fire; fox and hare watching from the edge of the circle of firelight.

There was bile in Mackenzie's throat; his stomach knotted with the hot sour pain of acute hunger. He watched the flux and flow of Jay's expressions—Jay's grip on reason was failing; he was swaying with the conflicting pressures of raw feelings. It was inevitable and

116

Mackenzie felt the same temptations in himself: the physical reduction to elemental atavism demanded a parallel reduction in emotional behavior but it was something they had to fight because if they gave in to it they were lost.

Jay laughed dispiritedly. "What difference does it make. I'm sorry, Earle—I'm taking it all out on you. Forgive me."

"I don't mind, Jay. It's circumstantial influence."

"What?"

"The Pavlov experiments." Earle's eyes were shut; his voice wasn't much more than a whisper. "Present an animal with an insoluble problem—put a rat in a maze that's got no exit. He'll hallucinate eventually. Isn't that what Duggai's doing to us?"

"How the hell do you ever reconcile religious nonsense with that behaviorist nonsense? Seems to me the two are mutually exclusive."

"Never mind." Earle's head rolled back. "I'm too tired."

Mackenzie heard the frightened squeal when something hit one of the noose snares.

Jay gathered his legs.

"Keep quiet," Mackenzie murmured.

The squeal from the darkness had agitated the fox; it backed away to the very rim of darkness so that the bright dots of its eyes were surrounded by nothing more than shadows suggestive of its outline. The jackrabbit sat up alert, ears twisting.

Mackenzie kept his face averted from the fire and his eyes squinted down to slits: he didn't want night blindness. What had the snare trapped? Rabbit—or only a mouse?

He pushed two small logs deeper into the fire. There was the distinct hoot of an owl not far away. He watched the jackrabbit. It carried its forepaws high and

117

limp-wristed; the nostrils and ears kept wiggling. Irrationally Mackenzie kept listening for the truck again.

Shirley murmured, "We ought to be telling ghost stories."

Silence again and then it was broken when the jackrabbit made its heel-and-toe tattoo. It made Mackenzie think of the ceremonial dances: the repetitive hypnotic chant, shuffling horny feet stamping the beaten earth, heads jerking, arms pumping, outcries to the knee-high gods of the pantheistic world.

For Mackenzie's paternal grandfather, whom he'd never known, it had been a twenty-five-mile walk to the trading post; the old folks had to carry water in buckets from a well half a mile away from the hogan. And their son, Mackenzie's father, the silversmith, had never been a citizen: in Arizona Indians only got the vote in 1948. Tsosi was dead by then.

Why am I thinking about all that?

He heard the swoop of movement in the air, a brief falsetto squeak; the labored beating of wings. The owl had nailed something.

The night was alive all around them: things grunted and moved through the brush. Through hooded eyes he watched the lone jackrabbit. It hadn't moved from its hypnotized place.

Then there was the definite smash of something big enough to make a racket in the bush: a sudden scrabbling—something had been hooked. It scratched to get loose. Not far away.

The racket was enough to break the jack's spell: it bolted away into the night.

Mackenzie gripped the knife and walked away from the fire.

14

One of the snares had been torn away, nothing left but a broken branch. Perhaps the owl had taken the catch. But there was a half-strangled jackrabbit twenty yards down the trail and there was a bonus nearby: another noose had trapped a half-grown one. He killed them both with the knife and carefully removed the loops and reset his snares. Then he heard something struggling and he went down the path to search out the source of the noise.

He couldn't identify it at first. Its struggle with the snare had sent it into the thicket of the manzanita's center and Mackenzie was reluctant to reach blindly through the tangle. He moved around the bush until starlight picked up the scaly shine—a lizard, a very big one, as big as his forearm. If it was a Gila Monster he wanted no part of its poisons. He spread branches apart carefully to get a better look and the lizard thrashed until its face came into the light.

Chuckwalla—eight or nine pounds in weight. Mackenzie's hand shot in through the spiny twigs; he killed the lizard with the blade and untangled the snare with precise caution because one of them had already been ripped away and he had no more string.

He carried the three carcasses to the fire. Earle was awake again. The three of them looked upon his booty;

he caught a telltale dart of Shirley's tongue, a twitch of Earle's cheek muscle. Jay only watched empty-eyed.

Mackenzie skinned the lizard and cut chunks of meat, skewered them on green twigs and passed them out. "Make sure it's cooked before you eat it."

Shirley regarded it with revulsion.

"And forget your prejudices," Mackenzie added mildly. He attended to the two hares: he lined a little pit with the lizard skin and drained the blood into it; then he disemboweled the jackrabbits and skinned them with slow care to retain the hide. He took the meat off the bones carefully and sliced it into strips; he cut seams in the ears and opened the skins out flat; he broke leg bones and ribs off and threw them directly on the fire.

He gathered up the lizard skin cupped in his hands. "Drink." Nothing in the world was more nourishing than fresh blood.

He sent them foraging and they returned with a harvest of salad makings: grass tips and saltbush—they would need a great deal of that; until they found an animal lick it would be their only source of salt—and maguey greens mashed to pulp on rocks.

Savaged by hunger they consumed the three pounds or so of meat on the chuckwalla in the course of an hour, cooking it spitted over the fire a bite at a time.

Mackenzie poked around in the fire with a stick, found the burnt rabbit bones, scraped them out into a maguey leaf. "We eat these bone ashes. Dysentery preventive."

"All that rabbit meat—it'll spoil, won't it?"

"We'll hang it dry."

"Don't you need salt to cure meat?"

"The sun does the job."

They stripped the spines off an arm of Senita and quenched their thirsts on its pulp.

Earle ruminated on a mouthful of chuckwalla.

120

"Tastes like curried chicken. You set a good table, Sam."

He felt mildly pleased with himself.

His belly churned: unaccustomed food, unaccustomed fullness after long hunger. The satisfaction of simple bodily needs made room for an awareness of other hurts and it was his feet that concerned him most. With the edge of one of the splintered quartz fire-rocks he scraped the rabbit hides as clean as he could; then while they were still pliably soft he sliced narrow strips off them lengthwise to use for lacings later on. He showed Shirley and Jay how to hang the meat where the sun would dry it; he was back at work on the skins while they did that job and gathered more firewood; then he heard again the twang of a tripped snare, the angered lungings of something in the brush, and he lurched out of the fire's circle to retrieve the catch.

Another jackrabbit: a small one no more than a few months old. It told him he'd made a mistake and he set all the snares a few inches higher so that the loops hung nine or ten inches above the ground; possibly he'd missed catching several full-grown jacks because his snares had been set too low.

Before he skinned out the new catch he had to sharpen the knives again. The brass alloy took a fairly good edge but wouldn't hold it long. He'd bent one of them doing something; he didn't straighten it—a bent knife was preferable to a weak one.

Tidbits of memory kept drawing him along the path of knowledge like crumbs scattered before a pecking bird: he visualized his father's moccasin-work and the beaded rabbit-skin jackets they'd made forty years ago and this time he remembered to remove the hare's sinews intact and to clean out the insides of the ears without slitting them open; once the flesh was removed it was possible to turn them inside out, scrape them clean, hang them for a sun cure. It was the most rudimentary curing system and would leave them with unsatisfactorily hard leathers but these would be far better than bare-ass nakedness—it was a matter of protection, not prudery. If they could keep the snares working for a few more nights they'd accumulate enough skins for essential clothing. It would be stiff and it would stink but if they were to have a chance of outwitting Duggai they needed to have mobility and that meant shoes, hats to keep the glare off, clothes to protect their privates from injury and their skins from the sun: there were things you simply couldn't do at night, you had to be able to move about in daylight more than they'd done today— otherwise this might take months and none of them was going to survive that long on rabbit meat and cactus: if nothing else they'd die on account of the simple lack of salt. You could eat saltbush until you were stuffed and it would do about as much good as a pinch of table salt.

If I were alone out here, he thought, I'd make it. Duggai and all, I'd make it.

But he wasn't alone and Jay and Shirley were greenhorns; and the broken leg anchored all of them. Of course Duggai had broken Earle's leg deliberately with this in mind: Earle had given him the excuse but it might just as easily have been any of them. Duggai wasn't the sort of avenger who left anything to chance.

Thinking of Duggai as an avenger—it was a turn of phrase that occurred to him now for the first time— made him recall Duggai's parting speech to them: it had been just over twenty-four hours ago. *Now maybe you find out how much of a crime it is. Maybe you find out how crazy you got to be to want to live. I tell you one thing—whatever happens to you out here ain't half as bad as what they do to a man in them hospitals.*

Ordinarily if a man nursed the dream of vengeance on account of his capture and imprisonment he vented

122

the dream against policemen or prosecutors or witnesses who identified him as guilty. Duggai hadn't gone after any of those. His resentment was aimed at the practitioners who had searched around inside him and concluded that he was not responsible for his actions. By making that statement they diminished him. And they put him away in a place that was to a man like Duggai infinitely less tolerable than a penitentiary. In prison the rule was brutality and Duggai could have lived with that—it would have been a finite sentence, he'd have been able to look forward to parole. For a misfit like Duggai a commitment to the state mental hospital must have looked like a one-way ticket and it wasn't the kind of place where a man could sustain himself on immediate physical hate: the attendants and doctors would treat him with professional competence rather than contemptuous ruthlessness. There was no object in sight on which to focus rage; therefore it focused on something more distant but less elusive—the four psychiatric witnesses who'd sent him to the place.

But there was more than that. There was the heritage of witchcraft and shamanism.

Mackenzie had felt the glancing edges of it in his own childhood. Now and then there was a witch-hunt—sometimes when someone got sick, sometimes when someone ran amuck. Either way it was the same: sick or drunk he'd been witched; people had a duty to find out who was responsible and deal with the witch. There was only one way and that was to hire a shaman whose powers were stronger than those of the witch. Then you had to bring the witch—by force if necessary—into the presence of the shaman and the shaman would make medicine to drive the spirit out of the witch. They didn't advertise it but the Navajo were firm believers in exorcism. In a good many cases it wasn't all that much different from psychiatry. The jargon differed but the objective was the same and the methods were not totally dissimilar.

It was something Grandfather Mackenzie had always tried to combat: his rigid Presbyterian mentality had loathed superstition and psychiatry alike—"They don't call them headshrinkers for nothing."

Duggai had been witched. He could escape from the hospital and he might break to freedom—there was always Mexico—but he would remain a doomed man unless he could exorcise the demons from inside him. You didn't get rid of demons by simply killing the witches who had injected them into you; you had to crush the witches' power. Only when their power was squashed could you gather enough strength to expel the demons.

That was why Duggai hadn't simply killed them and dumped the bodies. And it was why Duggai was still out there. Otherwise he'd be deep into Mexico by now. But he was a Navajo and he'd been witched and he had to take care of that first. He had no medicine of his own. He had to rely on nature's medicine: the gods of the desert: they would provide his justice.

Duggai would not interfere with their attempts to survive but he would wait out there and he would watch and he would terrorize them. If they lived and tried to get past Duggai then he would have to kill them for simple practical reasons—revenge and the prolongation of his own freedom—but if it came to that Duggai would kill them without pleasure because he would know that their power was too strong for him and therefore his demons were still intact; he would know he was doomed.

If Duggai ended up having to kill them with bullets he wouldn't live long after that. He'd try to shoot up a town or he'd walk into a police station and start a battle. Driven by the demons he'd be forced to precipitate his own destruction.

I lived out there that time because I was Innun.

124

Maybe you can live too. If you make it I'll be waiting for you, Captain.

No comfort in it but there was the knowledge that if it came to that, Duggai would score a Pyrrhic triumph.

It was the key to Duggai's tolerance. It was also a weakness they could exploit: Duggai would give them room to move around.

Understanding Duggai's motives was one thing. Understanding his evil was another. The more he thought about Duggai the more fervid became Mackenzie's rage. He hated Duggai with all the fury in his soul.

It was no good forgiving the enemy; a raging hatred was necessary: it was the spur to survival. Passions of rage consumed Mackenzie and he made no effort to resist them.

Toward morning the snares netted them a brace of jackrabbits. It was all they could expect from this worked-over patch of ground; the snares would have to be moved to a new hunting ground by tomorrow night.

Shirley volunteered to skin out one of the hares and her initiative shamed Jay into tackling the other. Mackenzie monitored the work, made a monosyllabic suggestion now and then, fought down his reluctance to let them handle the knives: he couldn't afford botched work but he no longer felt inclined to deny them their authority—his obsession with tyranny had burned itself out. At first he'd undertaken the experiment in benevolent dictatorship with shameful eagerness—not often in a lifetime was a man allowed to decree every move in the lives of his companions—and perhaps it had been necessary or perhaps he had only rationalized its necessity but the subtle brief groan of the pickup truck had changed all that. Duggai.

If Duggai was watching them through some telescopic device then he understood that they were being sustained by Mackenzie's leadership. If Duggai got a little impatient or a little more desperate he might think about putting a bullet into Mackenzie: kill him or disable him. Mackenzie would be the first target. It was only sensible to share the responsibility out; if he became a casualty the others might still have a chance.

The next time he went out to check the snares he took Jay along and showed him how to set them.

15

In the gray light before dawn they worked with concentrated silent industry. They smashed bones and ate the marrow for its nourishment. Mackenzie made a sack from entrails to hold blood from the night's kill.

A light scatter of cirrus clouds hung very high in the west but the sun would dissipate them early; there was no chance of rain until the brief season of cloudbursts of early autumn. If anything was predictable about the Southwestern desert it was drought and the fact that the early afternoon temperature would reach a minimum of 115 degrees and might go as high as 140 degrees. Equally predictable was a nighttime drop of as much as 70 degrees; by dawn the four of them were chilled through.

While Mackenzie worked the skins he explored possibilities and plans. He'd thought of moving camp late in the day but now he rejected it: once they left they'd have to move fast and keep moving and cover their tracks. During the days they'd have to hide out from Duggai and at night they wouldn't be able to light a fire. It would require meticulous preparation. Earle had to be considered.

They hung strips of meat on cactus spines. A day in the sun should cure the jerky. With bone needles and sinews and narrow strips of hide they set about sewing moccasins. They fitted patterns by laying the hides out under their feet and tracing oval outlines with chalky stones on the skins; they cut ankle flaps and punched holes all the way around the edges and threaded thong lacings through them. They made the moccasins inside out, hair-lined with the raw flesh out. "Put them on and keep them on as much as you can. It'll dry out and harden—we want them molded to the shapes of our feet." And beforehand it was prudent to examine the hair for insects.

It took all the hides; there was nothing left over for clothing. But they'd increased their range of movement.

With the three of them working the job was done quite rapidly; for the first time in Mackenzie's recent memory Shirley showed that she could smile—the little accomplishment pleased and encouraged her.

Just on sunrise he took Jay with him down along the trapline. They dismantled the snares and carried them away. Mackenzie prowled along the foot of the slope and they had to walk half a mile before Mackenzie found a fresh jackrabbit run. He didn't speak at first; testing Jay, he waited, and it gratified him when Jay made the discovery for himself. "That's got to be a trail—look how it's pounded down."

They set the snares and climbed back toward the cemetery. The jerry-built moccasins abraded Mackenzie's ankles and provided inadequate armor against the desert surface; it was still necessary to pick footings with care but at least it was no longer an agony simply to walk.

Midway back Jay stopped him. "I want to say something."

Mackenzie waited for it. Jay was looking up toward the horizon; he brought his face grudgingly around; the low-level sun licked the surfaces of his eyes, putting a shine on them, rendering his face sinister. "We'd have been dead by now without you."

"Maybe." Without me how do you know what resources you might have discovered in yourselves? But he didn't say it.

"You and Shirley—"

"For God's sake, Jay, that's beside the point."

"It can't help color our emotions."

"Stop being a psychiatrist. It won't help us out here."

"Mackenzie, there was a time I wanted to kill you."

"I know."

"Well, I want to express my gratitude."

"Sure." He said it gently with a smile but Jay's thanks didn't mean much; he'd been groping toward equilibrium but he hadn't nearly reached it yet and any setback could spin him right off balance again. Any imagined provocation could turn Jay vicious. In normal constraints he tended to bluster toothlessly: his threats to kill Mackenzie had been empty. But out here the placenta of normality was ruptured. They all were poised on the brink of sanity; trust was in short supply all around; several times Mackenzie had felt his own temper slipping free and the next time he might not contain it. And because he fancied he owned a better degree of stability than Jay's he found no comfort in this temporary offer of the olive branch.

But he showed Jay his smile and they went on up into the camp; Mackenzie was thinking, If he was sure of those feelings he'd have thanked me in the presence of the others. This way if there was an inconsistency no one would know it but the two of them. He didn't credit Jay with malicious intent; the bet-coppering shrewdness was unconscious.

They cooked a last small batch of meat over the fire and Mackenzie decided to let it go out; there'd be no point feeding it through the day. Fuel was scarce and too dry to make smoke and in any case he had decided against trying to make any kind of signal. If they were spotted from the air and there were any attempt to rescue them it only meant Duggai would finish them off with the rifle.

It was time to carry Earle to his hole. Earle was twitching in his sleep. His skin was hot and dry. When they picked him up he uttered a low incoherent groan. They cleaned him where he'd soiled himself and lowered him into the trench. Shirley said, "I'm worried about him."

"He's suffering from shock trauma," Mackenzie said. "Can't expect anything much less."

"What can we do for him?"

"Not a hell of a lot without antibiotics. If he doesn't get salt fairly soon he'll develop violent cramps."

"Feed him saltbush?"

"Some. It may help. But too much of it, he'd end up worse off for the dysentery."

"Then what can we do?"

"Go out on a salt hunt tonight," Mackenzie said. "The odds aren't too bad. This desert was an ocean floor at one time. There's plenty of salt. Question is whether there's any right at the surface."

Shirley searched the horizon. "How could we possibly find it?"

"If it's there the animals know where it is. After dark I'll take a hike, see if I can pick up an animal trail, follow it along and see where it leads." And try to stay out of Duggai's sights, he thought dismally.

Churlishly it crossed his mind that they'd be in much better shape if Earle died. The leg was going to take at least six weeks to heal. Duggai wasn't patient enough to give them six weeks or any significant portion of it; another day or two and Duggai would begin to get nervous, start looking over his shoulder, working out the odds that a plane or helicopter might come by.

They had to find some way to survive not only their

130

nakedness and the desert but Duggai's high-powered rifle as well. Thinking about that as he sank into his trench, Mackenzie felt a dispiriting wave of hopelessness. It was like a hurricane to a man in a small open boat: even if by extraordinary seamanship he managed to conquer one giant wave there was another right behind it and another behind that. . . .

Anxiety dumped him into a fitful sleep; exhaustion devoured him.

His face felt dry; it was covered with dust and insect bites. A wind blew sand across the top of the trench. His bowels were knotted. He made it up out of the trench and stumbled toward the futile shade of a bush. He had forgotten the heat; when it hit him he recoiled.

He leaned against a branch weak and sweating. Diarrhea burned him and vomit pain convulsed his stomach: he catted up a bilious stream. Bathed in perspiration, scalp prickling, he reeled out under the merciless orange sun. He felt his hair scorch as if it were hot wire.

Far off in the sky a jet made a faint sound like ripping cloth. He caught a tail-of-the-eye movement imperfectly and turned and discovered a small gecko darting into the shade: the only time you saw a lizard was when it moved. Now it sat under the bush, the pulse beating in its throat.

He lurched back to the trench and collapsed into it. For a while he dozed in feverish discomfort: in the heat time had no meaning. The pains came and went, rumbling uneasily in his belly.

Suddenly it was sundown. He lifted himself on his elbows and saw one pale star. Chills swept him furiously; he sank back. Something thick on his tongue had the residual taste of stale sleep but it was heavy and harsh, a sickening pungency that tasted like death. He was afraid. His pulse was thin, weak, rapid.

Shirley's sudden silhouette above him: "How do you feel?"

He couldn't focus on her: his eyes wouldn't track. He muttered something. She swung her legs over, sat on the rim and dropped to her feet beside him. "You've got a fever, Sam."

He rubbed his face, felt the cracked parchment of his cheeks. "Where's Jay?"

"He went to look for salt."

Duggai. He stared off into the twilight. Well, maybe it would be all right—maybe Duggai would let Jay stumble around out there wearing himself out in fruitless search. Maybe.

He saw she was carrying something in both hands and when she brought it closer to his face he recognized it—a small transparent bag cut from the raincoat's sleeve; pendulous with water.

"Drink it. It's beautiful. Fresh and clear."

He took it into his swollen mouth a sip at a time. "Things I need to be doing . . ."

"Tell me. Jay and I will do what we can."

If Jay ever returned. "How much water did that thing make?"

"The bag was full. Nearly a gallon, I imagine. It's astonishing, Sam."

"It'll do the same tomorrow but you've got to feed it—by now it's sucked a lot of the moisture out of that ground. Ought to urinate in there—around the cup, not in it. Cut pieces of cactus, dump them in there. Dig moist earth out of the walls of these trenches—put that in too. Every night we drink the fresh water and clean the junk out of the bowl around it. Start over again, feed it for the next day."

"How does it work?"

"Sun heats the plastic. Draws moisture out of anything in there—the ground, cactus, anything. Principle of evaporation. Water condenses on the underside of

132

the plastic, drips down to the low point, drops into the cup. It's a solar still—it'll condense pure distilled water out of any moisture in the hole."

"It's incredible." She was behaving with deliberate composure that betrayed how close she was to wild hysteria: their lifeline was fraying.

He coughed; something dry rattled in his chest. "Listen—use some of that water to make clay pots. Bake them in the fire. Can you make a fire now?"

"It's already burning. Jay made it before he left."

"Make mud, shape the pots, bake them slow—not too close to the fire or they'll crack. Got it?"

"What else, Sam?"

"We've got to start making some effort toward hygiene. We'll end up with festering sores if we can't clean ourselves. Got to make soap."

"How?"

"Cooking fats and white wood ashes. Mix it up in a clay pot. There's potash and soda in the ashes—mix it with grease and you get good soap. Stinks like a bastard but it cleans. Use the hair side of a piece of rabbit skin for a washcloth. Sponge baths." He ran out of breath.

His consciousness skipped a few segments of time—instants or perhaps hours. When he looked up again she was gone; when he looked yet again he saw thin clouds scudding across the stars; next he awoke and heard echoes of a ranting voice that he recognized as his own and he knew he'd been delirious in his fever.

Shirley plied him with morsels of warm cooked jerky. He couldn't swallow them. He took several swallows of water and coughed. "Where's Jay?"

"He hasn't come back yet. I'm sorry, Sam, I can't lift you out of here alone."

He went dizzy and nearly fainted. His eyes rolled shut and he heard her climb out of the trench, heard the muted song of her distracted humming. Why was it so incredibly hot?

Then it went cold—bone-chilling cold that rattled him with a trembling violence: the skin of his chest jerked with a palsied looseness and it radiated out to the farthest reaches of his body.

Shirley was trying to haul him up out of the ground. "Come on—help me, Sam, we'll get you to the fire."

But it was no good; he shook uncontrollably. His teeth kept banging. He tried to curl up into a fetal ball, clenched his hands between his thighs, felt the rough cold earth against cheek and shoulder and hip. Faintly he heard her speak, a catch in her throat: "We haven't got blankets, Sam." Then she curled soft against him, warm against his back, her knees under his, arms around his chest; she rubbed his chest hard with the flats of her hands. He tried to speak but reality swam away before he could voice his gratitude.

The fever broke and he came out of it as flaccid as protoplasm. At first he thought it was midmorning by the long shadow but then he saw he'd got turned around: that was the north wall and therefore it must be well past noon. *Jay*—had he returned?

There were ashes beyond his feet and when he looked up he found another dead little fire above him in the head of the pit.

By his hand lay a plastic balloon filled with water, tied shut with woven strands of red hair.

He drank it with slow patience, measuring out the greed of his thirst; he drank it all—at least a pint—and reached gratefully for the jerky that hung spitted against the wall of his grave.

Chewing the thing set up an ache in the weakened muscles of his jaws but he masticated it as fine as he could before he risked swallowing. Afterward he lay with his shoulder propped against the wall trying to gather energy to get up for a look around. He drowsed while random images fled through his uneasy mind. It occurred to him without much force that somewhere in the run of the past few hours he had nearly died and that Shirley's body and the two fires had kept him alive. He pictured himself rising out of the grave and had an image of Duggai out there watching through field glasses with keen disappointment.

He almost slept again but Shirley's angry hoarse yelling aroused him. He managed to get his feet under him and stood with his arms on the rim of the pit.

She stood above her trench throwing rocks and yelling at the buzzards that swooped low over the strings of hung jerky. The racket scared them off and they went back toward the hills in long resentful spirals of movement.

Her shoulders slumped; she watched them plane away; then she saw Mackenzie and she came anxiously toward him, the thin moccasins kicking up little whorls of dust.

"How do you feel?"

"Rocky. You'd better not stand in the sun." The heat was a furnace blast.

She hesitated—still ten feet from him—and stopped; her eyes went toward the farther trenches. Now Mackenzie saw bruises on her face. There was an ugly blue patch under her eye and one cheek was discolored. It wasn't sunburn.

She saw his face change and she tried to dismiss it. "Do you want more water?"

"I can wait for sundown. Shirley—"

"You'd better not burn energy talking. Get back out of the sun." She went away too quickly, he thought; furtively.

He spoke to her back: "Get some sleep. I'll take a turn doing scarecrow."

He saw her nod quickly as she climbed into her hole. She didn't look back at him.

So Jay had returned. Jay must have found them

135

pressed together in the pit during the night. And rage had overwhelmed Jay and he'd beaten her.

If he comes after me tonight I won't have much strength to fight him.

He lay back in the trench and squinted at the sky.

16

Through the hot afternoon he dozed and made periodic surveillances of the hanging food; once it was a near thing but he shouted the buzzards away. The fever had wasted his strength and he felt coltishly fragile—the least muscular requirement meant a willed determination and his mind floated in an eddying pool of unformed anxieties.

The sun tipped over and lost strength. Voices roused him from his stuporous reveries. At first he didn't attend to the words. He found an obscure fascination in listening to the songs and qualities, the play of sound back and forth among them, the feelings revealed in their tones; it occurred to him that a baby or a dog would listen to human conversation that way and absorb the same meanings from it.

Then the words trickled into his awareness.

"You're just trying to insist that God doesn't exist because if God doesn't exist then your sins don't exist. But it's no good denying the obvious. Who made the universe?"

"Aagh. Who made God?"

Mackenzie closed his eyes and found the humor in it.

"If I'd known I was going to be imprisoned out here with this loony defender of the faith I'd have—" Jay's voice trailed off and then resumed at the same pitch:

"I'll tell you this—God wouldn't keep his authority long if he was ever around to answer questions. Crap. I'm going—it's cool enough. You can fend for yourselves until I get back."

Mackenzie tried to lift himself. "No," he muttered aloud; he wanted to tell Jay to give it up—Duggai was out there. But he went dizzy and fell back. He heard the crunch of footsteps. Jay called: "Maybe you can find some way to have a rational conversation with the official representative of God here." The fatuity of it made a reckless laughter bubble in Mackenzie. He tried again to rise but his body was lax and he hadn't the will. He heard Jay's slow footsteps diminish. Earle coughed and there was a broken stretch without sound; the light began to change.

Two buzzards slalomed overhead. Mackenzie felt gritty, his head ached, there was a miserable knot in his gut; he pictured himself dismembering Duggai, snarling, pulping Duggai's big face with his fists. The savage fantasy was vivid.

Sullen and pugnacious, he emerged finally from entombment. Sweating, he surveyed the world around him until it stopped swimming. The sun tumbled out of sight before he got his breath. Near Mackenzie's hole a crowd of red ants dragged a huge dung beetle stubbornly across the earth. He saw half a dozen jackrabbit pelts hung on bushes near the fire; Shirley was on her haunches, her back to him, working with tinder and kindling. Earle lay with his arms folded across his breastbone like a corpse. The buzzards made lazy portentous circles overhead. A mile away along the flanks of the barren hills a small figure crabbed diagonally toward the skyline—Jay.

There was a bone-clicking racket when Shirley tried to set fire to the kindling. He got down on one knee to fix the lacings of his moccasins and then made his way drunkenly between catclaw and ocotillo along the slope.

Her cheeks were dark and gaunt. Mackenzie said, "Let me take a turn at that." She gave the rocks up to him. He sat flaking off chips and sparks while Earle muttered incoherently beside them and Shirley's swollen eyes drifted off toward the skyline to the east where Jay had gone out of sight behind a fold of ground.

Shirley's expression was fixed, melancholy, imprisoned. "He found a trail last night. He followed it a long way but he didn't find any salt. He's going to follow it in the other direction tonight."

"If he's not careful he'll wear himself out. It was stupid going off on his own."

"Someone had to."

"What if he twists his ankle five miles from here?" He didn't mention Duggai.

"I almost wish he would." She said it with infinite sadness. "I shouldn't hate him for what this is doing to him. It's not his fault." She flicked a tiny stone with her fingernail: it rolled a few feet and stopped, becoming indistinguishable from all the others. "Better off dead."

"What?"

"All of us. We're just prolonging this. Duggai's never going to let us out alive."

Mackenzie said dryly, "Where there's life . . ."

"Don't patronize me with platitudes."

"Well you know there's one Duggai and there are four of us."

"I'm sure he's got at least four bullets, Sam."

"At least we ought to give ourselves a run for our money."

"It's so unfair." She stood up and walked away. Mackenzie didn't watch her go. He kept scraping the quartz pieces together and after a while the tinder nourished a spark and it grew; he let it take half the kindling before he pushed the thin red logs into it.

When it was burning to his satisfaction he had a look at Earle.

139

Wire-thin veins made circular smudges on Earle's wasted cheeks. His belly was swollen but his chest and limbs had shrunk; the skin hung in loose folds and his elbows and shoulders protruded like those of something already dead.

Earle's face twitched; he looked apologetic. He said, "I suffer, therefore I live," and grinned maliciously.

"How do you feel?"

"Terrible. But you know it's a little like being up against a grindstone. Either it grinds you down or it polishes you up. Depends what you're made of. Spiritually I feel much stronger than I ever did before. Whatever happens, I can take it."

"Sure you can."

Earle shivered. "Sorry. Ghost walked over my grave."

"Jay's gone looking for a salt lick."

"I know."

"If we can find salt you'll be all right, Earle."

"I'll be all right whether we find salt or not. The companions of God are looked after. I really believe that, you know."

Plainly he was clutching in desperation; but there would be no pleasure in the cruelty of planting doubt in Earle's mind.

Earle said, "Are you all right now?"

"I expect so."

"Good. You're the lifeline for the Painters, you know."

It made Mackenzie give him a quick direct look but Earle turned his face away; his eyes dulled. He had decided not to confide.

Mackenzie thought, he knows he's dying but he doesn't want to depress us. It made Mackenzie angry with Earle's empty heroics. Better for all of them if Earle simply got it over with. . . .

Mackenzie winced at his own callousness. He sat furiously blaspheming to himself. Then he faced the truth. "Earle, listen to me."

"Sure. I've got nothing else to do."

"Don't let yourself die for our convenience."

"What makes you think—"

"Suicide is a mortal sin, isn't it?"

"I'm not Roman Catholic. I'm Anglican—Episcopal."

"Sorry. I heard you talking about sins before."

"Hardly a concept exclusive to the Roman church."

"Earle, I just don't want to think you're fooling yourself into some idea of noble self-sacrifice."

Earle's eyes turned smoky and hurt. "Have you seen me trying to slit my throat? Have you?"

"I want you to fight, that's all."

"I am fighting. I'd have been dead long ago if I hadn't."

"You've got to start expecting to get out of this alive."

"You've always detested me," Earle said with practical sensibility. "Why are you so concerned about my survival?"

"Because there's got to be a difference between me and Calvin Duggai."

"Do you want to be cryptic?"

"We've got to prove we're better than Duggai. We've got to survive—*all* of us."

"So that's the obsession that's driving you."

"Listen, you God damned son of a bitch, I intend to have Duggai's head in a basket and I expect you to help me get it."

Earle went all colors at Mackenzie's profanity. Then abruptly he smiled. "You're a mystic after all. You believe in that Indian witchcraft just as much as he does."

"What do you know about that?"

141

"I know enough to figure out why he left us alive instead of shooting us. Devils and spells and demons. I read up on it when the lawyers asked me to examine him. Thought it might be a key. After all, he's had cultural implantations a lot different from mine."

"How the hell *do* you reconcile your religious faith with that behaviorist dogma?"

"God makes the laws. Our behavior is just obedience to God's laws. I don't see any contradiction, do you?" Earle coughed distressingly and then smiled. "You're trying to change the subject."

"What was the subject?" He was tired; he honestly didn't remember.

"Your mystical obsession with proving that your devil power is stronger than Duggai's."

Earle fell back exhausted soon after and Mackenzie left him to rest. He'd tried to dismiss Earle's speculations but their ripples disturbed him for a time.

Shades of lavender and lilac suffused the distance. He fed the fire and turned on his haunches to look for Shirley. He found her in dramatic silhouette: she stood on a boulder searching the horizons. Against the sky she was like a sculpted Diana. The picture was vivid and he held it, not moving, watching her and absorbing the sight: a wild dramatic work of graphic art.

Finally he went uphill toward her. She looked heartbreakingly beautiful.

He put his hands around her ribs and lifted her down off the boulder. She stood against him; she didn't draw away.

She didn't smile. "Can you feel my heart?"

"I thought it was mine."

"Sam—right now I feel about sex roughly the way I feel about eating ground glass. But I want you to squeeze me until it hurts. I want to draw your strength into me."

142

They cleaned themselves with wood-ash soap and scraps of rabbit fur; they sponged Earle down and he spoke softly of God's bounties. Mackenzie built up the fire higher than it had been on previous nights: Jay would want a beacon to find his way back. He went down along the new trapline that Jay had set but it was too early and there were no prizes yet. They drank from the still and bagged the rest of the water, cleaned out the pit and spent half an hour gathering cactus and cutting it up into the hole to provide tomorrow's water. Mackenzie found the tattered scraps of the moccasins Jay must have used on his expedition of the previous night; apparently Jay had made new moccasins for tonight's travel. Jackrabbit hide was too thin to last long on this terrain—and Jay was foraging a good many miles out. Mackenzie had an idea what Jay's feet must have been like by the time he'd returned to camp fourteen hours ago; it spoke of Jay's courage that he had gone out again tonight. Maybe Duggai would leave him alone again. . . .

The clay bowls were clumsy but they were serviceable: Shirley improvised a thick soup from meat and blood and water and chopped saltbush. Mackenzie wasted nearly an hour searching a widening area for poles long and thick enough to make a litter but the land didn't provide anything nearly substantial enough; they would have to carry Earle on their backs until they got into heavier growth somewhere.

When he returned to the fire he said, "We should plan to move out tomorrow night."

"To where?"

He pointed toward the hills to the northeast. "I've heard coyotes up there."

"I don't understand."

"There'd be water not too far away. Bigger animals. Maybe salt too. That's the way we'll go until we find what we need. When we can equip ourselves with more

143

clothes and better footwear. Then we strike out due north. We move all night and hole up by day."

"Why north?"

"There's a superhighway."

"How do you know that?"

"Senita. The little organ pipes. They only grow in Arizona west of the divide."

"Where does that put us?"

"East of Yuma. Luke Air Force Gunnery Range." He indicated the compass points. "That's east, more or less. There's a road that runs north from the Mexican border through one or two little towns, finally ends up at the highway junction at Gila Bend. We could strike out for that road but it might be a hundred miles from here."

"That far? My God."

"This thing probably measures five or six thousand square miles. That way's the Mexican border. Might not be too far south of us but I don't think there's anything down there. Lava beds, craters, a lot of dry mountain ranges. They could have built towns down there in the past twenty years but I doubt it. That country's even less hospitable than this." He poked his chin toward the west. "That way we'd hit the Colorado River. Sooner or later. But we'd have to cross the Yuma flats to reach it—sand dunes. And again we don't know if he put us down east or west of center—it might be only twenty-five miles from here to the river, then again it could be more than a hundred. From Ajo to Yuma it's about a hundred and forty miles. It's all gunnery range. No— our best shot's north. The main highway between Tucson and San Diego. It can't be more than forty or fifty miles."

"I didn't know there was any uninhabited area that big any more."

"There are no roads, no human existence at all. Travel into these areas is forbidden."

144

"And forbidding."

"Anyhow we've got to go north. It won't be just forty miles. You can't go ten miles without running up against a range of mountains—they look easy from here but that's steep rubble and they're bigger than they look—six or seven thousand feet. You can go around the ranges but it trebles the distance. We've got a lot of ground to cover."

"Don't they ever patrol with helicopters?"

"If they've got reason to suspect someone's out here. Now and then I guess they do a routine sweep. But Duggai can reach us with that rifle if he sees a helicopter."

"If it came to that he probably wouldn't mind shooting the helicopter to pieces."

Mackenzie closed his eyes and nodded agreement. "He's just the one to prove he can do it. He knows 'copters—he'd shoot for the radio first, then the rotor coupling."

"What chance have we got then? Honestly."

"What difference does it make? It's the only shot we've got."

She began to clean out the bowls with a handful of grass. "It's tempting to get maudlin, isn't it." Mackenzie watched the play of muscles under her skin. She sat crosslegged, spine bent in a hunched concentration, breasts pendant, lip between teeth. "If you scrub too hard you disintegrate these things. I ruined one last night."

Then she looked over her shoulder toward the hills. She held the gaze for a moment. "I keep looking for buzzards up that way." She went back to work; her voice dropped. "If you want to know the truth he's amazed me in the past day or two. Before this happened if you'd served him a stringy piece of beef or told him his plane was half an hour late he'd have measured it as a catastrophe."

145

"It's not his fault."

"I'm not criticizing him. He never had to face this before. I suppose I'm surprised by how brave he's turned out to be." She scoured the last bowl and set it aside, making an irked face, rubbed her eyes. Then abruptly she said, "Oh, what difference does it make?"

"Don't go defeatist."

She made a little bark of sour laughter.

He said, "We started out hanging from our fingernails—not thinking any farther ahead than the next drop of water. We've made a lot of progress. We're talking about crossing a hundred miles."

"Well, thank you for the pep talk. But how do I ignore Duggai out there?"

"Think of him as one more hazard. We've licked some others."

"They're not the same. The desert doesn't care—it's indifferent. You can't say that of Duggai." Her shudder was theatrical; she apologized for it with a smile that switched on and off peculiarly. "Maybe it's because we don't see him. He's got so much bigger than life-size. He dominates every instant of our lives now. Some mythic malevolent ghost—one of those eternal spirits that can't die until they get their doomsday revenge. You know I keep picturing him like a childish nightmare—something gigantic with a scythe." Her head swiveled away; she tossed it as if she still had her long hair.

Neither of them had anything to say after that. Mackenzie didn't have the strength to keep anything going. The irony touched him: maybe out there Jay was torturing himself with fantasies of what might be transpiring between them.

He found himself listening for the sound of the four-wheel drive but there was no sound at all.

146

17

For a while he dozed. Near morning he worked the skins, made spare sets of moccasins, sewed a water bag with a shoulder strap and lined it with the raincoat sleeve. There were a few pelts left over—not enough for much but he sewed them into brief breechclouts with thong belts: not much protection but better than nothing. He gathered up two brass knives; there was no sign of the third one—Jay must have it. He made a little pocket in his breechclout and tramped the desert for half an hour gathering up a dozen additional .30-caliber shells; they might find uses for them.

Dusk, then dawn; and Jay had not returned. He built up the fire to provide Jay a homing beacon.

Earle said, "It feels cooler this morning. Maybe the sun won't be so bad today."

"Sun hasn't changed. You have—you're in better shape today."

"I thought I was supposed to die without salt."

"We put a lot of saltbush in that soup last night. Maybe it was enough for the time being."

"Those extra moccasins—"

"We'll be moving out tonight. They wear out pretty fast."

There was fresh rabbit meat from the night's snares. They ate up the marrow of briefly cooked bones and the ashes of charred ones, drank the last of the blood from the clay bowl, drank plentifully of the still's bounty of clear water. Mackenzie mucked out the still and carved segments of cholla into it, sealed the plastic coat down and squinted obliquely toward the rising sun: that was where Jay would appear but there was no sign of movement.

He went down into each of the trenches and dug out a few inches of soil from the bottom to expose a new underlayer of cool damp earth. Shirley was taking down the dried strings of jerky from the ocotillo racks and packing them into rabbit-hide folds. The sun began to drill into them and Mackenzie had another long look at the horizon. "He probably went too far during the night. Got caught short and dug a hole for himself."

"Or Duggai stopped him," Shirley said.

"We haven't heard gunshots."

It seemed to reassure her. They lowered Earle into the ground; he managed to smile. "Might not hurt if we all prayed for him."

Shirley went a few strides away toward her bunker; she waited for Mackenzie and dropped her voice so that it carried no farther than his ears. "Duggai wouldn't have needed to shoot him. Jay's no match for him. All he'd have to do would be break his leg the way he broke Earle's. Or hamstring him with a knife. Leave the inevitable to those horrible desert spirits of his."

"Most likely Jay's holed up somewhere to ride out the heat."

"Is that what you really think?"

"Yes. If Duggai got close enough to ambush him then he'd see Jay wasn't carrying enough water or food to make a run for help. As long as we stay in the area we're no threat to Duggai—he'll let us scramble."

"I wish I knew whether you believed that."

"It doesn't much matter what I believe. We've got to search for him tonight."

"Of course."

"He knows enough not to expose himself to the sun. We'll probably meet up with him an hour after dark."

"Sam—what if Duggai's crippled him?"

"Let's try to face one thing at a time."

"That's evasive."

"No. We've got to be practical. What's the sense wasting time worrying about catastrophes that may not have happened?"

"All right." She gave him a long level glance and Mackenzie saw irony creep into her eyes. It was directed inward. "Did you want to get laid last night?"

"No."

"But the thought did cross your mind."

"Yes." Put it down to that ancient biological impetus to procreate in time of stress.

"It crossed my mind too," she said, "but if we'd found out that Jay was out there dying while we were screwing. . . ."

"Never mind," Mackenzie said.

She touched the back of his hand with her fingers: there was gentle gratitude and a good deal of warmth in the gesture. She went away then and Mackenzie looked around the horizon, confused by feelings he sensed but could not identify. Out there he saw no buzzards and no sign of Jay. When he turned back she was descending into the earth. He felt the heat of the early sun against the raw burnt flesh of his shoulders; he got into his own trench and hunkered to keep his body out of the light—and sat that way watching the hills until his muscles began to cramp. There was no further likelihood of Jay's appearing; the sun was too high. Finally Mackenzie lay back, feeling the tremors of weakness when he lowered himself, resenting the residue of his fevered illness. He knew there was little remaining stamina. Throughout the night he'd tried to do everything with conservative torpor; nevertheless he felt rickety and drained. He wondered how far he could possibly carry Earle.

I doubt we'll get far at all, he thought with dismal clarity.

To his surprise he slept most of the day through. A thin choking swirl of dust awakened him. The dust devil wheeled across the top of his trench; he closed his eyes and curled up protectively. Driven sand needled his flesh and there was a great stinging furor but it passed quickly as the pint-sized whirlwind moved on. He scraped grit out of his eyes and spat dryly and then shot bolt upright in alarm because it just occurred to him the twister was veering west and the solar still lay in its path. The dust devil could pick up the plastic raincoat and carry it miles away.

He saw the plastic begin to flap but the twister careened away on its drunken aimless course; it passed twenty yards below Earle's bunker and dipped its tail in the empty pit that would have contained Jay. Carrying sand and twigs it veered toward the flats, a great spiraling funnel, obscuring the sun for a time.

He emptied the sand out of his moccasins and laced them up and went to inspect the still for damage. A good deal of dust floated on the water but the cup was nearly full. Withered bits of cactus surrounded it. He peeled the raincoat back and laid it out dry-side down and rubbed his hands on its beaded surface until they were dripping; he tried to wash some of the grit off his face.

The dust devil made its weird dancing way out along the plain, leaving a tan haze smeared across the sky. The six-o'clock sun threw its shadow across rocks and bits of brush. The air in his nostrils felt close and heavy; the temperature still hung well above the hundred mark but it would dissipate quickly now. Mackenzie used a clay pot to scoop a few mouthfuls of water out of the cup; he drank slowly and savored it. On his haunches by the rim of the ravine he squinted out along the hills

150

and knew they would find Jay up that way; the question in his mind was what condition they'd find him in.

The jerky was safe because they'd wrapped it; there'd been no need for a buzzard watch on the meat but he was a bit surprised he hadn't been awakened at least once during the day by the flap of wings as a bird swept down to inspect the motionless humans in their graves. It gave him bleak pause to wonder whether the buzzards might have found in Jay a more likely source of carrion nourishment. He saw no birds in the sky but that signified nothing.

He tightened the drawstring of his breechclout and shoved the two knives under the belt to free his hands. The dust devil was blowing itself out against a hillside. He studied the folds and creases of the land, trying to think as Duggai would think, trying to spot the most likely place from which Duggai might observe them. You couldn't expect anything as obliging as a telltale wink of sunlight off his telescope; Duggai knew better than that. He wouldn't show himself inadvertently.

Rule out anything in a line with the sun's arc; it would have put the sun in Duggai's eyes, either evening or morning. He'd be to the north or south of them.

The slope along which they'd scattered their trenches lay in a rough northeast-to-southwest line; it wasn't very steep but it couldn't be seen from the south or southeast because the crest was above them there. So Duggai was somewhere along the northerly horizon.

Mackenzie looked north; his eye measured an arc from left to right, about 120 degrees to its limits—logic had narrowed the search to one-third of the visible horizon.

To the northwest the flat extended quite a few miles to the foothills of crumpled mountains. Ten or twelve miles of plain. Duggai needed something substantial enough to conceal the pickup truck. Bearing that in mind, Mackenzie ruled out the flats. It fairly well confined Duggai to the range of hills a mile away to the north and northeast—the area where Jay had disappeared. So Jay had walked right toward Duggai: right by him—or right into him.

The low hills were buckled into crazy involuted contours: the range looked like the surface of a brain. Whatever lay beyond it was concealed. Probably another bowl of flat scrub, foothills after that, mountains eventually—it was a guess but it conformed to the pattern of the district.

He kept prodding the image of the camper-pickup in his mind. Duggai would want to conceal it not only from the ground but also from the air. The camper was wide and high-bodied; a substantial bulk. You couldn't simply camouflage it with brush—it would make an enormous heap out of proportion with the standard of shoulder-high scattered scrub. Anything that big would be spotted easily from the air; it would be conspicuous enough to draw attention even from twenty thousand feet.

How would I hide something that big?

It would require an excessive run of luck to find a spot under a rock overhang big enough to conceal the camper. The hills ran to patches of bare earth separated by strewn fields of giant boulders but there weren't any dramatic cliffs or overhangs; it wasn't that sort of terrain. You had to go pretty far east or north to find red-rock mesa country. These were tan-gray boulders weathered round and smooth by erosion.

Well you could bury it, he thought, but he couldn't see Duggai doing that amount of work or rendering the truck that inaccessible. In any case Duggai was undoubtedly living in the truck. The cab was air-conditioned. You couldn't run it all day long but you could use it for temporary relief during the hottest stretches.

So it needed to be hidden but accessible. Probably in

the shade. There were no trees big enough to cast worthwhile shade.

I think I know what I'd do. I'd back it up into a high-sided ravine. Wedge it close to the wall under the shadow of a big rock if I could find it. Sprinkle rocks across the roof. Plant a couple of bushes on the hood and the roof to break up the straight lines of it. Paint it with mud. Make it blend. But keep a clear track straight ahead so I could start the engine and bust right out of there full-speed if I had to.

It suggested the sort of place where Duggai probably had his camp.

It would be in a wash or gully—something big enough to serve as hiding place and road. It would be in the steep boulder-littered part of the range. And it would be near a point of high ground to which Duggai could walk: a point he could use for surveillance.

The range slanted away. The near end lay perhaps three-quarters of a mile distant. It sloped from there toward the north, slanting along a tangent—its sinuous spine ran roughly from northwest to southeast—and the far end where the range petered out into the flats lay due north of Mackenzie about three miles away. There were some high humps of ground up near the terminus but he ruled those out from Duggai's point of view: too far away. Even with keen eyes and a good glass you couldn't see much at three miles at night. Duggai would be closer than that so that he could keep close tabs on them.

By that reasoning he ruled out the left-hand half of the range and now he had narrowed Duggai's probable location to a stretch of hills to the northeast in an arc measuring no more than a mile in width. He ticked off the criteria he'd previously postulated and concluded that there were only two summits in sight that could serve as Duggai's observation posts. One was a flat-topped ridge with boulders scattered along its western slope like hogans in a Navajo compound. The other had the highest peak in the range; it had the shape of a human foot cut off jaggedly above the ankle—a very steep slope to the right where the heel would be and a much gentler slope to the left trailing off into an uneven tangle of toes. It stood perhaps a hundred feet higher than the hogan-village ridge but it was a quarter of a mile farther away; the ridge appeared to be not more than a mile from Mackenzie.

One of those two. But what if I'm wrong?

The sun dropped; it stood briefly balanced on a mountaintop, a great bloody disc against the pale sky. Mackenzie's shadow lay far out along the earth like something in an El Greco and at the end of it Shirley's head appeared, her cropped hair standing out in red tufts. She didn't see Mackenzie against the sun until he stood up. His shadow covered her. She came down for water.

They ate a meager supper in twilight. Mackenzie built up a new fire. When it was burning he piled logs high on it. Earle said, "I thought we were leaving. What's the fire for?"

"To give Duggai something to look at. And give Jay something to home on."

"I don't understand. If we're leaving—"

"I think we can intercept him. The only way he's going to find his way back here is to follow the tracks he made when he left. When he comes in sight of the fire he'll walk straight toward it. We'll spot him."

"Seems to me we could pass each other in the dark."

Mackenzie shook his head. There were no clouds; there'd be light enough to see movement against the open ground. He said to Shirley, "Take a look at those hills. Just to my right you'll see a flat-top ridge with big boulders down the left side. Got it?"

"I see it, but what—?"

"Now off to the left a bit there's a peak that looks like a man's foot. See that?"

"Yes."

"I believe Duggai's watching us from one of those two peaks. They're the most likely places."

"Good Lord, then that means Jay—"

"Probably walked right past him last night, yes." Mackenzie went right on without allowing her time to think about it. "I want you both to memorize the shapes of those two peaks. When we clear out we'll keep to low ground and try to keep things between us and those peaks. If you can see the peak it means Duggai can see you. Keep them out of your line of sight when we move." He took a drink and passed the bowl to Earle. "We'll start in the ravine where we've got the raincoat pit. We'll bag the rest of the water and take it with us. We go up the ravine—it seems to notch itself right up to the top of this slope and it'll give us concealment that far. We worm our way across the top and down the back of this little ridge. That'll put us out of Duggai's sight. We'll cut northeast until the ridge flattens out and see where we go from there. If Jay turns up we'll be able to see him out on the flats."

"Won't we be heading straight toward Duggai?"

"It can't be helped as long as Jay's out there. Once we've linked up with him we can divert away from Duggai."

"But he'll know we're gone."

"If we do it right he won't know till morning. That may give us enough of a jump on him. If he has to wear himself out searching for us it'll give us an advantage we didn't have before."

He saw Shirley's troubled gaze move from point to point along the slope above him. She was visualizing the path. She turned slowly and looked out across the mile of flats between here and the hills. "Sam—what happens if Jay doesn't come?"

155

"Then we go to him."

"I'm not sure I understand."

"We know where he disappeared into the hills. It was roughly midway between those two peaks. If he doesn't turn up in the next few hours we'll have to get around behind Duggai and pick up Jay's tracks there. Follow them to wherever he is."

"Won't Duggai think of that too?"

"He will—but he may not think of it fast enough. The idea is to convince him that we're still here. If he doesn't get suspicious until morning we've got a good chance."

"How do we do that?"

"We put on an act for him," Mackenzie said.

18

First he made a show of setting his traplines along the jackrabbit run. What he actually did was to gather up the snares and loop them securely around the belt of his breechclout. From any distance it would look as if he were stringing new traps.

Shirley walked a hundred yards out onto the flats and peered out toward the hills: it was an act contrived to persuade Duggai that they were alarmed about Jay but in fact there was no fraud in it. After a while she returned to camp with a physical show of worried dejection.

They lifted Earle and set him down near the fire where he would be comfortable for the night. But Mackenzie made a point of interposing a heavy clump of fuzzy cholla cactus between Earle and the peaks. Setting Earle down he said quietly, "You'll have to make your own way into the ravine. Drag yourself on your elbows. Take it easy—take all the time you want. And go directly that way. Keep the cactus between you and him. If you keep low enough he can't see you. It's only fifteen feet. Remember—keep in a straight line. Crawl to that catclaw, go straight under it, slide right down into the ravine. Okay?"

"Wait—don't go yet. Something I want to say."

Mackenzie glanced at the fire. It would need more

wood before they left. Shirley began to sponge Earle down with ash-soap. Earle drew a ragged breath and spoke with matter-of-fact control:

"I've been thinking about this. Had a long time to think it out. It makes sense, so hear me out and keep your protests to yourselves until I'm finished."

Mackenzie knew what was coming but he only said, "Go ahead."

"I'm not going to apologize for being a drag on you. It wasn't my fault, this damn leg. But we haven't even got anything to make a crutch out of. You're going to have to carry me—maybe I can hobble along on one foot for a while but I still need somebody's shoulder for support. Now you just said we'll have to cross a lot of the ground pretty low. We'll have to crouch and crawl. I'm not much good for that, am I. I mean it's all right sliding ten or fifteen feet from here to that gully but that's not the same thing as miles and miles."

Shirley said, "Earle, for heaven's sake we're not going to leave you here."

"I asked you to hear me out. Will you let me finish?"

Mackenzie said, "Go on, Earle."

"I've seen how that plastic distillery contraption works. I assume if you made it smaller it would make less water, but it would still make water. Correct?"

"Yes."

"Suppose you were to cut off one-quarter of the plastic and leave it with me. I'd have enough water to live on. There's enough dried meat and saltbush and grass around here for me to stay alive for quite a while. I've got that pit in the ground to keep me out of the sun. I can live as long as you can—probably longer when it comes right down to it because I'll be staying put while the rest of you are wearing yourselves out. The Good Lord's provided for me so far—I think he'll go on providing. Long enough for you to get out of this desert and get a rescue helicopter to me. Now Sam, that fire can't

158

burn for more than two or three hours after we leave it. Even if Duggai doesn't come down here until morning he's bound to come. He'll see there's nobody moving and he'll come down to see if we've died or what. When he finds us missing he'll start following our tracks. It won't take him long to catch up, will it. But if I keep the fire burning and he sees me moving around in the morning he won't have any reason to come down here."

With baleful triumph Earle leaned his head back against the earth. "That's what I wanted to say."

Shirley touched Earle's chest. She lifted her eyes to Mackenzie. "He may be right."

"No. I'd thought of it but it won't work."

"Why on earth shouldn't it work?"

"For one thing, Earle hasn't got enough mobility. We've pretty much cleaned out the immediate areas for cactus and saltbush. He'd tear his leg to pieces dragging himself across this ground gathering food. For another thing there isn't that much meat. Even if we left him all we've got it wouldn't do for more than three or four days—and we won't be out of here that fast. But the main thing's Duggai. He's got a telescope on that rifle. He may have binoculars too. He'll see it's only Earle down here. He'll wonder what's happened to you and me. When we don't turn up he'll come down for a look. He'll find Earle here alone and I imagine he'd kill Earle before he came looking for us."

He shook his head. "I'm sorry, Earle. I'm grateful for the offer."

Shirley was staring off into the night—the dark mass of the hills. Mackenzie had been watching them for the past half hour hoping to see Jay but nothing stirred out there.

Earle said, "Survival of the fittest, Sam. Isn't it better that he kills one of us than all of us?"

"I don't think you can quantify that kind of thing," Mackenzie said. "I want us all to live."

"I still think my idea gives us the best chance of that."

Shirley said, "What if I cast my vote with Earle? It's two against one then." She regarded Earle gravely.

Mackenzie bit a chapped shred off his lip. "I told you. I'm not putting things to a vote."

She said, "There's another alternative, you know."

Earle looked up. "Let's hear it."

"I could stay with Earle."

"Don't talk nonsense."

"It's the sensible solution, Sam. You know it is."

"I don't know anything of the kind."

"He'll see the two of us here. If he notices you're gone he'll think you've only gone looking for Jay. It can give you and Jay time to reach the highway and get help for us."

"How long do you think he'd stay fooled?"

"Sam, anything's a risk."

He fought it bitterly. "You're talking about suicide."

"I'm not and you know it. I'm trying to give all of us the best chance. Sam—we don't know if Jay's alive or dead. He may be injured. He's already been out there through the heat of one day. We've got to find him as fast as we can—and you know Earle's right, we can't move quickly if he goes with us. There's only one choice. You go alone—find Jay, do what you can for him, take him with you if he's able. Get to the highway. Isn't that really the only thing we've got left?"

"And suppose Duggai ambushes me. Where does that leave you?"

"No worse off than we are anyway." She scratched her scalp violently. "You can't go by that—you can't decide on the basis of suppositions. What if Duggai

160

comes down here now and shoots us all? The only thing we know is we've got to make the best of what we have. Earle's right. You've taught us how to stay alive here. We can do it as long as we have to. The only thing Earle can't do is move. Now you've got to be sensible."

"I don't like—"

"What you don't like is the guilt you'll feel if you let us out of your sight. You'll feel you're not doing your best to protect us. You'll be abandoning us. You can't help that feeling, Sam, but it's the wrong emotion to be guided by. Please try to face that."

He stood brooding down at her and saw a tentative smile waver across Earle's tiny lips.

"Shirley's right, you know."

His heart resisted it; his mind acquiesced.

He gathered the things he would need. The water pouch, plastic lined: he took half the water from the still. A bag of jerked meat. One of the knives. He took Shirley along the jackrabbit run, pretending to dismantle the snares that didn't exist any longer; he took her along the slope two hundred yards to a new trail and showed her how to rig them. He spent half an hour talking to her, telling her everything that came to mind—every trifle of information that could contribute to survival. "As you accumulate pelts you'll get enough to make clothes. Soak them in animal fats and dry them in the shade—they'll stink for a while but they'll cure out a little softer that way. Wash them down with soap morning and night. Wear them hairside in against your skin. You'll sweat less. And don't forget to keep feeding the still with cactus."

He cut the raincoat evenly in half—regretted doing it but if he found Jay alive they'd need that much water. Dug a new pit for the still to accommodate the shrunken plastic roof. Tucked two extra pairs of moccasins under his belt. Knelt down by Earle and examined his wasted face. "Don't go hopeless. It could be a week—could be two weeks."

"Could be never," Earle said, "but I'll take whatever God dishes out."

Mackenzie stood up. He put his arm around Shirley's shoulders. "I'll walk you to the ravine."

Her hip brushed against him as they walked. At the lip of the ravine he turned her in the circle of his arm and held her roughly.

She looked up at him. He said: "That's for Duggai's benefit. Climb down here with me."

He took her hand and jumped into the ravine. Lifted her down. Took her in his arms and lowered her to the ground.

"We're out of his sight now. Stay here a while before you show yourself again. He'll think I've gone to sleep."

"Post-coital exhaustion," she said dryly. But she smiled with gentle warmth. "I wish we were really—"

"No you don't. Do you."

"If it weren't for Jay."

"If my aunt had whiskers she'd be my uncle."

"All right, Sam, whatever you say. I suppose I should wish you good luck or something. It seems awfully lame."

He left her, going up the ravine doubled over; he picked his way around the distillery pit and climbed toward the low summit. Just before he turned the bend he looked back. She was sitting crosslegged, watching him. He climbed away.

19

When he got near the crest he saw there was an open stretch he'd have to cross. It lay twenty yards long in plain sight of the hills across the valley. That was no good; Duggai might be looking this way. Mackenzie slid back down the ravine to consider his options.

On the eastward horizon a thin first-sliver of moon stood low and pale. It did nothing to brighten the desert; it would be four or five days before there'd be sufficient moonlight to make a difference. The stars made enough illumination to pick out the silvery span of the desert, the darker clumps of growth, the shadow outlines of hills and mountains. You wouldn't see a man out there unless he moved but you'd see movement quickly enough.

The air had cooled down rapidly since sundown; it was comfortable against his skin now. Another four hours and he'd be chilly.

He rubbed his stubble-bearded chin against the skin of his shoulder and searched the slope to either side. Nothing looked useful by way of concealment.

You never see an animal out here unless it moves, he thought, and it became clear there was only one way to do it. He fought down his impatience and made his start.

He emerged very slowly from the ravine and lay flat

against the earth. The back of his hand before him was hardly visible—the starlight failed to distinguish among colors and the shade of his skin blended well with that of the earth. His head of dark hair would be visible as a dot against the earth—visible perhaps; but noticeable only if it were seen to move.

He went up the slope an inch at a time, crawling with toes and fingers and caterpillar humps of belly and chest musculature. It was distressingly time-consuming but it was the only answer: he was out in plain sight and his only invisibility was his motionlessness. From a mile away his movement was no faster than that of the moon: imperceptible but deliberate.

He was thinking about Duggai's possible arsenal of equipment. It was remotely possible Duggai had a heat-seeking infrared scope but Mackenzie found it highly doubtful. Duggai would have had to raid a military armory for that. All the equipment Mackenzie had seen in the camper appeared to be the sort of things you could steal from a private dwelling. The rifle—he hadn't taken too close a look but he was sure it hadn't been a military weapon. It was some sort of big-game rifle, a civilian arm, scope-sighted and expensive.

Assume Duggai had a five- or six-power scope on the rifle. Assume—for safety—that he had binoculars as well. Ten-power? Certainly not more than twelve magnifications. The nearer of the two possible lookout positions stood a mile away by Mackenzie's rough naked-eye measurement. A twelve-power glass would bring that down to about 150 yards—but a twelve-power glass had to be tripod-mounted or rested because no human hand could hold it steady enough for practical use. Even so: how much could Duggai see, given a twelve-power lens with good night-resolution, at an effective distance of 150 yards?

Mackenzie looked to his left, turning his head with

infinite slowness. He picked out a maguey that he judged to be 150 yards from him.

If a man was lying beside that century plant would I see him?

He decided he could not.

Heartened, he continued his crawl.

When he was over the top he slid down the back of the ridge and had a look around. Nothing he saw surprised him. A flat pan of earth stretched away to the south and west; mountains stood around in small ranges and there seemed to be a fairly high sierra along the far southern horizon but that might be clouds. From this bit of elevation he probably was surveying distances of thirty miles or more; there was not a single light.

The air was so dry that the stars did not twinkle; they were steady incandescent chips. Mackenzie set off along the back of the ridge and followed its curve around toward the north keeping an eye on the horizon because he didn't want to blunder out in plain sight of Duggai.

His passage disturbed a few lizards and exploded an owl out of a bush. There was a patch of broken country—cutbank gullies and sand washes: he had to do a bit of scrambling and he abraded one knee climbing out of an arroyo. It was impossible to move swiftly because the ground was dotted with pincushions of miniature cactus and you didn't see them until you'd nearly trod on them. He moved as fast as he could but it was a stroller's pace. In the hours of darkness that remained he might be able to cover six or seven miles at this rate but that calculation was immaterial because soon he would have to start doubling in order to stay out of Duggai's range of vision.

The ridge petered out toward the flats and he went right down to its bottom. Soon he was bent double and then there was no cover at all.

He crouched behind a greasewood bush. To his left he could make out winking reflections of Shirley's fire against bits of growth on the slope.

It was going to use up time but he saw no alternative to a long sweeping circuit that would bring him around the flats and up into the main range of hills south of the higher peaks. It meant he'd be going behind Duggai's position but that was all right: his chances were better there—Duggai wouldn't be looking for anything behind him.

He had to retrace a hundred yards; then he struck out along a shallow arroyo that meandered into the plain. Half-dead brush lined its banks—it had been a long time since the last rain. The slow rise to his immediate left was enough to block out any view of the hills beyond; he moved quickly up the arroyo—if he couldn't see the peaks then Duggai couldn't see him.

Sun had cracked the hardpan arroyo floor and pulverized it into fine soft dust but there were rocks hidden in it and he had to set his feet with care: the jackrabbit moccasions were too thin.

The arroyo made a wide bend and cut its way south. He climbed out and went along the flats with high ground to his left obscuring view of the peaks. He'd gone a mile out of his way but it kept him out of Duggai's purview.

Then there was a dip in the ground on his left and he found himself facing fifty yards of exposed plain.

He sculled along the floor of a ravine and this took him half the distance but then the ravine doubled back on itself and there was nothing to do but cross the open. He did it as he'd done it before—an inch at a time on his elbows.

He had a clear view of the silhouette of the boulder-strewn peak. The peak was hardly half a mile away and at that distance Duggai might spot him even if he wasn't moving. But the alternatives were to quit or to waste the rest of the night making a far circle across the boundary of the plain. If he did that he'd get caught in the open by daylight. This was a risk but it would put him safely into the hills with at least three hours' darkness left in which to search for Jay. Mackenzie banked on the fact that Duggai had no reason to look in this direction.

Nevertheless at the back of his neck the short hairs prickled.

He fought down a cough and slithered behind the dead-black shadow of a rock. It was the size of a small car and gave him safety and breathing time but he listened cautiously for the scrape of scales that might indicate snake.

He peered around the far end of the rock. A shoulder of rising ground to the left blocked the peak from sight. Mackenzie dodged into the foothills.

The plan was to circle behind Duggai's position and try to intercept the line of Jay's tracks. He'd go northeast until he judged he'd crossed the better part of a mile and then he'd make a ninety-degree left turn which should take him behind Duggai and bring him toward the point where Jay had gone through the range. With luck—assuming Jay hadn't doubled back—he'd have to cross Jay's tracks somewhere back in there.

The foothills began to squash in against themselves and heave more violently. He had no trouble keeping land masses interposed between himself and the peaks but the ground was covered with fist-sized rocks and he couldn't move recklessly for fear of dislodging them and setting up a racket Duggai would hear.

He picked his way around boulders that weighed as much as battleships. In the boulder fields virtually nothing grew except trivial tufts of cactus that sprouted out of cracks in the rock. The surface of the earth was covered with layers of pulverized stone; it crunched softly underfoot but that wasn't noisy enough to carry. What worried him was the likelihood of kicking something loose that might roll downslope and start a slide.

He crabbed his way along the side of a talus hill toward the groined head of a dry canyon. Stepped around a boulder and climbed toward the dip in a saddle that appeared to give access to the hills above. But when he reached it he found an open bowl in front of him as regularly spherical as an inverted helmet.

If he crossed it he'd expose himself to view from the nearer peak. There was no option but to go around. He spoke a silent oath and turned to the right.

The detour ate up half an hour but then he was in the center of the range with the spinal divide directly in front of him. He had to cross it. That was a matter of choosing a pass through to the far side.

Pick wrong and it would cost an hour in false movement. He considered the high divide with patient speculation.

The highest peaks probably stood about a thousand feet above the desert floor but he'd already climbed several hundred feet through the foothills and it wasn't a mountain-climbing problem; it was simply a matter of avoiding box canyons. Most of the gullies that ran up toward the ridge didn't go all the way to the top. The trick was to pick the one that did.

It wasn't easy; the bends and humps of the earth made it difficult to determine whether the canyon that opened invitingly at the bottom was the same one that made a V at the top.

The thin rind of moon stood directly overhead. Mackenzie made his choice and struck out toward the divide.

The twisting canyon carried him up a dry-wash bed;

168

he walked along one bank of it to avoid the litter of rocks that had been carried down in flash floods. At each bend the bank cut close to the wall and sometimes the floods had carved little cliffs and overhangs.

At times he had to make heroic little leaps from boulder to boulder—that or squander a good deal of energy and time on descents and detours.

The high shoulders of the canyon narrowed the sky and reduced what light there was; there were points where he had to feel his way through the shadows. It was good likely rattlesnake country and he moved respectfully with his ears straining to probe each faint signal the night had to offer.

He'd made the right choice; the climb brought him to an open pass through the divide. He posted himself briefly in the heavy shadow of a looming boulder and had a look down his backtrail.

The foothills stretched out beneath him in pale silver lumps. He was surprised to see how much distance he'd covered. The campfire out on the flats seemed quite far away—much too far, certainly, to see any human movement with the naked eye. He could see a vast distance beyond it from this elevation. The landscape seemed as dead as something on the moon.

A tumbled mass of rocks hoisted itself above him and cut off all view of anything to the west and northwest—Duggai had to be up that way somewhere. Across the pass a gentle slope of barren ground made its way up to a stone promontory from which the spinal ridge continued southeastward; this pass had been a weak point in the granite backbone and the winds had eroded it away.

Ahead of him to the north the land gave way gradually. He saw strings of brushy foothills and a stretch of broken badlands at the bottom perhaps half a mile from him; beyond that was more of the familiar desert and on the horizon the vague outlines of another range.

It was what he'd expected to find. He looked to his left along a slant down the backside of the range: more foothills followed by more flats. Somewhere down there Jay had gone foraging and not returned.

He began to pick his way down the north side of the range.

20

The descent went faster because the north slope was a gentler one and there wasn't the clutter of boulders he'd had before; because of the angle of the spine he was in the lee of the prevailing winds here and the erosive forces had been less pronounced on this side. Winds in this corner of the world tended to come up from the Gulf of California and from the Pacific Ocean off San Diego: they were westerlies and southwesterlies. When they carried low clouds the ridgetop would break them and therefore on this slope there was more vegetation. It was the same in kind but it grew more densely and some of the manzanitas had substantial limbs. It meant more forage for bigger animals and that was why Jay had found a game trail back here.

He kept looking over his left shoulder as he progressed down the hillsides: he didn't want to blunder into the open where Duggai might spot him. But there was a mass of heavy rock up there and it looked as if Duggai would have to come across the divide before he'd be able to see anything out this way.

Mackenzie made good progress. In the foothills he made his left turn and followed the flank of a narrow little valley toward the northwest. After half an hour he began to search the ground ahead of him for an indication that Jay might have passed this way.

A shallow wash crossed his path. He looked up to the left before he entered it. The wash penetrated the range and made a bend out of sight, its walls growing higher and steeper.

Down in the sand he found tracks. Not Jay's tracks. Tire tracks.

He bent low and crossed slowly with his attention welded to the canyon into which the wash disappeared.

Duggai almost certainly was up there—the truck parked somewhere in the canyon, Duggai camped on a mountaintop above it. Could he command a view in this direction? There was no way to tell from here—the odds were blind odds but Duggai should have no reason to be looking back this way. On the other hand Duggai was wise to the wilderness and could be expected to spare occasional surveillance for his flanks and rear.

No choice but to take the risk.

He went straight across and holed up briefly in the manzanita along the bank.

If anything was moving toward him he detected no sign of it. After a moment he moved on, eyes to the ground.

It wasn't likely Jay had crossed the range this far to the south—if he picked up Jay's track it would probably be at least another quarter-mile north of here—but there was no purpose in carelessness; he couldn't afford to miss the trail and have to make a second sweep. There wasn't time.

He wasn't likely to find Jay anyhow: it was drawing too close to morning. How much darkness left? Two hours at a guess. Tracking in hardpan wasn't a job for nighttime but he had an advantage in the fact that Jay wasn't a woodsman and had no desire or ability to conceal his tracks. If you knew what to look for you might spot signs of his passage—it didn't need anything as specific as footprints. Mainly what Mackenzie had was

Jay's reference to the game trail he'd picked up. Find the game trail and it would lead him to Jay.

But two hours probably wouldn't be enough.

He hurried along, making the best time he could: if he didn't find Jay before dawn it would have to wait for nightfall but that could make the difference between Jay's living and dying if he were injured—or even if he weren't: he hadn't carried water with him and he'd already been gone too long.

Mackenzie passed a long toe of earth that grew out of the hills like the exposed root of a giant tree. Once past it he stopped in a thicket of creosote and had a look uphill.

As you moved around the compass it was natural that configurations of terrain had to change. But the hill with the boulder slope that had reminded him of a hogan village was beginning to come in sight around the edge of the stone ridge; it was behind him by now—he'd come past it by going around behind it.

That meant the other peak had to be ahead of him and off to the left. From this angle it would no longer resemble a human foot but he thought he'd still recognize it if it were in sight. It was not; nothing up there was high enough—the nearer hills blocked off that part of the range. In any case he'd already crossed the camper's tire tracks. It meant Duggai probably was behind him on the boulder-studded peak.

From here Mackenzie saw its slope; the top remained invisible behind an intervening ridge. He wasn't going to be able to advance much farther in the open before he would emerge into Duggai's sightlines.

He decided to cross the foothills to the north in order to interpose them between him and Duggai; then he would proceed along the edge of the range in search of Jay's game trail.

He turned to the right and walked between the two low hills. A startled jackrabbit flashed away and Mac-

173

kenzie froze bolt still in a shadow of catclaw because the jack's sudden movement might draw Duggai's attention if Duggai were positioned to see it.

Mackenzie gave it five minutes before impatience boosted him forward again.

He walked from bush to bush, trying to blend into shadows when he could; he kept hunched low to the ground. The knife in his waistband was beginning to slip through and he repositioned it.

He thought about taking a drink but decided against it; not knowing how long the water was going to have to last. He'd been moving for about three hours; it was quite cool and he hadn't worked up too much of a sweat; the system didn't require water yet.

He walked out between the hills and bent his course to the left, striking out along the flanks of the foothills. Above him he could no longer see the range itself and that meant Duggai couldn't see him. He moved along quickly until he brushed a cholla and a segment attached itself to his calf. The needles immediately worked their way into the flesh and he had to stop to knock it off with his knife; then he had to pick a dozen spines out of the skin before he moved on—if they worked their way in they'd fester.

He passed a notch between hills and searched for any sign that Jay might have come this way but there was nothing like a game track and nothing seemed to have been disturbed. He stopped to empty a pebble out of his moccasin and went on.

Somewhere in the course of the next half hour he found a well-beaten trail. Relief flooded him.

Animal hoofs had packed the earth along a single curvaceous rut. Scrub pincushions that tried to grow across it had been trampled; overhanging twigs of catclaw and manzanita had been gnawed bare of leaves up to the level of Mackenzie's thigh. It couldn't be mistaken for anything but an animal path. Something a

174

good deal heavier than jackrabbit. Probably a variety of animals used the trail.

It was not a path new to this season; it had been here many years because there were no seedling plants along its flanks—they'd sprouted but they'd been eaten immediately.

A perennial game trail meant one of three things: there was water, food or salt.

He couldn't conceive of any food succulent enough to draw animals endlessly along this rutted path—there weren't any cornfields or orchards out here to draw the constant attention of game herbivores. So it was water or salt or perhaps both.

Which way? The trail came out of the foothills and threaded the brush out along the flats.

Jay had said he'd followed it several hours but found nothing. Mackenzie wished he'd asked Jay whether he'd gone up into the hills or out on the plain.

Logic decided him. Jay probably had followed the trail first up into the hills because to the greenhorn there'd be nothing attractive on the flats: automatically he'd have concluded that if there were a water hole or a salt lick it ought to be up in the broken hill country rather than out along the featureless plains.

In his first night's foraging Jay had intercepted the path somewhere around here and must have followed it up into the hills, where Mackenzie had no doubt it branched out into various tributaries and finally dwindled to nothing.

Because the animals that used this trail weren't plains dwellers. They had to reside in the foothills in the narrow band of heavier vegetation along the slope where the occasional rain broke.

As he looked out on the flats he saw the vegetation grow steadily more sparse. Nothing bigger than jackrabbits out there.

The big animals lived in the hills but they came regularly down this trail and out into the plain—because there was something out there that drew them.

Jay had struck out that way on his second expedition. He hadn't come back. It meant one of several things: he'd crippled himself or got sick or he'd followed the trail until daylight and holed up and continued the trail tonight. Or he'd gone out into the open to a point where Duggai had spotted him and Duggai had come after him and left him maimed or dead out there. Or—it was far-fetched—he'd run into a pack of pigs or coyotes and been jumped. Or maybe he'd been too tired to dig a pit at sunrise and had broiled in the deceptive shade of a bush.

It could be anything. But the odds were strong that Jay was out on those flats. Maybe fifty yards from here and maybe five miles.

Mackenzie set out along the game path. He hadn't gone far before he got confirmation: a decapitated barrel cactus—Jay had cut its top off and drunk the pulp; and there was a little heap of fishhook spines that he'd carefully removed one by one before attacking the plant.

Mackenzie looked back toward the hills. You still couldn't see the summit from here. Another quarter-mile out and he was certain it would rise into view.

He scanned the desert floor. His eyes stopped to examine everything that might be a human form. Each time he rejected the possibility and moved on to the next lump.

Nothing. He moved on along the trail.

Thirst was getting to him; he had a short drink from the bag, rolled the water around in little mouthfuls for quite a while before swallowing, put a pebble on his tongue and sucked it to keep the membranes moist.

One thing was certain. Out at the end of this trail was a water hole or a salt lick. Sometimes you found them together.

The population of these hills couldn't be very great—it took a good many acres of this sort of scrub to support much life—but there'd been enough traffic along this path to groove it deep and hard. That meant almost constant travel. If it extended any distance at all then it had to exert a very strong lure. Water alone wouldn't do it: there were always pockets in hills like these where a man might never find water but a coyote could easily smell it out and dig for it. On the other hand salt alone wouldn't do it either; a pack might wander to a salt lick every week or two for a treat but it wouldn't venture such a journey every night.

If animals were beating this track every night or two it meant a potently seductive attraction at the far end. He concluded there must be ground salt and fresh water quite close together.

If that was the case and Duggai knew about it then a lot of possibilities fell into place. Duggai might have picked the spot deliberately if he knew he'd have ample water for himself—all he had to do was make sure his victims never found the water hole. If Jay had headed out that way last night then naturally Duggai would have been keeping an intermittent eye on his water supply; he'd have spotted Jay; he'd have had to prevent Jay from returning to the others with the news.

How much darkness left? Half an hour? An hour?

He was several hundred yards away from the protection of the foothills. The desert plain receded away from him in all directions, its undulation so gentle there hardly seemed anywhere Jay could be hiding.

Mackenzie stopped and measured the hills behind him—trying to determine how much farther he could proceed before he walked into Duggai's line of sight.

It was sheer guesswork because he wouldn't see the peak until he was out where Duggai simultaneously would see him. But the contours of the slopes at either

177

end gave him a hint to the altitude of the summit and he felt strongly that he was quite close to the limit of safety here. It might be fifty yards and it might be a hundred and fifty but certainly it was no more than that.

And if Duggai spotted him on this trail that would end it right here. Bullets in both kneecaps would do the job handily.

His feet were bruised and raw. The moccasins were beginning to shred but he resisted the thought of changing to fresh ones because of the fifty or eighty miles he'd have to cross to reach the highway—assuming he could get beyond range of Duggai's eye.

He was having trouble walking: his breath came in short gasps and the muscles at calf and ankle felt spongy and his knees had developed a wobble. When he thought of the highway and the miles that lay between he didn't think he'd have the strength for it.

He ate a string of jerky because it might perk him up; and moved on, scanning the brush to either side of the game run, searching the flats, looking back with each step to see whether Duggai's summit had climbed in sight, ticking off the array of imponderables and obstacles that loomed before him, seeing not much hope at all.

A voice rocked him back in terror:

"Mackenzie. . . ."

21

Jay had dug himself a pit on the north side of a manzanita twice Mackenzie's height. The hole was invisible under its deep shadow. Mackenzie homed on his voice and didn't see him until he was within arm's length.

Only head and shoulders; Jay was down in the pit.

"Are you all right?"

"More or less. I stepped on a fucking cactus. Better keep your voice down. He's right up there."

"You've seen him?"

"Several times. He doesn't know I'm here."

"You're sure?"

"I'm still alive, right?"

Mackenzie opened the water bag. "Here."

"God. Thank you."

"Don't guzzle it."

He watched Jay critically. The Adam's apple lunged up and down but Jay reluctantly lowered the bag after three swallows. "I pulped a cactus but it's not the same thing. Right over there—that's a juicy barrel cactus but it's right out in the open—I didn't dare demolish it. He'd spot it right away."

"I saw the one you cut open back up the trail."

"He can't see that one from up there."

"How bad's the foot?"

179

"Not too bad. I got all the splinters out. Spines. It swelled up some and I couldn't walk on it last night. I've experimented—it still hurts but I think another twelve hours should do it." His voice was rusty, tired. "I let you down."

"Forget it."

"No. I wasn't looking where I stepped. It's entirely my fault. I'm responsible—you can't pass it off as an accident."

Mackenzie wondered if Jay had spent the past twenty-four hours flagellating himself with self-humiliation.

Jay said, "This is as far as I got but you look at these tracks, you know there's got to be something out there."

"Water hole and salt lick, I imagine. You did a good job finding this trail."

"Sure—sure." Jay's breath ran out of him. "When you were a kid did the other kids ever take you on a snipe hunt? That's what I've been feeling like since last night. All I need's a burlap sack and a flashlight to complete the picture." Jay humped himself up onto the lip of the excavation. His face came into stronger light and Mackenzie saw unhealthy blisters under his eyes.

Jay had to wait to get his breath before he spoke again: "I started out with the best intentions but I'm a stinking amateur. It's a wonder I'm still alive. Lying here all day in this grave—I couldn't get to sleep. All that resolute ambition drained right out of me. Then I heard you coming—thought it was Duggai. I made myself as small as I could. I didn't recognize you until you'd gone right by. Thank God you came. I'm not sure I could make it back alone."

"We're not going back," Mackenzie said.

"Once in a while he takes a turn along the top of the ridge up there. He's got field glasses. He searches the whole area. Takes his time. Two or three times I could have sworn he was looking right at me."

180

"Any pattern to it? Does he show up at regular intervals?"

"Not that I could tell. Twice yesterday—maybe more than that but I saw him twice. Once tonight since sundown. For a while he had a campfire up there. I couldn't see the fire but I saw the flicker on the hillside. It's gone out now, or gone down."

"He's got to sleep sometime," Mackenzie said.

"I wonder about that. With him anything's possible."

Mackenzie was thinking: if he's using hand-held binoculars then they're not stronger than eight-power. It was useful knowledge.

"What are we going to do, Sam?"

"Find that water hole after dark."

"He'll see us if we go out there."

"Maybe. Right now I've got digging to do."

"I'll give you a hand."

They picked a spot behind a greasewood clump. Mackenzie scraped a pit for himself while Jay dug a still.

By the time Mackenzie had gone thirty inches down it was dawn and he was worn out. He kept his attention on the hilltops waiting for Duggai to appear. They stretched the half-square of plastic across the still and weighted it with a stone. Mackenzie divided his ration of meat with Jay. "Get as much sleep as you can."

"Hard to sleep not knowing when he may take a notion to wander down this way."

"If he does there's not much we can do about it."

By noon his eyes felt sticky and the hovering glare had given him a headache. He had slept a few hours and been too keyed up to sleep any more after that. His tired lids took longer to blink as he watched the summits through the lacework of creosote branches.

Concern for Shirley and Earle rubbed against him.

He hadn't wanted to leave them behind; he'd had to face the necessity; but bitterness made him irritable. If we get out of this and they don't. . . . It was something he doubted he'd be able to live with.

The inimical desert was leaching him of strength; it was a steady deterioration that no amount of primitive ingenuity could halt and what worried him was the knowledge that he was the strongest of them: if he couldn't resist it then what chance did Shirley and Earle have? Even if he managed to drag himself and Jay beyond Duggai's range they would still have endless miles to crawl and by the time they reached the destination it might be too late for the others.

Something moved on the summit.

The distance was perhaps a thousand yards and Duggai's figure was tiny against the sky but the silhouette was etched in crystal-sharp outline and Mackenzie saw it when Duggai lifted the binoculars to his eyes and began to search the flats. There was no sky reflection off the lenses and that meant there were rubber antiglare hoods around them. Duggai was wearing a wide cowboy hat and his shirt and trousers were pale and loose: Mackenzie could see the shirttail flap in the breeze.

He knew logically that Duggai couldn't see him. He was behind a thick bush; there was nothing above ground but his eyes and hairline; he was in shadow. But he understood the coppery dry fear Jay had expressed: Duggai was looking straight at him.

Duggai was only being sensible—keeping a check on his rear—but the terror couldn't be denied. Suppose I left visible tracks last night?

It was mitigated by the fact that Duggai kept turning the glasses steadily, sweeping in slow arcs. But still it was like one of those paintings: wherever you stand in the room it stares you in the eye.

182

He must have seen Jay come into the hills. He didn't see him leave. He knows Jay's got to be around here somewhere.

He's giving us rope, that's all.

Then he thought: is it possible he didn't see Jay the other night?

Had Duggai been asleep during that hour?

It would explain why Duggai hadn't made any effort to come looking for him. It was the sort of coincidence that easily could have happened but Mackenzie was reluctant to credit it.

In any case they'd have to predicate their actions on the assumption that Duggai knew he had at least one of them behind him.

Duggai walked up to another vantage point, a fifty-yard hike to the west, and repeated his scan.

From the corner of his eye Mackenzie glanced at the plastic still. They'd heaped earth around the edges and it lay to the north of the catclaw fifteen feet from him but they had to put it out where the sun could hit it. To look at it Duggai would have to be able to see through the catclaw but the sky might make enough of a reflection on the plastic. With luck he might take it for mica or pyrites or quartz—the desert made a blinding glitter anyway.

Now Duggai put his right shoulder to Mackenzie and began to search the country to his west. It was then Mackenzie realized he'd nearly stopped breathing. He drew a long hot dry gust into his lungs.

Shortly thereafter Duggai walked back behind the ridge and Mackenzie didn't see him again until late in the afternoon when Duggai repeated the ritual.

It was full dark before they ventured out of their cool graves. "How's the foot?"

"A little tender, what the hell. I can walk. You name

183

the program, I'll follow it." Jay regarded him eagerly but his face had a gray tired look and folds of trenchant weariness bracketed his mouth. He'd been remarkably agreeable ever since Mackenzie's arrival—that was partly relief and gratitude but mostly it was the sense that Mackenzie had some sort of magic that was going to save his life. There was a toadying obeisance in the way Jay looked at him. Jay must have persuaded himself that he didn't have to obey but that he would comply because if he argued or refused he'd be letting Mackenzie down.

It was a reversal of Jay's earlier attitude and it could make matters easier for a while. Mackenzie played along: he took a tone of stern command.

"We wait until he makes his next sweep. After that we move out of here."

"All right, fine. Whatever you say."

They uncapped the still. Mackenzie folded the plastic with care and put it in the pouch with the remaining jerky. There was a quart of water in the plastic bag; they took a drink and Mackenzie bagged the rest of it inside the rabbit-skin sack. They made a slow hard-chewing meal of the dried meat and sat together on the lip of Jay's trench under the big manzanita waiting for Duggai to appear.

Mackenzie said, "I was up there last night. If there's a water hole you can't see it from there. It's got to be hidden down in a cutbank. Once we get that far we should be out of his view."

"And between here and there?"

"We take a large chance."

"On what?"

"Duggai. I'm counting on a supposition that he sleeps through the night in catnaps. Rouses himself every two or three hours to have a look around. I don't think he sleeps in the daytime—he'd have to be worried about helicopters and planes. He knows they're not going to fly search patterns at night so he'd feel safe sleeping then."

"But how do we know when he's asleep and when he's taking a look?"

"What time did you come through the hills night before last?"

"I don't know. Right on sunset I think."

"He was probably asleep then. Sleep an hour or two, have a look around, sleep some more."

"I don't know how you can assume that but I don't feel like arguing with you. Go on."

"Another supposition—he's not right on top of that peak."

"Why?"

"Too windy. It gets cold up there at night. He'd be down in some sheltered spot where he can keep an eye on the campfire. That puts him on the opposite side of the hill from us. That's why he comes out and makes those periodic surveillances in this direction. If he could see these flats from where he's camped he wouldn't have to walk the ridge."

"You've got something there."

"We've got to risk it. Otherwise he's got us pinned down here."

Last night Mackenzie had told him the outline of the plan to reach the highway. It occurred to him now that Jay hadn't once asked about Shirley.

He watched the summits as the last of the twilight died. We probably could go now, he thought. But it wasn't worth taking that much of a chance. He said, "Once we're out of Duggai's sight we can make ten, fifteen miles a night. We'll hit badlands here and there, can't be helped, and we'll have to go the long way around some mountains. I'd guess five days to the highway with a little luck."

"Be nice if we don't shove an ankle down a gopher hole on the way."

185

Duggai came with the moonrise. They watched him stalk the ridgeline. He seemed to pick random vantage points from which to survey the desert; he didn't stop at the same places where he'd stopped during the day.

The moon wasn't perceptibly stronger than it had been in the previous night's sky. There was a scatter of light clouds against which Duggai's silhouette disappeared two or three times as he walked the summit. Finally he went back toward his camp and when he was gone Mackenzie stood up. "Come on."

22

The game run carried them briefly northward, turned past a low pile of rocks, lifted them over a swell of ground and dipped into an arroyo with steep banks and a wide desolate bed. Mackenzie thought they'd found the trail's destination but then he saw where it emerged on the far side through a notch in the bank and continued out across the flats.

He picked up the rumor of movement—perhaps through his ears, perhaps through the soles of his feet. He touched Jay's elbow and made a quick silent gesture: they dropped low and crab-walked off the game trail, fled along the wash, squatted against the cutbank wall. He heard the rapid shallow breathing of Jay's fear.

The sound grew with approach: a crisp fast rataplan. Mackenzie loosened up. Small hoofs on short legs moving fast—several animals. His ears told him that much; his brain sorted possibilities and told him the rest: *javelina*. Peccaries—wild pigs. Couldn't be anything else.

The leader came into the arroyo and looked suspiciously to both sides and ran on across; the others followed in convoy and Mackenzie counted seven animals in the pack. The miniature boars of the desert: they stood no higher than a man's knee. He caught the faint glimmer of starlight on exposed tusks. They ran with little sonorous grunts.

It was a fast determined trot and they were gone quickly. Jay expelled an explosive breath. "Mean little bastards. What do they weigh?"

"Thirty, forty pounds." You heard yarns about *javelina* ganging up on humans. *Macho* hunters laughed at greenhorns who tried to hunt peccaries with small-caliber rifles—in legend the pigs had armor-plate hide that deflected bullets. Mackenzie didn't put much stock in tall tales: peccaries were grass eaters—leaves and succulents—their ferocity was no greater than it needed to be for protection against coyotes.

Just the same I'd rather not tangle with them.

They moved on warily in the pigs' wake. Dust hung where the sharp hoofs had kicked it into the air. Mackenzie kept looking at the skyline behind him. He might too easily have reached the wrong conclusion about Duggai's routine: it fit his own needs, therefore it was an attractive supposition; but it was based on random fragments of evidence.

Mackenzie walked past the high stalk of maguey and stopped short.

"What?"

He stared back along the trail. "We should have filled in the damn holes."

"Oh Christ."

"If he comes down off the mountain he'll know we came this way."

"We'd better go back and fill them in."

They'd come nearly a mile. "No. It would cost us half the night and then we'd have to wait for him to do his next reconnaissance."

It put a driving urgency in him and he forced the pace until Jay began to limp on his bad foot; Jay spoke no complaint but Mackenzie dropped back to an easier gait and in that manner they went on.

A low pile of hills bubbled to the left and the track circled behind them and when Mackenzie followed the turn he saw that the wind had cut the backs off the hills and left a vertical cliff thirty feet high and perhaps seventy yards long.

The track arrowed along the base of the cliff and Mackenzie was persuaded to a certainty that the game run would end here.

Now he heard the snuffle and grunt and hoof-thud of *javelina*. How far ahead? Fifty feet? A hundred?

It was full black under the cliff and they moved ahead in isolated paces, fingertips trailing the wall. It was a slab of granular stone. Some seismic contortion had tipped it on end. Around to the southwest the winds had drifted piles of earth against it to make hills. But here in the lee of the weather the rock stood nude. The cliff was a barrier between them and Duggai; they were safe from discovery as long as they remained in its shadow.

Mackenzie moved cautiously past a jutting angle of rock. He could see the plains but the immediate foreground was opaque.

He stopped and lifted one arm to bar Jay's advance.

He didn't know what had made him halt.

He heard a snout disturb the silence of water: a pig nuzzling—there was a snort and a lapping of tongues.

Artesian, he judged; it couldn't be a rain trap—it would have dried out since the last storms.

Hoofs kicked at the ground; he heard scrapes and thuds that had to be pigs rooting for salt with hoof and tusk. The aural sensations reached him with extraordinary clarity but it wasn't an alarm of proximity—he wasn't that close to the pigs: the sounds were crisp on the still air but there was a forty- or fifty-foot distance. It was something else that had stayed him. What? He had to know before he could advance.

189

The fear with which he lived had revived fundamental instincts. On a therapeutic couch he'd have diagnosed his condition as atavistic regression: an abnormal mental imbalance the symbol of which was hyperacuity. Under some circumstances it was an unhealthy condition; under others it was not. The organism had a responsibility to react in environmental danger. Adaptive compensation: the deaf man learns to hear with his flesh; the blind man to see with his ears. The endangered man learns to take nothing for granted. Sensory information that can be ignored by the unafraid must be examined from all aspects before it can be dismissed or acted upon.

Some undefined sensation had gone through the nervous system and the data system had analyzed it and the analysis had been fired into the decision-making executive. The neocortex without thinking had reacted instantly in self-protection: the motor muscles were stopped, warning signals were flashed to the cerebrum, the conscious thinking apparatus followed along in its clumsy way and tried to catch up.

A quick tally to rule out alternatives: Scent? No—his olfactory talents were not particularly keen; he smelled nothing unusual. Sight? No—nothing. Tactile information? No—nothing remarkable except perhaps the hint of dampness in the air.

Therefore it must be something audible.

He listened again; heard nothing he hadn't heard before.

Then the slow conscious mind informed him.

It was a shift in direction. The rooting noise was coming up to reach him—up from a level beneath him. The water was in a depression.

He put his foot forward and lowered it without taking his balance off the other leg.

Nothing there.

If he'd kept walking he'd have pitched right over.

Maybe not much of a fall—ten feet—but it could have broken a bone. His ears had told him the pigs were ten feet lower than he was.

Therefore I am not yet dead.

They withdrew along the trail and emerged into marginally better light. He made out the strain on Jay's drawn features.

"They're digging salt down there—we'll need it. And I'd like to try and kill one of those pigs. It'll give us enough food for the rest of the hike. If we lose a day here we'll make it up—we can bag quite a bit of water and stretch our marching hours. What do you say?"

"You mean lay over here all day?"

"We'd have to. To dry the meat."

"What's the alternative?"

"Keep going. We might get beyond Duggai's sight by daylight."

"You think we'd be better off if we stayed here until tomorrow night, don't you."

"I'm still kicking it around," Mackenzie said, "but we've got to make up our minds."

"My foot's starting to give me hell. Another day's rest would help a lot. But you decide. You know best."

"All right. We'll stay."

"How the hell can you kill one of those things?"

"Ambush it out here where we've got enough light to see by. We know the route they're going to take."

Mackenzie set it up as best he could and while he worked on it Jay sat nursing his foot and watching Mackenzie's every move, waiting with doglike patience for any morsel of attention Mackenzie might toss at him: Jay's mind hadn't gone soft but he seemed to have settled into the new role he was trying out as devoted sidekick. Mackenzie had a feeling it would last only as long as he didn't make a serious mistake. As soon as he

191

damaged Jay's desperate faith in him that would end it: Jay would feel betrayed. He might sulk or he might explode but either way he'd be hard to deal with after that. It surprised Mackenzie that Jay hadn't already started to rail about the open pits they'd left.

To herd the pigs closer to his chosen ambush Mackenzie rolled a rock across the trail, narrowing the opening. The cliff started here, rising out of the earth; it was no more than five feet high. They would be more likely to look for danger in their path and on their flanks; less likely to look up—and the wind should carry his scent right over their heads.

He didn't know how long it would be before they came out. He had two minutes or he had the rest of the night.

He instructed Jay and posted him across the trail in the brush; they assembled a pile of throwing rocks.

It would have been simpler to set a snare but they had no rope capable of restraining a strong forty-pound animal nor would they be able to lift a rock that would be heavy enough to stun or kill a pig from a triggered deadfall trap. Mackenzie was going to have to get close enough to kill the pig by hand.

His only weapon was the trivial brass-cartridge knife and he didn't think that would do the job. Their hides would resist the soft metal and he couldn't count on getting an eye.

The nearest manzanita was a good distance off the trail. He sent Jay to break off a branch; Mackenzie remained on the cliff with his knife and a stone in case the peccaries came. He kept his eye on the trail where it disappeared under the opaque shadow of the cliff and heard the rending crackle of twisting wood on the plain behind him. The stuff was not easy to break.

Jay brought him the prize. "I hope it's all right."

"It'll do fine."

Jay beamed at him and retreated to his post and

Mackenzie hefted the branch: it was a strong stick with a crook in it, a little shorter than a baseball bat and considerably lighter in weight; not heavy enough to do service as a club. A twisted strand of flexible bark hung from its end where Jay had had to rip it loose. Mackenzie wondered if the bark had enough tensile strength to make a thong. Then he rejected it; he couldn't afford to experiment and have it fail. Instead he set the food pouch beside him on top of the ledge and pulled the hide drawstring out of it. Pouch, string, breechclout and moccasins all were stiffening to an uncomfortable hardness and his shoulder was badly welted where the tough strap had chafed it. He foresaw no improvement in that situation; they'd just have to make the best of it. Even if they did manage to kill a *javelina* its hide would be far stiffer than the jackrabbit skins and in any case they'd need the pig hide for a water bag; it would harden up to the consistency of wood but that wouldn't affect its usefulness as a vessel.

He pulled his mind back to the immediate problem and focused on the attempt to solve it. There was no point speculating about the use of *javelina* skin until you had a *javelina*.

Jay's efforts to tear the club off the bush had left one end of the stick split clear through. The split ran down into the wood a few inches and one side of it had curled back. Mackenzie took the split ends in both hands and pulled with steady pressure. The split ran farther along the wood and he pulled the ends apart carefully with continuing effort until he judged it deep enough.

As an interim weapon he'd been clutching a stone; he'd picked it up from the foot of the cliff. It was a shale slab with the shape of a wedge—butt end as thick as his wrist, blade considerably thinner. It was irregular and not quite as heavy as he'd have preferred but he didn't want to waste time hunting for a better one. He rammed it down into the split stick and used the rawhide thong to tie the wood tight around it. If he struck a bad blow the rock probably would fly right out of the wood but in the meantime it made for a rudimentary ax—stone blade, wood handle. Not as effective as his ancestors' tomahawks but then he hadn't had weeks to craft it.

He gripped it in his right fist and clutched the knife in his left and lay along the cliff above the game trail waiting for the pigs to finish their pleasure.

23

Time ran by—the slice of moon gave him a rough gauge—and it was midnight and Mackenzie listened to the approach of the *javelina*, small hoofs clicking on the rock as they came.

His muscles gathered and he saw Jay cock an arm, ready to throw if the peccaries tried the wrong side of the rock they'd rolled across the path.

The leader came into the light and paused when it came on the rock: snuffled and swung its neckless head from side to side. The pigs bunched up behind it and finally the leader came into the passage between rock and cliff: it burst through quickly and trotted under Mackenzie's position and went on to the open where it began to run sideways, circling, making a little dance of agitation while it waited for the others to brave the pass.

Mackenzie's scheme was artlessly direct: to fall with his club upon the last pig in line.

But the bunch herded together and he regretted having moved the rock; they knew the trail and the alteration had nerved them up—now they hesitated and finally they all tried to squeeze through at once.

The weaker ones gave way; the bunch came crowding through the neck. Mackenzie poised to spring. But the last two pigs came through abreast, hurrying to catch up.

Mackenzie swung the club ferociously. It tipped him off the ledge and he fell. But the head of the ax took the nearer pig somewhere on the shoulders; it was still underneath when Mackenzie fell on it.

It wasn't much of a drop and he wasn't hurt but confusion welled in him and he wasn't certain of his bearings for a moment: he was in a tangle with the stricken *javelina* and he felt something strike his flailing ankle. It must have been a hoof of the second pig: he had a glimpse of it reeling out, dodging away from the cliff, bolting toward the rear of the pack, and then the pig under him began to squirm: it got free and its short legs scrabbled with frantic energy—it got away from him amazingly quickly.

Mackenzie brandished the tomahawk and slithered for footing.

The pig was clattering along the base of the cliff like a crab on a rock jetty: pushing itself along the face of the cliff, crippled, sliding its shoulder along the wall.

He went after it and felt a stab of squeezing fright that maybe the other peccaries were after him from behind but he leaped at the struggling *javelina*. He gripped the ax in both hands and brought it down with all the might in his shoulders.

He felt it jar his hands when it broke. The light was poor; he wasn't sure whether it had hit clean.

There wasn't time to examine it. Mackenzie whirled in a crouch, knife in his left hand and broken stick in his right to meet the assault of the pack.

But the pack was making a run for it: Jay across the trail hurled rocks at them with mighty overhand heaves that flew in wild directions and clattered like enfilading fire. The commotion spooked the mob into a brief terrorized gallop that soon became a disorganized trot. Mackenzie watched the pack dwindle up the run until the night absorbed it. He dropped the stick and examined the stricken peccary and saw that he'd broken its neck with his blow.

A neat kill after all: a blaze of crafty preternatural pride made him lightheaded and he looked at Jay with fierce excitement. "Old-fashioned redskin ingenuity does it every time. Stick with me, son."

Jay gave him a strange frightened glance and Mackenzie laughed to show he'd been joshing him.

He laid out the carcass on its side. Let's see now: you cut slits down the hind legs between the bones and the strong tendons. Then you jam the front legs through the slits. Break the forelegs and turn them sideways like cross-pins: you've made a sling of the animal—put your arms through and carry it on your back like a knapsack. Leaves your hands free.

Then he brought himself back from fantasy. No need to sling the pig for a long carry: they'd be skinning it out right here.

He remembered how his father had carried deer that way. The silversmith's teachings were close to the surface now: he realized what was happening to him—more and more he was finding the capacity to make the right moves without having to stop and think them out first. It pleased him. "—but you can't take the desert out of the Navajo."

"What?"

He realized he'd spoken aloud, dismissed it with a gesture and went in search of a stone flat enough to hone the knife. He moved off the trail and began to skin the *javelina* and dress it out. Jay said, "How about the water hole?"

"No point risking our necks trying to get down there before dawn."

The meat was tough and the knife too flimsy; in the end they had to tear the meat. They ripped it into strips as thin as possible so that the sun would dry it quickly.

Mackenzie pegged out the hide fifty yards beyond the game trail—they didn't need to be trampled. They scraped the hide, working with knives and rocks, and it consumed muscle and time because they had to be certain they left no traces of fat or meat on the skin: anything that went rancid could spoil the water or rot a hole through the bag.

At random intervals an animal or a small group would enter the *tanque* for a while and then emerge from the cliff shadows and return toward the hills. Two coyotes came; later a fox and finally something that moved with quick dark stealth—Mackenzie thought it might be a bobcat.

After three o'clock they dug their pits to survive the coming day. Mackenzie placed them some distance north of the cliff where they wouldn't be affected by its reflections of heat. He selected positions where they were screened by the cliff from Duggai; but by crawling a few feet Mackenzie would be able to peer through the base of a catclaw bush and keep a periodic eye on Duggai's summit.

He saw no need to dig a still and cover it with the plastic—not with a source of fresh water at arm's length. He left the plastic folded inside the food pouch. They strung the pork on cactus spines and then with the first predawn hint of color they went to examine the *tanque*.

It lay in a forty-foot bowl of streaked black-red rock. The sloping walls had been smoothed to a mottled gloss. Animal hoofs over an incalculable span of time had worn a grooved trail that curved back on itself twice in sharp switchbacks on its way to the bottom and he was glad they hadn't attempted it at night.

The little pool at the bottom was obsidian-black, an indication of depth—probably it had never gone dry: artesian pressures far underground kept it forever at a level.

The worn hoof trail circled the narrow pool and went down to the water along the shallowest gradient. Along the slope was a wide fault in the rock where mud and brown clay had flowed down like a paste from the desert floor above, after every rainfall; the mud slope was crosshatched with white scratches that had been left by animals in search of ground salt. The tongues of generations had worn the salt lick down until it had assumed the shape of a trough.

Above it the cliff was a dramatic monument of crags—from this perspective it loomed alarmingly although it was of no real size—and Mackenzie saw how if you came at it from the north you'd spot it from quite a distance.

Likely that was how Duggai had found the water hole in the first place. The brass-scavenging expedition in California that had led to Duggai's arrest hadn't been his first such adventure. He'd explored most of the gunnery ranges by then. Certainly he knew this one; that had been apparent all along—Duggai wouldn't have dragged his prisoners out here if he hadn't known where he was going.

The water was startlingly cold. Its minerals had stained the rocks around the edge of the hole; the taste was faintly metallic. Mackenzie drank his fill out of cupped hands. When he looked up there was a small scorpion in the crevice above him, tail-stinger curled over its back. He made a sudden motion and the scorpion fled back into the crevice.

Mackenzie said, "These rocks will be full of those. Keep an eye open—don't step on a scorpion, you could die from it."

"Listen, Sam—"

But Jay didn't resume immediately; his eyes wandered in bashful irresolution. Then finally: "I'm not such a shit, you know. I'm really not such a total loss."

"No."

"Listen, I was the best student in my class and the most maladroit oaf you ever saw. Stereotyped bookworm. You get older, you learn how to camouflage insecurities—you compensate for the inferiority complex, you learn how things work, you grow up to be a mediocre psychiatrist and you think you know all your own weaknesses. Well at least I think I know some of mine. But knowing how emotional aberrations work isn't necessarily a cure for them. I know I'm unreasonable about things. I even know why. But a lot of the time I can't seem to do much about it except just live with myself. I'm talking about Shirley now. Maybe it's all a long way in the past—unreasoning jealousy. I can't help it. It's the way I am. I'm trying to be honest with you."

Mackenzie went up to the salt lick and began to dig with the knife. "What do you want me to do about it?"

"I'm not asking you to do anything. Just try to see my side of it, that's all." Jay followed him up, started digging, searched his face with inquiring intensity. "Maybe I'm asking you a favor, come to think of it. You're so much stronger than I am. I used to hate you because you were always so sure of yourself."

"Did you really think I was?"

"Come off it, Sam, I've never seen a hint of self-doubt in you. You exude self-confidence like musk. You've got the composure of a sphinx. All right, for all I know maybe it's compensation for all kinds of turmoil inside—but that's not the image you project."

He felt uncomfortable under the glass of Jay's scrutiny. "What's the favor you want?"

"You know what it is."

"I'm sorry. I don't."

"Leave me room with Shirley, Sam."

They ate the dirty salt, bagged a chunk of it, went back to the pool and drank deep. Jay dipped water with his cupped hands and splashed it down his face. With his eyes shut, dripping, he looked like a tearful suppli-

200

cant. "You could take her away from me without half trying. If you did I might even try to kill you for it—I might be capable of that—but I'd probably decide against it. Because it wouldn't get her back to me."

In sudden embarrassment Jay started to wash himself busily, scrubbing his face and chest and arms.

It was an extraordinary performance. It didn't astonish Mackenzie but he had to walk away to keep his contempt from showing. He stood at the base of the switchback trail and watched light pour into the sky; he rolled the taste of salt around his tongue.

Mackenzie thought: it's the first time he's mentioned her and all he can say about her is that he owns her and he doesn't want me to steal his possession. He still wants to keep her but he can't even remember why. And he talks as if we're in San Francisco unaffected by any of this.

And then reluctantly he granted the alternative: maybe Jay didn't talk to me about her but that doesn't mean he hasn't been thinking about her, worrying. I'd be the last one he'd confide in, about her.

"Sam."

He turned. Jay was waiting for his answer.

Mackenzie came back down to the pool. "You're a chronic worrier. We're not out of this alive yet."

"You'll get us out. Look how far we've come already."

"The sun's come up. Eat some more salt—we're starved for it. Then we'd better get underground."

"You don't care about her the way I do," Jay insisted. "It just wouldn't be fair."

"Stop obsessing yourself with it, Jay. We don't even know if she's still alive."

It shocked Jay into silence. Mackenzie took satisfaction from that—and the satisfaction displeased him: it was petty. Disliking himself, he went up the trail on fingers and toes.

He slept in snatches. Now and then he had to throw rocks at buzzards around the hanging salt pork: it worried him because the circling scavengers were bound to draw Duggai's attention to this spot but a great many animals used the water hole and Duggai would have to assume there was an injured or dead one on the ground. But that was a risk too: suppose Duggai was running low on meat?

He could still taste the acrid filthy salt in his mouth; it was as if he could feel his grateful organs soaking it in.

Some time before noon he posted a watch at the base of the catclaw and in time he was rewarded by the distant movement of Duggai's patrol along the summit line. It reassured Mackenzie to know Duggai hadn't come down off the mountain. The man's malevolent patience amazed him. Duggai seemed prepared to spend the rest of his own life on that rock if that was what it would take to extinguish his victims.

How much simpler it would have been for Duggai to have murdered them all with his rifle and left them for the buzzards. But to Duggai that would have been pointless and too merciful.

Heat drove him back to the dugout.

Clouds heavier than usual built up during the late afternoon along the western skyline. When it was cool enough to climb out of the pit Mackenzie gathered the pigskin sack which they had left to dry in the shade. It had stiffened so much that he wasn't sure they'd be able to draw it shut with the hide laces they'd prepared. It wasn't crucially important except to the extent that evaporation would be minimized if the bag could be sealed.

He'd thought about sending Jay back to the others and continuing toward the highway on his own. He'd ruled it out—Jay might be seen by Duggai and that might lead Duggai to search northward for Mackenzie;

and with two of them striking for the highway the chances of success were doubled; he had other thoughts as well but he wondered if they were shabby rationalizations—perhaps he wanted to keep Jay away from Shirley.

It was a possibility he had to reckon with, but it came to a choice between guilt and sending Jay back and that was no choice at all. He kept Jay with him.

By evening a great toppling tower of cloud loomed overhead. There was no sunset; the light simply faded from the gray air: sky merged with earth along the uncertain twilit horizons. It was a great boon for them because the clouds obscured nearly all the stars and there was no possibility that Duggai might see them cross the open plain.

As soon as it was dark Mackenzie took Jay in tow and they struck out into the soul-sucking darkness.

24

Those first miles were painfully slow because of the bad light. The clouds pressed residual heat back against the earth; it remained warm for hours. Dust rose into Mackenzie's eyes and teeth, carried on wanton gusts of eccentric wind. There was a thick dampness in the air but it didn't bode rain.

They had to pick their way with infinite caution. Several times they blundered against shrubs; twice they had to stop to extract spines from their ankles. A portion of sky to the northeast remained clear for a long time and Mackenzie, having memorized a pattern of stars there, guided on it—kept it ahead of his right shoulder.

There was a range of low mountains ahead of them and he wanted to go around its western flank. Once past that buttress they would be permanently out of Duggai's sight; but there remained miles to cross.

It was too dark to make out the mountains but Mackenzie knew where they were. They settled down to a flatfooted weary march and he realized they were not likely to get beyond the flats by daybreak. The pace was too slow and in this blackness there was no way to crowd it.

It meant another day holed up under Duggai's jurisdiction and he wasn't sure he had the patience for that. They would lose precious hours of cool traveling time:

they'd have to stop an hour before first light, dig their pits and get out of sight. If it weren't for Duggai they'd be able to keep walking at least two hours longer before stopping to dig in; and the digging would go faster by daylight.

He was carrying the water sack and they'd filled it with three or four gallons; it was a heavy burden. Jay had taken all the other accoutrements—these consisted pitifully of the food sack, the two brass knives and the spare moccasins. In the food sack were several pounds of dried pork, the remaining shreds of jackrabbit jerky, a few clots of rocksalt, a pair of small thick clay bowls and the folded square of transparent plastic. Like Punjab beggars they lugged their worldly possessions across the flayed arid landscape.

The clouds tumbled eastward on high winds aloft; along the surface of the earth dust devils whirled and greasewood bushes clattered like cicadas. As the slim moon moved west it passed beyond the thicker body of cloud; it began to throw a hazy glow through the trailing sky-fog and this pittance of illumination helped them move faster: no longer was it necessary to test the ground with a prodding toe before putting one's weight down. Cactus and rocks became vaguely visible against the paler surface of the desert. Several times Mackenzie stubbed a toe against things unseen but they were making a good walking pace now and he revived his hope of passing the end of the mountain range before first light.

It had been sixteen hours since his body had ingested the first mouthfuls of rocksalt; its beneficence had ramified through his system and the muscles no longer had a tendency to cramp. They had consumed the blood of the *javelina,* its raw marrow and its sun-dried flesh.

His legs were tired but it was not the loose-kneed weakness he'd got used to. He'd lost a good deal of weight and for a time he'd been feeding on his own muscle but it hadn't gone beyond restoration. Jay had suffered more because he'd begun with less: now his jut-ribbed gauntness was macabre but he was keeping up with the pace: salt and the meat had revived him.

When they reached the edge of the mountain range he judged the moon's westward angle and saw no suggestion of light to the east. The clouds had gone on toward Tucson, El Paso, the Gulf.

"We'll go through the foothills instead of around."

"Won't that slow us down?"

"A little. But it'll put high ground between us and Duggai."

"Good idea."

So they climbed, striking through canyons and passes, skirting clumps of sandstone boulders and igneous rock. At the trailing end of the range the foothills were of lackadaisical proportion: above to one side the rock cliffs sprouted and the razor spine of the range stood several thousand feet higher than the plain. The low crumple of foothills bordered the range all round; staying within its folds they pressed on. Where canyons narrowed into deep shadow Mackenzie elected to go up and around rather than through: it made for stiffer going but they had light and it minimized the risk of accident.

With the first spread of morning they paused to eat and drink but they were up again and moving within ten minutes. Mackenzie looked back and had a last brief look at the arid plain that had sustained them. Shirley's campfire winked ten miles away beyond the flank of Duggai's hills and Jay said explosively: "Thank God."

"They've made it so far," Mackenzie agreed. Then they went on across the sandy hogback and when they began to descend its northern slope they were beyond any further view of the plain behind them—and beyond Duggai's view as well: a smile stretched Mackenzie's lips until the chapped skin split painfully and he felt his shoulders lift as they marched steadily downhill in the growing dawn.

The land out ahead was more of the same and that was no surprise but Mackenzie was vaguely disappointed. In a corner of his hopes had rested the improbable chance that they'd been marooned just out of sight of salvation. All the evidence stood against it but it had remained there until now. The span of sand-whacked plain to the north only fulfilled his expectations but it was enough to sunder the relief he'd felt on discovering Shirley's fire.

They made good time in the freshening light—down the backslope through inconsequential hills and onto the plain. Rock ranges encircled the district but there was a gap between them to the north and they set out toward that passage. It was six or seven miles away and Mackenzie knew they wouldn't get that far today but they were making better distance than he'd anticipated. At sunrise he stopped to parcel out a ration of water and searched Jay's physique until Jay blushed.

"I'm trying to judge how many miles you've got left in you."

"You don't have to put it brutally."

"If you look at your skin you'll see what I mean. The sunburn's starting to tan. The blisters have gone down on your shoulders."

Jay tucked in his chin to examine himself. "So?"

"If we can add two or three hours' walking time to each night we can cut a day off our travel time."

"You want to keep going a few hours, that it?"

"It won't get scorching hot for another four hours. If we walk for three hours and dig holes under scrub shade we still should be all right. Then start out again a couple of hours before sunset. If our feet hold out we may make it in three nights."

"I can stick it as long as you can." There was jealousy in Jay's defiance; but he didn't hold Mackenzie's glance. "I'm just as eager as you are. If we can shave a day off it'll make a lot of difference."

So they continued until the sun was well up; dug their holes with the sun strong against their backs; and tumbled into their damp earth beds with a twitching of overtaxed muscles. Mackenzie had a final look back toward the mountains they'd crossed. He saw nothing remarkable and he was asleep instantly.

He awakened once with the sun just past zenith: it was the rush of a jet that had alerted him but by the time he lifted his head the plane was retreating toward the horizon. He saw no buzzards, no Duggai; he sagged into the cool bunker and slept.

He was awake again by three or so; he spent an hour repairing his frayed moccasins with rawhide but they wouldn't last the night and there remained only one spare pair each.

Well, we'll keep the ruined ones and try to stitch them together to make new ones.

They were fed and moving again well before sundown; by nightfall they'd crossed several miles; moonrise found them in the passage between ranges.

It was going better than he'd hoped: if their muscles and moccasins held out they were going to make it. But he itched terribly where the sun had baked his already punished skin and he was conscious of the dry scratch of the hard leather breechclout.

They walked without hurry, not letting impatience force the pace; they'd settled down to the march of soldiers, one pace at a time and no thought of anything beyond it. The water sack swung from Mackenzie's fists, the palm tacky with sweat, and every hundred yards or so he shifted it from hand to hand.

They emerged from between the ranges. The moon was perceptibly stronger tonight: it threw a steel-hued glow across the flats and by its light Mackenzie could make out distinctly the canyon contours of sierras some miles away. To the northeast the plain stretched away to a level horizon many miles distant. At other compass points there were cairns and hummocks and mountain ranges that brought the horizons closer. Due north stood a forbidding rampart of boulder cliffs. No point going up against that: they struck off to the right and followed the flats.

Underfoot they traversed pebbles and clay and the dry-rotting remains of crumbling plants. The trick was to stay a good distance from any shrubbery big enough to cast a shadow. The bare earth ran in contours of washboard unevenness but it made firm footing and the journey was easy so long as you watched where you were putting your foot down.

The occasional coyote yapped distantly; the occasional rodent or jackrabbit bolted away. Mackenzie thought of the bonepiles of bleached remains that had been strewn across this desert a hundred years ago— pioneers trying to reach California across the infamous Jornada del Muerte: the trail had been signposted with cattle skulls and human skeletons.

Well, they didn't have plastic raincoats in those days.

Judderingly weary; but he felt good. Triumph filled him, kept him moving even when spasms ran uncontrollably along his punished legs. Jay kept up—it was an evident struggle but he voiced no complaint and halted only when Mackenzie called a rest.

By midnight the moccasins had given out; they changed to the last ones. The new footwear was stiff and painful but they kept on.

As they approached the horizon a massive range climbed into sight and Mackenzie diverted the course again, swinging west of north. They were zigzagging in long arcs and it was adding to the distance but it wasn't as severe as he'd expected: the ranges stood far apart and rarely extended more than a few miles in length.

Off to the west he could see a great humping granddaddy sierra that covered an entire quadrant but it didn't lie across their path. When they stopped to drink he said, "I think we may strike the highway sometime tomorrow night."

"That soon?"

"We've covered at least twenty-five miles since we left camp. A lot better than I expected. It may not be much more than fifteen, twenty more miles."

It perked Jay up. When they continued Mackenzie saw him searching the plains ahead for headlights.

Toward morning the earth began to tilt; they faced a gradual upward climb. It was a shallow slope but it extended miles and they could see nothing beyond it but sky.

The climb sapped them; they had to stop every quarter hour, then every ten minutes.

"Maybe we should call it a night?"

"I want to see what's on the far side."

"You're stumbling like a drunk, Sam."

"So are you."

"If we burn ourselves out we won't get far tomorrow night."

"Earle needs help as fast as we can get it to him."

"All right. You know best."

Dawn, then daylight. He'd long since stopped counting the days of the ordeal. The earth ran uphill endlessly in front of them: they would reach something that ought to be the top but beyond it they would find a shallow dip and then more climb. The horizon was never more than a few hundred yards away. It was as if the demons were putting them to the ultimate test of patience and endurance.

"It's getting hot. . . ."

"Keep going."

They must have climbed at least a thousand feet, he

thought. A wind soughed across the desert; dust rose into his teeth. Twice Jay spoke to him and went unheard. Finally Jay struggled around in front of him, flapping both arms in his consternation. "We've got to stop. We'll broil."

"All right. The top of that rise right there—we'll stop there."

"No farther," Jay warned.

"No farther." His unfeeling feet propelled him toward the top. Long steady climb: Jay scuttled behind him, hands on knees to thrust against the tilt of the earth, knees splaying every which way. Mackenzie switched the water bag from right hand to left hand. He could feel the skin frying on his back: his mind must have gone away for a while—he didn't remember the past two hours. It had been dawn, sunrise, then abruptly it was midmorning. Jay was right. We ought to stop right here. We'll kill ourselves.

But he walked. Just to the top there. . . .

Agonizing to walk. But the top was in sight—he homed on the tufted flagpole stalk of a century plant. That's as far as we go. A hundred feet, seventy-five, fifty.

Beyond the top was a trough that ran crosswise to their course: it was half a mile across; beyond it another ridge rippled right to left.

But there was a gap through the ridge and he could see the long dry plains beyond. This was indeed the top.

And far out across that desert he saw an object crawling at steady speed. A tiny rectangle rolling eastward.

"Look."

"What—where?"

Mackenzie's arm lifted, trembling. He sighted along his extended finger. "That's a truck."

"The highway."

They stared for the longest time. The truck disappeared behind a roll of ground. Something winked then—a flicker of painful light that appeared and disappeared along a westward trajectory. Sunlight against a car's rear window. Then behind it another.

"Sam—"

"Forget it. We'll dig in here."

"But the highway. . . ."

"That's twenty miles away."

"But we'll make it tonight, right?"

"Bet your ass we will."

They grinned at each other ludicrously.

He tried to dig in the shade of a bush but the roots stopped him and he kept having to slope the pit farther out until the sun again cooked his back but he closed his mind against it and kept clawing earth out of the hole: sunburn could be treated.

"That's got to be deep enough."

"No. At least another six inches. You don't want to die this close to the end."

"I can't even pick up this rock anymore."

"Dig, damn you."

Eventually the pits were done to his satisfaction and the bottoms were invitingly damp. They sat mostly in shade now; they portioned out meat and salt and finally a good deal of water. It left only a couple of quarts in the bag but that would do—they'd drop the bag somewhere along the downslope and cover the last few hours without water. They wouldn't need to carry anything on the last lap.

He put a pebble on his tongue and smiled. Jay laughed aloud in response. The taste of joy overcame Mackenzie's weariness: it ran sweet and strong through his veins.

"By damn." It was an expression his father the silversmith had used. "By damn, Jay."

"Shouldn't we get some sleep?"

"Aeah.. Go ahead, stretch out. I'll just have one look down the backtrail."

It was only an excuse: he was too nervy to remain still—he'd passed beyond fatigue into jittery alertness. He splashed a handful of water over the back of his neck and felt it run deliciously down his spine. Then he climbed out on doddering legs and limped back past the maguey stalk and crouched in a catclaw's futile shade to look back the way they'd come and try to estimate the distance they'd covered.

They were on high ground here and he had a panorama before him: where the sky touched the earth it was perhaps as much as forty miles away. None of it looked familiar: they'd never looked at any of it from this angle. He saw going down the hill the ragged faint imprint of their foot tracks. The tan-gray slope ran down toward a bottom four or five miles away, tiered ridge below tiered ridge. Then the flats and the serrates of indigo mountains in random crumpled piles. The sky seemed very thin. He counted five vultures above a rock cairn out to the west eight or ten miles from him.

He was looking south toward the mountain clumps; he was thinking about Shirley. Just hold on—another twenty-four hours we'll have you out. Hold on.

He'd won. He knew it with a sense of savage victory.

He got up to return to the dugouts. As he began to turn away he saw in the far southern distance a hint of risen dust.

He looked away, looked again and it was still there.

He gaped at it, squinting; shaded his eyes with his palm. Dust devil? Windstorm?

It was miles away. But it came straight toward him.

It was Duggai's truck.

25

He scuttled back to the pits.

From a half sleep Jay roused himself irritably. "What?"

Mackenzie had only to point to the south. His voice broke: "Duggai."

Jay boiled out of his pit and stood in the hard sun staring at the plume of advancing dust.

Jay's eyes windowed his terror. "What can we do?"

"Not much."

"We can hide." Jay dived back into the pit. "Maybe he won't see us. Maybe he'll go right by."

"He's following our tracks, Jay. They lead right here. They stop here."

"For God's sake we've got to do something."

Mackenzie's toes curled inside his moccasins. Everything ran out of him: he felt exposed, vulnerable, weak of soul.

"Sam, we can't just give up."

"Ambush him," Mackenzie muttered; he felt a scalp-tingling madness. "Ambush him."

"With what?"

"Give me your knife."

Armed with two knives he straightened up and looked down the slope. The truck was out of sight now behind a ridge near the bottom but the dust still hung in its wake.

"Stay here. Distract him when he comes. When he gets out of the truck I'll jump him from behind." He knew it wouldn't work but you couldn't always go by that: he had to try.

He backed away from the pits and with each step he swept his moccasin back and forth to smooth out the tracks. He made his way to the nearest object that gave enough shadow to conceal him: a creosote bush four feet high. It was ten yards from the dugouts.

Over his shoulder he looked through the notch in the ridge and saw a string of cars pass across the horizon.

That's how close we got.

Jay stood up in his hole. "Maybe we should run?"

"No."

"I'm frightened."

Jay's head disappeared. Mackenzie got down behind the creosote. He made himself small and clutched both knives. Maybe this could work after all. Maybe this would end it.

He waited for the truck.

He heard the straining engine and then he saw it come. It emerged over the last ridge and lurched right toward him. When it was still a hundred feet away he made out Duggai's big face through the dusty windshield.

They'd made a confusion of tracks in the area with their digging and eating and exploring. The truck went right on across it, right to the top of the ridge. For a moment Mackenzie thought it would keep going right by. But Duggai stopped the truck.

Mackenzie shrank. The truck's door opened. Duggai stepped out, shook one leg out and pulled the Levi's down from his crotch; he hitched at them with the flats of his wrists and reached into the truck. Mackenzie saw him lift out the rifle.

A pair of binoculars hung by a strap from Duggai's thick neck. His filthy shirt clung to him like the skin of a prune. His dark wax face was neither angry nor anxious: it had a strange vacancy. The eyes were opaque. The desert had exacted a price from Duggai as well.

It was dazzling hot. Mackenzie itched horribly. He squatted motionless against the bush. Through its tangle of little leaves he had a fragmentary picture as Duggai walked to the tailgate of the truck and examined the area. Duggai took his time, knowing they were right around here somewhere.

He must have seen those open trenches we left. He must have picked up our tracks by the water hole.

One more day and we'd have beat him to the highway.

Duggai went back toward the driver's door. It heartened Mackenzie: he waited for Duggai to get into the truck.

But Duggai only opened the door to toss the rifle inside. Then Mackenzie saw him lock the door. Duggai came away from the truck lifting the big Magnum revolver out of his belt.

He knows we're not far enough away for him to need the rifle.

Duggai went prowling around very slowly. He didn't go near any bushes from which he might be jumped. He stayed in the open and kept moving around to see things from new angles. He took his time: he had plenty of it. He tipped the hat back on his head.

The silence made it that much more unbearable— that and the flat expressionlessness of Duggai's high cheeks. The twanging stillness brought the hairs erect on Mackenzie's neck. The knives grew slippery in his fists.

Duggai would stand motionless for minutes at a time, jaw slack agape, nothing moving but the eyes set back in their deep weathered folds. Then he would move ten feet and search again. He would examine the earth right around his boots and then he would enlarge the circle.

Mackenzie breathed shallowly in and out through his open mouth. He remembered attacking the *javelina*. Just give me one chance, Duggai. One chance is all I need.

Terror got all mixed up in him with raging hate. He was willing, eager to kill.

Duggai moved so slowly. He was reading the things that the earth had to tell him. Sorting out tracks. By now obviously he knew exactly where the dugout pits were. He hadn't approached within twenty feet of Jay yet. But he knew the excavations were there: he kept looking back at them.

The slow circles of Duggai's progress hadn't brought him near Mackenzie; Duggai now stood beyond the pits. He was looking the other way. If I had a gun I could blow his head off.

Mackenzie glanced at the truck. The rifle. . . . But he'd seen Duggai lock the door and pocket the key. What about the other door? No—Duggai wasn't careless.

Get around behind the truck, he thought. Duggai's got to come back to the truck eventually. Jump him then.

But Duggai would spot him if he moved.

Now Duggai turned and searched again, facing Mackenzie. After a time he seemed to satisfy himself that he knew the placement of things. He walked straight over to the pits and aimed the revolver down. Mackenzie thought he was going to fire.

Duggai jerked the barrel in a peremptory upward gesture and reluctantly Jay appeared, head and shoulders. His trembling was visible. Duggai jerked again.

Jay, never taking his eyes off the gun, climbed quaking out of the pit and stood up.

Duggai came around the pit and jammed the revolver against Jay's neck.

Then he spoke. His voice was matter-of-fact. "All right Captain, show yourself."

There was nothing to do but obey.

He walked forward in slow defeat and tossed the brass knives to the ground and waited for Duggai to do whatever he intended to do. Mackenzie's mind had gone blank now: he thought of nothing—he only watched.

"Good try, Captain. Real good."

Jay pulled his head around toward Mackenzie, showing his tears. The fists at Jay's sides were clenched like a child's.

"You think I want to shoot you?" Duggai said. "That ain't the way this works. Get on over to the truck now." The Magnum came away from Jay's neck and waggled toward the camper.

He wasn't sure his legs would bear him. He staggered toward the truck: all muscular control was gone and his consciousness served only as a vessel for the reception of impressions. There was no will.

Duggai said, "Now strip."

Mackenzie sat on the tail bumper of the truck and pulled the moccasins off. He had trouble untying the bow knot in the stiffened thong of the breechclout. When it came off he saw distractedly that it had left a deep red welt around his waist.

Duggai still had the coathanger wire with which he'd trussed them before. "I guess you know the drill by now. Right wrist."

Mackenzie went blank then and was not aware of anything until he came half awake in the stifling box of the closed camper. He was sitting where he had sat before and Jay was on the cot beside him and they were tied to the truck hands and feet as they had been before. They were not gagged this time. Nor were they clothed. The truck was a furnace and it pitched him hard against his wire lashings but he didn't feel the pain. He felt nothing at all. After a brief semiconscious interval he passed out.

26

He had been in a dark place. The sudden daylight whiplashed his eyes. He was aware of it when he was dragged from the truck and pitched to the ground on flank and shoulder and the back of his head: aware but as if it were in a nightmare—divorced from physical sensation. A boot in his kidney rolled him over on his face and he knew the texture of hard ground against his cheek. His eyes were opened to slits—he saw the blazing earth, out of focus. His wrists and ankles were freed. Footsteps tramped away: heavy boots treading hard. The mesh and whine of an engine. Chittering, it drove away. Then there was silence.

He rolled over and the pebbled ground was agony against the charred flesh of his back. That was what woke him: the pain.

The sun was straight overhead. It filled the sky, blinding him. His head lolled to the side. He saw the desolate earth—sand, clay, rock, scrub, cactus. A flat plain stretching miles. Dry weathered mountains. Pale haze of sky.

How long had he lain unconscious in the noon sun?

The rage to survive pried its way into him. It propelled him across the desert on elbows and knees to the shade of a bush. His arrival spooked a tiny lizard: it scooted away.

Dig, Mackenzie.

No thought of past or future; no awareness of the cause of his presence here. He thought only of life. He searched the ground and found a stone and began to scrape unthinkingly at the soil.

Dusk; but the intolerable heat lingered. He lay on his belly, his cheek on his bicep—the arm had gone to sleep and tingled when he stirred.

He dragged a hand across his mouth and felt the prickly beard and mustache. His eyes had no moisture in them: he lifted himself and peered through painful wedges.

The empty land stretched away in all directions. He turned a full circle. It seemed he had seen this landscape before. Was it familiarity or only the fraud of *déjà vu?*

The rusty brain began to function after a fashion. Duggai dumped me out here. Alone. Dumped Jay somewhere else. So that we can't help each other. Punishment for our attempted escape. We'll die quickly now—Duggai must be losing patience.

Shirley—Earle. What's he done with them?

What difference does it make?

Lie back, Mackenzie. You may as well die fast.

He blinked rapidly, trying to moisten his eyes. Yawned. It worked a bit; he was able to keep them open. In the fading light he inspected the horizons.

In the west the twilight silhouetted a sawtooth skyline he knew he'd never seen before. In the south nothing—flats fading away into darkness. To the north some nondescript mountain clumps, nothing to distinguish them. To the east—he gazed that way a long time. Something nudged his memories. It was only a range of hills five or six miles away but it held his scowling attention.

It took the sluggish mind a long time to work it out. There—the summit dotted with boulders; there beside it the adjoining summit that sloped up to a flat crown and fell away steeply on the far side. The angle of view made the contours different, foreshortened them; but he looked again—finally he was certain. That was the place where Duggai had his camp. Swing around to the south and it would assume the shape of a human foot. The one beside it was the summit that had resembled a hogan-studded village.

It stood to reason. Duggai wanted to keep his victims in range.

So he brought me all the way back.

It meant Shirley's camp was east-by-southeast from here. Four or five miles.

The burned skin of his back had been tightened by the sun until it felt as crisp as fried bacon: every movement was shockingly painful. His buttocks were too raw to sit on and the sole of his right foot had been exposed as well because of the position in which he'd fallen.

He stood on one foot in his cramped foxhole and closed his eyes tight: he had to fasten his will like steel hoops around his emotions—he had to drive fear and pain from him.

Then he climbed out of the hole and began to walk.

In an ungainly manner he lurched across the desert without thought. He was no longer rational. He simply hated. Any object excluded all others from the space it occupied: there wasn't room for anything else: his hate filled every crevice. It kept him alive.

Dimly it occurred to him there was no campfire ahead. But he kept going.

His feet were puffy and splitting. He trod pebbles and spines. Moonrise and a tracery of clouds behind him gave a hint of time's passage. He walked toward the moon.

After a while he realized he'd been talking out loud—he didn't know how long he'd been doing it; he heard the steady lackluster monotone, rhythmic blasphemous oaths—a dark fugue of profanity, a dirge. He didn't silence himself. The metered curses were like a drummer's pace.

Intransigent rigidity kept him upright and moving. He had no objective and no defined purpose—journey for its own sake. He knew the objective would make itself known to him when its time came.

Thirst swelled his tongue. Now and then he stumbled. He moved slowly but he moved. The moon climbed; its light changed the hills—their shadows settled and shifted; now and then he looked up at the summits and marked his progress by the disappearance of another star behind the hills.

The prints he left behind were darker now: his feet were bleeding.

From a low well of instinctive information came the realization that the organism had to be sustained—that self-destruction was not an acceptable answer. He stopped.

He knelt at the altar of a barrel cactus with a stone in his hands: it was large and heavy, requiring both hands and the remaining strength in his arms to lift it overhead. He slammed it down, crushing the top of the cactus, pulverizing it. Gently with his fingers he plucked the big hooked spines out of the mess. Then he scooped up cupped handfuls of pulp and sucked the juice from them.

He broke fronds off a creosote bush until he had an armful of them. He carried them twenty feet to a scrubby manzanita and began to wrench small branches

223

off the red-barked bush, twisting and tearing them. He was able to strip lengths of bark off the branches and he used these cords of bark to bind the creosote fronds to the soles of his feet. The small oval leaves of grease-wood were brittle but they crushed quickly underfoot and the fronds filled with dusty clay as he walked, cushioning the ravaged feet: the fronds flapped like snow-shoes and every so often he would pick up a jagged pebble which he would have to remove.

At intervals of two hundred or three hundred feet the manzanita lacings would break and he would replace them: he crossed the desert from manzanita to manzanita.

The flats were never flat: it was uphill and downhill always. He would lose sight of the hills for a while and climb to a height from which they were visible and descend through another blind trough.

At normal walking pace a man could cover three miles in the space of an hour. Mackenzie had started walking when darkness came. The moon had risen. Midnight had come and gone. He kept walking. Perhaps he had crossed three or four miles.

There was urgency but it wasn't the kind that would be assuaged by hurry: if he burned his machinery out too soon it would defeat the purpose. The pace had to be steady but slow enough to conserve the pittance of fuel remaining in the engine. His speed across the desert was that of an infant just learning to walk. But it was enough.

The configuration of the hills became familiar and this informed him he was near the camp. He didn't know whether he would find anyone alive there. He had no expectations. It was something he had to do; he did it without curiosity.

He found his way to a point of ground a few yards higher than its surroundings. From here he examined the land ahead of him in order to locate the camp: it had to be nearby.

It took time and minute examination but finally he placed the site off to his right. He could see the outline of a ridge and knew it was the high ground over which he had crawled the night he'd crept out of the camp.

Therefore the camp lay beneath it just out of his range of vision: one hump intervened.

He went that way, lurching from foot to burning foot.

Perhaps half an hour later he came up out of a shallow dip and crossed a rising wave of earth and saw the familiar slope before him. Down there to the left they had strung their jackrabbit snares; a bit above and to the right he identified the paired clumps of brush that marked the ravine where they'd dug the still. The ravine snaked up toward the top—that was the route he'd taken when he'd left.

He still had several hundred yards to cross. It was too soon to make out human figures in the moonlight unless they moved. He glanced at the mountain foot: was Duggai watching him now?

He came up into the camp on his tottering raw feet. A twinge of alarm quivered in some distant part of him. He was certain he was going to find them both dead.

There were no snares along the jackrabbit run. He climbed. The pit of the solar still was still there where they'd dug it in the floor of the ravine but the plastic sheet was gone. He went across the ravine toward the foxholes they'd dug: he could see the dark rectangular outlines like shadows on the ground.

The trenches were empty.

He blinked very slowly and looked all around him. There on the ocotillo they'd hung jackrabbit strips to dry. The solitary barrel cactus they'd pulped. The manzanita they'd half destroyed to make splints for Earle's leg.

Something drew his bleary attention. He moved to one side to get a better view past the greasewood clump.

He found them there.

27

They lay naked, the three of them curled up, very close to one another; at first he thought they were dead. Then he saw Jay stir.

Jay?

Jay shot bolt upright with tight expectant eyes, ready to cringe. Then recognition changed the skeletal features behind the dark beard. "My God. . . ."

It woke Shirley. She blinked and scowled. "Sam?"

"We thought he must have killed you."

Mackenzie dropped to his haunches, braced a palm against the earth, rolled onto the side of his hip and lay with them. It was the first time he'd taken his weight off his feet since nightfall.

Both of them stared at him as if at an unfamiliar object. Shirley's eye sockets had gone charcoal black. The flesh had sunk to pits under her cheekbones. She was very old—shriveled. "Sam."

He'd spent himself. He let his head drop onto his arm. Shirley croaked at Jay: "Get him some water. A cactus—something."

Gray streaks rippled above the eastern horizon. Mackenzie tried to speak. It came out in a hoarse whisper. "Earle."

"He's alive," she said. "Barely."

In sleep behind the tufted beard Earle's mouth was

composed into a spasm of clenched teeth and drawn narrow lips. The splinted leg was propped on a bed of creosote boughs.

The cropped red hair lay matted on Shirley's skull. In the early light her eyes burned like gems. She spoke with difficulty. "He came in the truck. When was it? The night before last it must have been. He took everything. The meat, the hides, the knives you made. He took our shorts and moccasins. And the plastic."

So Duggai had got suspicious when he'd seen only two of them moving around in camp. He'd come down to find out. He'd stripped them of everything and then he'd taken up the trail. It had taken him thirty-six hours to track them. Over the hills, down the game track, past the water hole, north along the desert. He'd found them and he'd brought them back like truants.

"He came back yesterday. He dumped Jay out of the truck and drove away. He never said a word to any of us."

Mackenzie's vision blurred. He closed his eyes. It occurred to him that it was the end of his life and that death was simply the end of a long journey around himself: it had not gone from place to place but merely from one point in time to another. There should be more than that, he thought.

Then he was aware of an important fact.

Duggai had brought Jay back to the others but he'd taken Mackenzie far out on the desert and isolated him there. Why?

Because I'm the one he's scared of. I'm the one who can beat him. I'm the alter ego of his schizoid fear—I'm the Navajo.

Jay returned, hobbling on the outsides of his feet with bowlegged pain, treasuring in his palms a heap of cactus pulp. "Here." His eyes were strained with some emotion or other, his mouth was tight and straight, he looked cross and sulky.

While Mackenzie savaged the pulp Jay sat looking at him, twisting his knuckles while his face slowly became a twisted venomous ugly mask of fury.

It was enough to astonish Mackenzie. "What's the matter with you?"

Jay raised a fist as though to strike him—not as a man ordinarily lifted a fist but high above his head: as though it held a wrathful righteous sword.

Then a great sob burst from Jay and he plummeted away, rolling on the earth until his back was to them. He curled up fetally: his body shook with its outpouring. The sound of his weeping pulsed and shook.

Shirley glanced at Mackenzie. He saw a fleck of something there. Then she went weakly to Jay; she cradled him and Jay subsided into quietude. Stroking Jay's head she watched Mackenzie—it was almost defiant.

He blames me, Mackenzie thought, and she's picked her side.

"Why didn't you build a fire?"

"There didn't seem any reason to." Her expression was stained with hopelessness. Prefiguration of death. "Nothing to cook. And we hadn't the strength."

"You've given up," he said accusingly.

"We've had it."

"No."

"What's the point in lying?"

"One more day," he said. "Make it through one more day."

Jay rolled his face toward Mackenzie. "What for?"

"One more day. Please." He begged them, pleading with his eyes.

Jay averted his face then. He clutched at Shirley and she held him: together they looked as awkward as beings that might have crawled out of a wreck. Neither of them looked at Mackenzie; neither of them responded to his plea. He said again, in desperation, "Just one day more."

Through the suppurating day he lay half awake in the pit. The pit had become the familiar chamber of his environment: it was as if he had always lived in it—a troglodyte in the exclusiveness of his castaway cave of pain.

Degraded to cave-floor essentials his body did nothing more than absorb oxygen and send halfhearted signals of agonies along the nerves. The mind, reduced to its underpinnings, groped toward occasional contact with existence and cognition.

Now and then lucidity welled up in him like a seismic bubble in a sulfur pool. It stretched its skin and burst; he waited then for the next one. In such moments he had bemused visions of himself. He pictured himself as something with primitive claws and no eyes—scrabbling blindly at the hot stone walls that confined it. In a fantasy he felt himself adrift: the floor of the pit became a raft on which he floated gently across calm water until it was drawn into the tubular eye of a whirlpool—then it fell and he continued to lie on it and above him the sky dwindled to a dot of pleasantly pale blue light. Another time he saw himself as a half-crushed dung beetle with half its legs crippled dragging an immense burden across an endless barnyard.

In a moment of sanity he reflected on the passage of images through his mind and it occurred to him that in all these fantasies there was a common aspect: in each of them he had pictured himself as *life*.

Rickety with weakness he climbed from the pit into starlight with no recollection of the passage of evening. It was not yet late: the moon hadn't risen.

There was a heavy breeze. It whipped sand against

him, stinging the sunburned flesh. He repaired his creosote shoes. Somewhere inside the rigid cloture of his mind a purpose had been provoked: he knew what it was with such intimate completeness that it didn't need articulation and never lifted to the surface of his consciousness. It was simply the engine that drove him and it was not to be questioned.

In the sound of the wind he didn't hear Shirley's approach and he was startled when she said, "Sam?"

The wind batted the tufted remains of hair around her forehead. She kept pushing it back with her hand. He could almost see the bones of her fingers and wrist.

She said, "You're alive."

"I am."

"Can you have a look at Jay? I'm worried about him."

He crossed the slope with her. Jay lay in his hole and it was too dark down there to see anything. Mackenzie climbed down and lifted Jay by the shoulders.

Jay's head rocked back loosely. He stared at the sky, his eyes comatose.

"Is he—?"

"He's breathing."

He did not have the strength to lift Jay bodily out of the foxhole. He left him propped there sitting against its interior. He climbed out and went off a few paces. Shirley followed him until he put out a detaining hand. Then he turned and spoke: he kept his voice right down. "Keep them alive."

"How?"

"Build a fire. Cut cactus. Do what needs to be done."

"What for?" she wailed.

"Do it. *Look at me when I'm talking to you.*" It was a savage whisper.

"I can't. I just can't any more." Her eyes came up; her mouth worked—she was screaming soundlessly. Arms dangling, she cut a shabby hunched figure.

"Do it. Stay alive. Keep them alive until I get back."

"It's no use."

"Do it." He walked away from her.

He found his way to the dugout where Earle had interred himself. Earle had hiked himself up by his hands and sat on the rim of the pit with his bad leg outstretched along the ground. Somehow he lived. The fair skin was mottled with open sores; the small mouth was cracked away from the teeth; loose flesh hung without resilience from throat and belly and arms; yet he looked upon Mackenzie with recognition.

"Want you to stay alive, Earle."

"It's God's will, I believe."

"That's right—that's right. Maybe you can help Shirley build a fire."

"Fire. Yes."

"Wait for me," Mackenzie said. "I'll come back." Then he shuffled out of the camp with his eyes fixed on the summit where Duggai lived.

28

He went toward the hills straight up: Duggai would know anyway. Duggai would see him coming no matter which way he came. Duggai saw everything. There was no point trying to fool him. You couldn't fool the mountain; you could only climb it.

Purpose drove him. His feet plodded uphill and down. This first leg had to be crossed gently in order to conserve fuel for the climb. He knew quite precisely how much fuel was left in the machinery. He knew it was enough.

He struck the hills and began to climb. He would come to a steep canyon and he would put a foot up on a rock and place both hands on the knee and thrust himself upright. Then the other foot onto a higher foothold and another boost up. Occasionally he had to descend before he could climb again.

The shadows were tricky but the moon helped. Once he heard the rustle of something that might have been a rattlesnake. He diverted around the sound and proceeded, forgetting it instantly.

Behind him he saw the twinkle of a tiny fire in the camp. Perhaps it would hold Duggai's attention or some part of it. In any case it hardly mattered. He'd wanted the fire mainly for his own purposes: while it burned it meant they were alive down there. It justified his progress up the mountain.

Now he needed to summon what cleverness he had left. It wouldn't do to stumble straight into Duggai's lair. Duggai would only wire him up and drive him back down to the desert and leave him there again. He knew that now. Duggai wouldn't shoot him unless he left Duggai no alternative. The game had to be played all the way to the end by the rules that Duggai's demons had prescribed. It was obvious that the singleminded obsession had cleared everything else from Duggai's consideration.

My purpose and his are almost the same. But then that was almost always true of mortal enemies.

This is what I should have done in the first place.

But up to now it hadn't made sense. Duggai was a soldier trained to kill. Mackenzie was not a fighting man.

But he was a hunter. The silversmith had trained a hunter.

As he climbed higher in the range the terrain became more rocky. He began to slip. He had to discard the footpads. Now he climbed with bare feet and his soles soon began to bleed again.

Everything wasted but his will, Mackenzie made a few yards' progress and had to stop, then a few more yards and another halt. The night wore on. But the top wasn't far now—two hundred yards, perhaps less. He was on the instep of the mountainous foot, going up the open gentle slope of it. He went from boulder to boulder, trying to keep abutments between him and the top, trying to stay in shadow.

Impulse and caution chased each other elusively through the remains of his rattled mind. There was the raging urge to go in straight up: challenge the monster in the open, fight it out, answer Duggai's vast strength with a greater strength of his own—the strength of his fury.

But he would lose that way. Beyond doubt. It required strategy: stealth.

Now Duggai knows I'm up here batting around someplace. He must have seen me come into the hills.

And he knows I can't move very fast and I'm not very strong.

He's expecting me. He's too smart to come down looking for me because he won't leave the truck unguarded. Even if he leaves it locked I might get it open. I might know how to wire up the starter and drive it without the key. So he's got to stay with the truck to keep me from stealing it.

He'll hang around the truck and when I don't turn up by daylight he'll wonder whether I passed out in the rocks or whether I'm creeping up to drop a boulder on his head. He'll worry a little. Finally he'll figure out the best way to handle it. What he'll do, he'll get in the truck and drive down the back of the range out through the desert, out to the water hole and he'll spend the rest of the day out there taking a bath and keeping himself cool. Sure. Let me fry up here in these rocks.

But right now he's still up there with one eye on the truck and the other eye on the rocks around him. Maybe he's even sitting inside the truck.

Only the one way to handle it, for sure. I hope I've got the fuel for it. It's a God damn long walk.

The yucca plant had broad leaves like those of a giant artichoke. Each leaf was the size of a man's forearm. The edges were serrated with spines.

He broke off eight big leaves and rubbed their edges against the coarse surface of a boulder until he had removed the spines. Again he made lashings of tensile bark. Again he had shoes: yucca-leaf soles layered four leaves thick. They lasted, amazingly, clear to the bottom

235

of the range before they shredded away. Then he made footpads from creosote as he had done before—the yucca did not grow down here—and he continued. One foot before the other: one measured advancement after the last: goal and purpose fixed precisely in the dwindling bright core of his consciousness.

Nearly dawn and he had to hurry. He'd intercepted the game trail a while ago; he'd followed it past the point where he'd found Jay in the pit. The holes were still there. The game trail took him a pace at a time through the ravine where they'd first seen the *javelina* pack.

When the footpads wore away this time he went on barefoot.

He kept listening for the sound of the truck. If it came now he was lost.

When he dug the pit he broke off a half-dead catclaw bush near the ground—it was brittle enough to give way. He climbed down into the pit and placed the bush above him across the opening to conceal it.

The light grew and he watched the sky through the interlaced branches. He licked fresh water—from the water hole—off his shriveled lips and let his eyes drift shut. Suspended in unthinking existence he listened to the wind. The cold damp earth enveloped him. Possibly he would not be able to rise from it. He was beyond worrying about that. He would do what he could; no one could ask more than that of him.

But he thought, I have not yet failed.

There was lucidity enough in his mind for thoughts that ranged far beyond his body and the hole in which he lay buried. Without willing it he speculated that there might be a future. He rated the chances at about one in a hundred but the possibility was there and he had nothing else to think about and he couldn't afford to sleep because he had to listen for Duggai.

Thoughts jazzed like butterflies and he couldn't hold onto them. He wondered if he would return to the mountain station and find the dog waiting. He pictured the fire tower and the table of solitaire cards. If I have a chance, if I live, will I go back to that?

He'd go back, if only to find out about the dog, but would he stay?

The sensible thing to do would be to settle in the middle of the biggest city he could find and surrender to the comforts of civilization. A tap that provided water whenever you wanted it. A refrigerator with an automatic device that made ice cubes endlessly. Air conditioning. Bedsheets on a king-size mattress. Butter-soft steaks from a butcher's frigid meat-storage room. An air-conditioned car with a thermos of water kept freshly filled at all times. A woman to ease his nights and make inconsequential talk: someone with whom he'd never again have to pry straight through to the rock bottom of existence. The freedom to be trivial, the luxury to take comfort for granted.

He would clutch at it—greedily, just as he'd clutch now at a filled canteen—but the brain in his dehydrated skull throbbed with a glowing residue of desperate health and the knowledge seeped through it that his brain would need more than comfort: it would need stimulus, challenge. This thing of Duggai's had bred restlessness in him. He couldn't settle for anything: he couldn't go back to the solitaire pack.

No way to foresee what form it might take. Adventure came in many ways. Duggai's weren't the only demons: there was an endless variety against which a man could pit himself.

But he couldn't go back to forestry. Or psychiatry. Or even to Shirley.

Shirley. That had been another world. In any case she'd decided at the last to make her peace. She and Jay had found each other again. Mackenzie had left them comforting each other like children in the dark: holding hands while the world ended. If it didn't end after all— if they lived—they would go out of this place fused into unity. They weren't Navajos, they weren't built to play Duggai's games, but they were whole, within themselves. Mackenzie had seen them grow stronger. The final setback had shocked them into temporary surrender—they'd given up, accepted the fate Duggai had decreed, but they'd resolved to do it together and that was the thing they'd remember when it was over.

It's not that I don't want her. Maybe I always will.

But the memory of all this would make it impossible. The same experience that had welded Shirley and Jay together would pry Shirley and Mackenzie apart. She would look at Jay and remember how it had brought them together, how they'd found the strength in each other; then she would look at Mackenzie and remember how he had come between them; and any warm feeling she had for Mackenzie would be destroyed, in time, by the awkwardness of gratitude. It would get in the way of anything deeper.

In his dank grave, waiting silently, Mackenzie felt eased by fatalism.

There'll be another woman somewhere, sometime.

He could wait.

He was getting good at waiting.

When the truck came he listened to it with critical attention. His body was lax in the shaded hole. Messages of pain from his feet threatened to drive everything else from his awareness and he had to force pain from the arena. There was no leeway now for anything but the two contestants: gladiators in the sand.

He sat up until the top of his head lodged against the

branches of the catclaw. He couldn't see the truck from here; he hadn't expected to; but his ears placed it and in his mind's vision he watched the truck.

It went along past him, below his level. Growling slowly along the uneven ground. A dry axle-spring creaked disrhythmically. At its closest point it probably wasn't more than twelve feet away from where Mackenzie sat hidden. It went on, went as far as it could and then stopped. The engine switched off. In the sudden silence he heard the metal ping with heat contractions.

The truck door opened. Springs creaked. The door chunked shut. Mackenzie heard a dull click—Duggai locking the door?

He was neither surprised nor gratified that Duggai had obeyed his prediction. The luxury of such emotion was far behind him: he had room left now only for pragmatic objectivity.

When he turned his head he could see the sun and he judged the time: probably around eight o'clock. Not hot yet. He heard Duggai's footsteps. They didn't alarm him; Duggai wouldn't come this way. Coming to this spot Mackenzie had eradicated every footprint behind him. In any case he'd left no spoor on the rock. There'd been a smear of blood but he'd scrubbed it off.

A wave of faint dizziness toppled him against his shoulder; he rested against the wall of his foxhole and drew long deep breaths. He felt the engine skip a few beats, then pick up again. Not yet, he thought. Not just yet.

Duggai made random noises; it wasn't possible to tell what he was doing. Mackenzie waited in mindless patience.

When he heard the splash he made his move.

He pushed the catclaw aside and got out of the hole and sculled on elbows and knees and toes to the rim of

239

the cliff. Inch by inch he lifted his head until he could see down the face of the sheer rock.

Beneath him and to his left was the water hole. The salt lick threw scattered reflections at him; the pool itself was out of the sunlight. Insects jazzed around above the *tanque*.

Duggai was naked in the pool, floating, paddling.

The truck was in the shade under the cliff, its tailgate overhanging the *tanque:* out of habit Duggai had backed it in.

Mackenzie hadn't realized Duggai would be able to get the truck that close to the pool.

Bleak realization desolated him. The truck was in Duggai's sightline. There was no way to get to it without being seen.

He looked at the pool again.

Duggai was looking right at him.

Mackenzie let his breath trickle out slowly through his mouth. It occurred to him after a moment that with the bright sky in his eyes Duggai couldn't see him. Duggai floated around, splashing lazily, benign. By the bank of the pool his clothing was heaped and the Magnum's blue gleam came from the top of the pile of clothes. Duggai was within arm's reach of it.

Duggai stiffened and listened to something and then relaxed, having identified and dismissed it.

The rifle wasn't there.

So the rifle was in the truck. But the truck was visible to Duggai and probably the door was locked.

When Duggai rolled over in the water and began to wash his face Mackenzie backed away from the rim, moving by inches. He had to fight a cough down. He slithered back along the slope until he was concealed from below. The sun blasted him into the ground but he found his feet and got upright and swayed when the last strength tried to run out of him as if a drainplug had been pulled.

He tightened everything. Massive effort. Down to raw quivering nerve ends he walked the tangential incline to the point where he'd ambushed the *javelina*. The cliff ended here. He stumbled out onto the game trail. The splintered ground punished his feet into an agony that was almost blinding.

Rich light streamed across the desert, its color too bright: it made his head swim. Hot wind soughed through the brush. Mackenzie feebly went up along the game trail in a silent crippled crouch.

He went past a dispirited mesquite and around the jutting rock. The truck came in sight, its snout facing him. Beyond it he heard splashing in the pool.

He put his shoulders against the cliff and inched toward the truck until he could see the far rim of the *tanque* beyond the narrow passage between truck and cliff. Past the rim he could see the desert and pale blue mountains far away. Forward another few feet and he could see halfway down into the *tanque*. If he were to step forward as far as the truck's door he'd be in plain sight of Duggai.

Duggai, he thought, all this time through all this anguish we have dueled with each other at long range until now and I've longed to get within reach of you, you God damned cocksucking motherfucking miserable pissing son of a bitch, and now we stand within thirty feet of each other and I can't get at you.

He sagged back against the wall of the cliff and brooded at the dusty drab hood of the truck. Through the windshield he could see a pillow scrunched up in the slot behind the driver's seat. Duggai probably used it for dozing through the heat of the day, sitting in the cab with the air conditioner running.

Mackenzie worked forward another foot, stepped out in front of the truck, put his palms lightly on the hood and stretched forward on tiptoe trying to see if the rifle was in the cab. The bulk of the truck blocked him from

241

Duggai's view but if he stepped on either side he'd be seen.

He saw the front sight and the muzzle, tipped up against the inside of the passenger door. So Duggai hadn't slung it in its rack under the camper roof. He'd kept it in the cab. It stood, no doubt, with its buttplate on the floor, the stock wedged firmly between seat and door so that it wouldn't carom around inside the cab. If Mackenzie could only get that passenger door open the rifle would fall right out into his hands.

It was that easy. And that impossible. The rifle might as well have been in Texas. The lock buttons on the sills of both doors were punched down in the locked positions; and the windows were shut.

He backed silently away from the truck and leaned against the cliff and tried to think.

Beyond the rock lip he heard Duggai grunt with pleasure and splash gleefully, slapping the surface of the water like a child learning to swim. Mackenzie scowled at the distraction and tried to focus his thinking on the truck, the problem of the truck, the Chinese box puzzle dilemma of the truck. Then something tickled his foot and when he looked down he saw the scorpion.

It was a small one not more than half an inch high with the whiptail stinger curled up over its golden back. It's the little ones that kill, he thought dispassionately. The little ones had the most virulent poison. He watched it move alongside his foot, coming out away from the base of the cliff where it must have been holed up in a crack between the rocks. He stood absolutely still in his terror and watched it. The scorpion stopped, one tiny leg pressed against the knuckle of his little toe, and he thought perhaps it was licking up the blood by his foot. The curled stinger twitched back and forth.

His mouth twisted with the irony of it. Stretch the scorpion out straight and it might not measure three inches from antennae to stinger but it was deadlier than

Duggai's two hundred-odd pounds or Duggai's engine-block-busting Magnum.

It was one of Duggai's demons. Mackenzie knew that without thinking anything through. Nothing mystical about it. Sheer logic. Duggai had posted the scorpion here as a sentry.

He wanted to laugh.

The scorpion leaned momentarily away from his foot, following the trace of the blood Mackenzie had left. Mackenzie whipped his foot away, hopped mightily away along the face of the cliff—more than a yard in the single jump and then he kept retreating until he saw that the scorpion had scuttled back into its hole, startled by his sudden movement. When Mackenzie stopped he felt the pain flood up through his feet but it wasn't the pain of a poison sting, it was only the same pain as before; anyhow he'd been watching the scorpion when he fled and he was sure it hadn't had time to whip him.

Frozen against the cliff he waited: had he made noise?

The water rippled once or twice. Then he heard nuzzling snorts: Duggai playing in the water. So he hadn't heard anything.

Mackenzie watched the scorpion's hole with abiding suspicion but the creature didn't reappear for a while and finally he switched his attention to the truck again, the truck and the rifle locked inaccessibly within it.

He stood there for a very long time filled with nagging frustration because his mind had gone blank.

Duggai's voice startled him: his heart seemed to stop. Then he realized Duggai was only singing. Chanting a Navajo song softly to himself. The voice was too soft for the words to reach Mackenzie but he knew the song. It was a young boys' campfire song of no particular consequence. White Painted Woman and Coyote and legends from faraway times—a sort of nursery-rhyme song.

Perhaps it was the song that drew the scorpion out of its hole. Mackenzie saw it venture into sight and stand just outside its rock crack, tail up over its back, little claws opening and closing like lobster appendages. When it moved it moved quickly but not very far—across the game trail in front of the truck, claws rattling audibly like a crab's. After some insect, probably, but Mackenzie couldn't see the prey. The scorpion disappeared into leaf shadows under a ball of scrub.

Sluggishly Mackenzie's brain began to work. He had one advantage although it wasn't much: Duggai wouldn't be expecting him here. Duggai wouldn't credit Mackenzie with the strength to get this far and probably he wouldn't believe Mackenzie still had the presence of mind to think ahead of him. Duggai had it all mapped out and knew his victim's limitations and knew he was safe here: this was R&R, not a combat zone. Therefore Duggai would be just a shade slower to react than he'd have been if Mackenzie had come at him last night in his hilltop lair where Duggai had been expecting it.

But it wasn't enough of an advantage to be reassuring. It was a factor but there were plenty of factors in this and most of them were set dead against Mackenzie. And above them all loomed the simple fact that Duggai could get his wet hand on that Magnum faster than anything Mackenzie could do by way of getting near the rifle.

He thought, half panicked, of getting back up onto the cliff and somehow dragging a boulder up there with him and dropping the boulder on Duggai's head in the water but he knew that was no good because it was too chancy—he was so weak he certainly couldn't trust his aim and anyway Duggai would probably hear him struggling with a rock long before he got into position to launch it.

He thought of trying to disconnect the brakes from underneath the truck, then pushing the truck over the lip so it would roll down and crush Duggai in the water but that was a fevered pipedream: even if he knew some way to disengage the gears and cut the brakes from underneath the truck, Duggai would hear the noise.

He thought of trying to pick the lock but he didn't know how; anyhow he had no implement.

He kept watching the ball of brush where the scorpion had disappeared because he didn't want it taking him by surprise. And that gave him an idea.

It was a slim chance, perhaps no better than some that he'd discarded, but he had to do something quickly before Duggai got tired of the pool and decided to come back to the truck for lunch or a towel or a look around.

He backed away painfully toward the half-dead mesquite he'd passed on his way up. Under it lay half a dozen dead branches and he selected one. It was the size of a broom handle, gray and gnarled and brittle; he tested it gently to make sure it wasn't broken. All the time he kept watching the ball of brush for the scorpion to reappear. He saw a spider run out across the clay. It disappeared under a catclaw. Something had frightened the spider; it meant the scorpion was still under there. Mackenzie hefted the stick and quickly searched the ground nearby until he found a loose rock twice the size of his fist. He picked it up but it was stratum-cracked shale and that was no good; he needed a rock that wouldn't shatter. He kept half his attention on the ball of brush while he continued to seek a suitable rock and finally he found one that satisfied him: it appeared to be honest hard stone and it would have to do.

Mackenzie padded forward, feet curling in agony; he had the rock in his left hand and the stick in his right, holding it by the butt-end like a saber. He worked his way past the ball of brush until he was crouched in the trail with his back nakedly exposed to the truck and whatever might come up behind the truck; he was facing the ball of brush, as far away from it as he could get and still remain within stick's-length of it. Then he began to prod silently.

Finally the provocation succeeded. The scorpion came out of hiding, lashing at the offending stick with its tail. When it was out in the open Mackenzie poked the stick under the scorpion, resting the point on the ground. Predictably the scorpion grabbed hold of the stick in a tight-clenched grip and went to work at it, flailing away overhead with its stinger. Mackenzie whipped the stick into the air, holding onto the butt-end, flipping it hard when the tip reached its apex—like a fisherman casting with a fly. The scorpion flew off. He watched it sail over the top of the camper and disappear.

Mackenzie put the stick down soundlessly and moved as fast as he could. He transferred the rock to his right hand and gripped it securely and went up alongside the truck, dropping to his knees as he went past the right-side front wheel; he was in shadow here, between the truck and the cliff, and unless Duggai was looking right at the spot and expecting to see him probably he'd go unseen if he didn't move too abruptly. Mackenzie slowed and moved forward until he could see the edge of the pool below him; he kept pushing his head forward an inch at a time until more of the water came in view and Duggai finally appeared.

Duggai was staring narrowly at something Mackenzie couldn't see on the rock face to the right. It had to be the scorpion. Mackenzie saw Duggai paddle back through the water toward the pile of clothing. Never looking behind him, Duggai reached the edge of the pool and his hand groped along the rock behind him while he kept his eyes unblinkingly on the scorpion. Mackenzie moved his foot and leaned forward six inches farther; now he could see the scorpion, crawling on the rock to one side of the pool. Probably it had been shaken up by its flight but Duggai wouldn't know that; Duggai would know only that it was deadly and alive and he would think it was after him—a personal thing, just as Mackenzie had automatically tagged it at first as one of Duggai's deliberately conjured demons. In Duggai's mind there would be no question but that the scorpion was after him.

Behind Duggai the big brown hand reached the pile of clothing and patted it blindly until it found the Magnum. Mackenzie lifted his arm and cocked the heavy stone in readiness.

Duggai brought the Magnum around overhead and settled it in both hands. Mackenzie saw him cock the hammer and take careful aim across the quarter of the pool to the point where the scorpion made its slow scuttling way across the bare rock.

Mackenzie tensed. He saw the flesh of Duggai's finger whiten slightly on the trigger. All his fibers twanging, Mackenzie watched and clenched his muscles.

When the revolver went off Mackenzie smashed the truck's window.

29

The scorpion was replaced by a white streak on the rock.

Simultaneous with the roar of the gunshot Mackenzie slammed the heavy stone with all his remaining strength against the side window. It was safety glass and it didn't shatter; the stone punched a great hole through it and left the remainder starred and frosted. There was no falling tinkle of glass shards.

The explosion of the Magnum's cartridge kept booming around the bowl of rocks, reverberating, dying slowly. Deafened by it, Duggai certainly hadn't heard the smash of rock against glass above him. Mackenzie was in plain view but Duggai only put the Magnum back on the pile of clothes and braced both palms on the bank of the pool to lever himself out of the water. It put Duggai's back to Mackenzie and now Mackenzie reached inside through the hole in the window and found the handle inside the door. As silently as he could he unlatched it.

His mind was hurtling forward in anticipation. Certain things he had to be aware of. The rifle was scope-sighted and probably zeroed in for a range of not less than 250 yards and that meant, at this short range, he'd have to aim low. A combat-trained rifleman like Duggai would keep a round chambered and ready to go but he'd make sure the safety was engaged so it wouldn't go off accidentally. Mackenzie wouldn't need to work the rifle's bolt action but he would have to kick the safety off before pulling the trigger; otherwise nothing would happen.

All this went through his mind in the time it took him to free the door lock.

Duggai was still clambering out of the water, his back to Mackenzie, and Mackenzie with a rough uncaring need to finish it yanked the door open and caught the rifle as it tipped toward him and lifted it to his shoulder in a smooth synchronous motion, found the safety with his thumb and flicked it off, and saw by the sudden tensing of Duggai's back muscles that Duggai had heard something—some sound Mackenzie had made. Duggai began to turn and began to fall to one side toward the Magnum where it lay only a few feet from him on the bundle of clothes.

In the circular telescopic lens Duggai's profile was immediate, point-blank, and Mackenzie lowered it, remembering that it was sighted in for longer ranges than this, but suddenly there was too much rage in Mackenzie for this—a bullet through Duggai's head wouldn't even make the down payment—and so, as Duggai reached out for the Magnum, falling toward it, Mackenzie shifted his aim. It was guesswork because he didn't know for what distance the scope was sighted but the target was big enough and close enough—it wasn't more than thirty feet from him; he hardly needed sights—and Mackenzie squeezed the trigger quickly until the big rifle slammed back in recoil against his bare shoulder and the earsplitting racket exploded in his ears and the bullet knocked the Magnum spinning halfway up the salt lick far out of Duggai's reach.

Duggai reacted with blinding speed. He pushed himself backward and slid into the water and ducked under.

Mackenzie worked the rifle bolt. The empty cartridge case flipped out and rolled down the rock with a tinkle like something they rang at the altar between incantations, and Mackenzie watching it had time to think: it was one of those that started all this.

Duggai had a big chest and stayed under for a long time but then he came up, sputtered, raked hair from his eyes, stared at Mackenzie and finally went still, his head above water, looking like nothing Mackenzie had ever seen but something crossed the mind crazily:

John the Baptist on a silver tray.

The water reflected silver barbs all around Duggai's decapitated face. He said nothing—only stared into the muzzle of the rifle. Mackenzie put his eye to the scope and he could count the bloodshot veins in the eyes.

Mackenzie did not speak or move. He wanted terror to reach into Duggai and spread through every fiber.

After a long motionless time Duggai finally turned to the shallow side of the pool and climbed onto the slope of rock. Then without even looking toward Mackenzie he began to walk up the salt lick toward the revolver.

Mackenzie spoke.

"Both kneecaps if I have to. You'll never walk again."

It stopped Duggai in his tracks. He turned to face Mackenzie and his face lifted, jaw jutting—*Get it over with*.

"You don't think I'm going to make it that easy, you rancid bastard son of a bitch."

Duggai's eyes closed down as if he was bored. Insolence settled over his features. He merely waited, demonstrating his courage.

"Come up here. Bring the truck keys. Never mind the clothes, you won't need them."

Naked and powerful Duggai climbed the switchback rock trail. Mackenzie backed away, never letting him come in jumping distance: he had no reserves left but it didn't take much strength to pull a trigger and Duggai knew that and Mackenzie kept the rifle aimed at his privates so that Duggai knew he couldn't be panicked into a hasty kill shot. Even if it missed it would tear up his pelvis or his abdomen and he'd be a long agonizing time dying. No: Duggai's illness of the mind wasn't that kind. He hadn't forsaken his shrewdness. Like his victims he would bide his time and wait for an opening— he wouldn't fight the drop.

Mackenzie said, "You knew I was Navajo. You should have thought about that."

"Half Navajo. *Beligano*."

"White man hell. I put myself in your moccasins, Calvin. I knew what you'd do. I got here ahead of you. We played your game and I won. You hear me?"

"I hear you, Captain." Duggai stood dripping, all hard dark musculature—mammoth and unbowed. He gaped at Mackenzie in that maddening way of his. "You can kill me now."

The rifle was so heavy he could hardly hold it. He stopped Duggai at the tailgate and shuffled painfully around him in a wide circle. He got the truck open and found the pieces of wire where Duggai had tossed them inside. He threw two of them at Duggai and got his hand back on the rifle.

Mackenzie's lips peeled back viciously. It came out in a whisper of rage: *"You know the drill."*

Duggai's eyes went a little wider. He bent down and picked up the wire. While he was bent he hesitated a moment and Mackenzie knew he was thinking about making a try—throwing dirt in Mackenzie's eyes—but it was too far for that and finally Duggai twisted the wire around his wrist and sat down on his naked butt and wired his own ankles together. Then rolled over on his belly and put both hands behind his rump.

Mackenzie approached him very slowly and put the muzzle of the rifle against the crotch between the buttocks and held his right hand on the trigger. With his left hand he wired the hands together behind the small of Duggai's back.

He had trouble standing up after that but he made it. "Get in the truck."

"How?"

"Hobble it."

Duggai hopped like a farmer's kid in a potato-sack race. Then he sat on the tailboard and lifted his legs and swiveled himself up inside.

"On the bunk now."

He wired Duggai's feet to the floor cleat as his own had been wired. He jammed the rifle against Duggai's hip and again held the trigger at arm's length while he leaned behind Duggai and wired his hands to the steel crossbrace of the wall.

"You fixin' to leave me out in that desert, Captain?"

Mackenzie slammed the door in his face.

30

The truck came strenuously across the ravaged earth. Approaching the camp it tipped clumsily through a gully that almost rolled it over. It righted itself and advanced, gears snarling.

Shirley came out of her hole hollow-eyed and hesitant. She stood with her arms folded as if she were cold and stared at the truck with the face of a prisoner awaiting execution against a wall.

Drawn by the hated sound, Jay arose from the grave and sidled toward Shirley. He touched her hand and they stood together, watching.

The truck whined slowly up the slope and finally stopped. Mackenzie in shirt and shorts and boots opened the door and stepped out, all his muscles twitching. He had to keep a grip on the door to keep from falling over on his face but he managed a grotesque smile.

They stood behind the truck watching while Mackenzie opened the camper door. Inside Duggai sat wired on the bunk. He gaped at them with that idiot vacancy he used to mask the ceaseless wild hatred that filled his soul.

Jay coughed horribly and found his voice. "I'm glad you didn't kill him."

"It would have been too easy."

"Yes. Better to leave him the way he left us."

"No," Mackenzie said.

"What?"

"We're taking him back." All the fury of the desert climbed to a screaming pitch in him. *"We're taking the son of a bitch all the way back."*

Jay slumped against the truck, terrorized by Mackenzie's sudden venom. Shirley reached for Mackenzie's arm, her face alarmed, but he veered toward the truck: he took a canteen off the bunk and tottered past them toward Earle's trench.

Earle blinked up at him.

"You're still alive, then."

"I never doubted I would be," Earle said. He even smiled. "Providence, Sam."

Mackenzie lowered the canteen to him. "That's all yours. There's plenty more. We've got the truck—we'll leave as soon as it cools down. By midnight we'll be on the highway. Have you in a hospital before you know it."

"God be praised."

"God and Samuel Mackenzie."

"That too. I won't begrudge your strength. It's God-given."

Earle's God or the silversmith's gods. One or another—Mackenzie believed it.

Shirley brushed past him with the first-aid kit. Jay lurched behind her, his arms flapping as if broken. He'd put a hat on his head but he stood stark naked under it—an awe-inspiring scarecrow. "What do you mean, take him back? For God's sake, take him *back?*"

Mackenzie felt too weak to stand. He stumbled toward the truck. Jay chased him with comic alacrity; caught him at the truck, hauled him around. "What did you mean, take him back?"

Mackenzie felt the pinch of Jay's weak grip on his arm. He didn't push Jay away. He put both hands on

Jay's shoulders and gripped them hard, feeling the strength surge into his hands.

He measured his words out with infinite effort. They fell with equal weight; like bricks.

"This desert was our hell. But the one thing he can't stand—that's Duggai's hell." He pounded Jay's shoulders happily, taking cheap pleasure in vindictiveness and feeling no shame for it. "Think of the worst thing we could do to him. The worst thing we could possibly do to him."

Jay's face changed with slow comprehension.

Shirley whispered, "The hospital?"

"The hospital," Mackenzie replied.

They both began to nod and Mackenzie turned to see her better but the red haze washed her out. He had something to tell her. With stubborn determined effort he tried to form the words but then for a while he passed out.

"A spine-tingling page turner."

—Mary Higgins Clark,
author of <u>Where Are The Children?</u>

OUTRUN THE DARK

CECILIA BARTHOLOMEW

A four-year-old boy is found dead. His eight-year-old sister, Billyjean, is accused of the murder. This is the story of Billyjean—thirteen years later.

Now she is twenty-one, and going home. She had finally confessed to killing her brother. That showed she could face reality. She could live on the outside.

But Billyjean didn't really remember killing her brother, no matter what she confessed—and someone else knew that too!

She had outrun the dark....and now she must run for her life!

JOVE

$2.25   B12046488
Available wherever paperbacks are sold.